GW01372413

CLIVILIUS
WHERE CREATION MEETS INFINITY

First Edition, 13 March 2024
ISBN 978-1-4461-1356-1
Imprint: Lulu.com

Step into Clivilius, where creation meets infinity, and the essence of reality is yours to redefine. Here, existence weaves into a narrative where every decision has consequences, every action has an impact, and every moment counts. In this realm, shaped by the visionary AI CLIVE, inhabitants are not mere spectators but pivotal characters in an evolving drama where the lines between worlds blur.

Guardians traverse the realms of Clivilius and Earth, their journeys igniting events that challenge the balance between these interconnected universes. The quest for resources and the enigma of unexplained disappearances on Earth mirror the deeper conflicts and intricacies that define Clivilius—a world where reality responds to the collective will and individual choices of its Clivilians, revealing a complex interplay of creation, control, and consequence.

In the grand tapestry of Clivilius, the struggle for harmony and the dance of dichotomies play out across a cosmic stage. Here, every soul's journey contributes to the narrative, where the lines between utopia and dystopia, creator and observer, become increasingly fluid. Clivilius is not just a realm to be explored but a reality to be shaped.

Open your eyes. Expand your mind. Experience your new reality. Welcome to Clivilius, where the journey of discovery is not just about seeing a new world but about seeing your world anew.

clandestine world of Guardians, Beatrix must navigate a labyrinth of secrets and moral dilemmas. Caught in the crossfire of legacy and destiny, she faces choices that could redefine the boundaries of her world and her very identity.

Jamie Greyson (4338.204.1 - 4338.209.3)

Haunted by shadows of his past, Jamie Greyson navigates life with a guarded heart, his complex bond with Luke Smith teetering on the brink of collapse. When Jamie is thrust into a strange new world, every moment is a test, pushing him to confront not only the dangers that lurk in the unknown but also the demons of his own making. Jamie's quest for survival becomes a journey of redemption, where the chance for a new beginning is earned through courage, trust, and the willingness to face the truth of his own heart.

Luke Smith (4338.204.1 - 4338.209.2)

Luke Smith's world transforms with the discovery of a cryptic device, thrusting him into the guardianship of destiny itself. His charismatic charm and unpredictable decisions now carry weight beyond imagination, balancing on the razor's edge between salvation and destruction. Embracing his role as a Guardian, Luke faces the paradox of power: the very force that defends also threatens to annihilate. As shadows gather and the fabric of reality strains, Luke must navigate the consequences of his actions, unaware that a looming challenge will test the very core of his resolve.

4338.209.1 - 4338.214.2

SARAH
LAHEY

CLIVILIUS
WHERE CREATION MEETS INFINITY

"As mysterious disappearances grip Hobart, I stand on the precipice of my first potential homicide investigation. The thrill of unmasking shadows echoes the dreams of my youth."

- Sarah Lahey

4338.209

(28 July 2018)

UNFORTUNATE TRUTHS

4338.209.1

"Oh, Karl," I whispered, my voice barely more than a breathless sigh. Across the dimly lit room, the silhouette of Karl stood framed in the doorway, a vision that quickened my pulse. His white shirt hung loosely, carelessly unbuttoned, revealing the contours of his muscular chest, evenly trimmed and gleaming faintly in the low light. My eyes lingered on him, taking in every chiseled detail, as a wave of anticipation washed over me. "I've been waiting for you."

Lying on the soft bed, I felt the bare mattress yield to the contours of my body. Each fibre of the fabric seemed to whisper against my skin, heightening my senses as I waited for Karl to approach. The room was hushed, the only sound our synchronised breathing, creating an intimate rhythm in the quiet space. With each deliberate, slow step Karl took toward me, my heart seemed to beat louder, echoing my yearning.

He moved with a deliberate grace, his presence commanding yet tender. Another step, then another, until he stood at the foot of the bed, his figure casting a long shadow that melded with the darkness of the room.

I ran my hands over my naked breasts. They were smooth and heavy to the touch. "Do I please you?" I asked, my voice laced with a mix of vulnerability and desire.

"Yes," Karl replied, his voice a deep, resonant timbre that resonated within me. "You always please me." The sincerity in his words wrapped around me like a warm embrace, reinforcing the deep connection that always seemed to exist between us.

Without any warning, Karl knelt on one knee, the gesture so sudden that it caught my breath. He rested his left arm on the cold iron bed frame, a contrast to the warmth in his eyes. Rolling to my knees, I leaned forward, curiosity piqued as his right hand slid into his trouser pocket with an air of mystery.

In that moment, my heart seemed to stop, suspended in a bubble of hope and expectation. My mind raced with possibilities, each more enchanting than the last. *Could he be about to reveal a small box, its contents a glimmering testament to the depth of his feelings? A piece of jewellery, perhaps, made to fit my finger perfectly, a symbol of a future together?*

"Oh, Karl!" I whispered again, my voice trembling with a cocktail of emotions.

Suddenly, Karl's bright blue eyes widened in surprise, or was it mischief? In a swift, unexpected motion, he fell onto his back with a loud thud that echoed through the room. Concern flooded through me as I peered over the edge of the bed, my heart in my throat.

But there he was, lying on the hard floor, a grin spreading across his face that was both boyish and endearingly charming. In his large, strong hand, he held a small box, its lid open to reveal the treasure inside. Nestled on a soft silk pillow in the centre of the box was a piece of rose-gold jewellery, its gem catching the scant light and flashing like the fire of a distant star, a beacon of promise in the soft darkness of the room.

"Oh, Karl," I whispered softly, my voice a delicate murmur in the stillness of the room. The sensation of my own touch brought a surge of yearning, a longing intensified by the thought of him. "I love you. Yes! Yes, of course!" The words tumbled from my lips, a confession of my deepest emotions, echoing in the quiet.

Karl's movements were a slow, mesmerising dance of love. He sat up, his eyes locked onto mine, a look so deep and full of emotion that it seemed to reach into my very soul. Gently, with a tenderness that made my heart swell, he slid the diamond ring onto my slender finger. Its weight was a tangible promise, a symbol of our connection that glinted softly in the dim light.

He leaned in, and his lips brushed against my forehead in a kiss so gentle it was like a whisper, a touch that sent shivers down my spine. It was a moment of pure connection, a sealing of our shared affections.

"I love you," I whispered gently again, my words a soft caress in the air between us. "Oh, I love you... I love you," I continued, each repetition a deeper affirmation of my feelings, my voice fading into the warm air that enveloped us, a tender serenade for the only man who had ever truly touched my heart.

But then, like a cold breeze sweeping through a warm day, a wave of fear crashed over me. The enchanting spell shattered, leaving a stark, jarring reality in its wake. The realisation of where I actually was flooded my mind, washing away the beautiful illusion. The vision of Karl, that beautiful man ready to profess his love and desire, to ask me to be by his side forever, evaporated like a mirage.

As consciousness clawed its way back, a reluctant awareness creeping over me, I didn't dare open my eyes. But deep down, I knew it was too late. The heat rising in my face was a telltale sign, a burning tide of embarrassment and disappointment washing over me, leaving me exposed and vulnerable in the wake of my dream. My heart ached with the longing for what could have been, and the harsh reality of what actually was.

"Are you alright there, my dear?" The voice, gentle and tinged with years of wisdom, belonged to an old woman. It came from the bed, just a few meters away from where I lay. I was curled up in my late grandfather's favourite recliner, a familiar and comforting spot filled with memories. Her voice, though frail, still carried the comforting tone that had always made me feel safe.

"Hmm?" I groaned innocently, trying to seem oblivious. As I stretched my arms widely, I executed a perfectly timed, yet entirely fake yawn. A strategy formed in my mind: *Maybe if I pretend not to remember, my grandmother will let it be.* I hoped to deflect any further probing into my embarrassing dream.

"You were making quite the noise over there. I was beginning to worry about you. All that moaning," she said, her words laced with a subtle playfulness. I noticed the slightest of grins pulling at the corners of her tired mouth, a hint of mischief in her otherwise serene expression. Her words were teasing, yet filled with an underlying layer of understanding and empathy.

"You may be nearly thirty now, but don't you worry. Your time will come." Her voice was reassuring, a gentle reminder that life had its own pace for each of us.

My heart melted at her words. Slowly, I took my time, allowing myself to really look at her. My grandmother's eyes sparkled with a blend of love, wisdom, and a zest for life that age had not diminished. Their warmth spread across her wrinkled face, a testament to the many years and experiences etched into her skin. Each line told a story, a narrative of laughter, sorrow, and love.

Lit up by my own sleepy foolishness, her smile was a sight to cherish. In that moment, I realised that the embarrassment was worth every second. To see my ninety-two-year-old grandmother smile like that, with a glint of youthful playfulness in her eyes, was a precious moment. It reminded me of the strong, unbreakable bond we shared, one that transcended generations and was rooted in unconditional love and understanding.

It had been five years since my grandfather passed away, his life richly lived until the ripe old age of eighty-eight. In the wake of his absence, my grandmother had moved into a small retirement home nestled in the heart of Hobart. I often wished I had the time and energy to care for my ageing grandmother full-time, but it simply wasn't an option for me. Life had dealt its cards differently.

My parents had been taken from me and my older brother, Oscar, many years ago during an overseas trip. I was only nine then, lost in a world suddenly too big and too cold. My mother's parents, the anchors in our storm, had generously taken us in, filling the void with their unwavering love and support. Oscar, seeking his own path, had moved to London, chasing after a love interest, leaving us with little more than sporadic calls twice a year. My father's parents had departed this world a decade ago, leaving us to navigate life's complexities without their guidance.

So, in essence, it was now just me and my grandmother, the last of our once larger family.

"I don't know what you're talking about, Jane," I said, my voice laced with a playful denial as I grinned from ear to ear. I wrestled myself out of the recliner, feeling the stiffness in my muscles as I stretched. The chair, a relic of my grandfather's, had become my temporary refuge during these visits.

I collected my shoes scattered across the floor, their placement a testament to the hurried, carefree way I had discarded them earlier. Approaching the edge of my grandmother's bed, I bent over and kissed her softly on the cheek. "I've got to go home and get ready for work," I told her, trying to keep my voice steady. "I'll let the reception staff know on my way out that you're awake and ready for your morning routine," I added, attempting to maintain a semblance of normalcy in our morning.

"Thank you, dear," Jane said, her voice frail yet filled with love. She took my hand in hers, her grip gentle yet firm, a silent testament to the strength that still resided within her.

As I left the small, neatly kept room, a warm smile plastered on my face to mask the turmoil inside, my finger quickly wiped at a tear that threatened to betray my emotions. Jane hadn't mentioned anything to me herself, but I knew. She had to have given her consent to the doctors, aware that I was now privy to her condition. Last week, the specialist had informed me in hushed, solemn tones that Jane was riddled with cancer, her time measured in weeks rather than months. The suddenness and the inexplicable nature of it baffled everyone; it was as if the disease had materialised out of thin air.

Even more peculiar was that my grandmother didn't seem to be in any pain or discomfort, a small mercy in an otherwise heartbreaking reality. I clung to the hope that it would remain this way, that she would be spared the agony so often accompanying such a ruthless disease, for however long we had left together. My steps were heavy as I walked down the corridor, each footfall a reminder of the limited time remaining, a countdown to an inevitable goodbye.

SERGEANT & LOUISE

4338.209.2

I arrived at the police station early that morning, the events of earlier still lingering in my mind. After my grandmother had caught me unwittingly revealing my dreams, I felt a need to immerse myself in work, to escape into a world where I had control and purpose. Living alone, without even the company of a goldfish, suited me just fine. I thrived in the solitude, finding solace in the quiet. It was in these silent moments that I felt most connected to my passion for solving mysteries, preferring the thrill of unravelling a crime over the echo of an empty, silent home.

As I exited the changing rooms, ready to dive into the day's work, my path led me towards the open-plan office. My desk, cluttered with case files and notes, beckoned me from afar, a familiar mess in the midst of organised chaos.

"Detective Lahey," a deep voice called out, slicing through the hum of the busy corridor. I recognised it instantly and halted in my tracks. Turning, I faced Sergeant Claiborne, the source of the voice. A shiver of apprehension skittered across my shoulders, an involuntary reaction that felt like a foreboding chill.

"Yes, Sergeant Claiborne?" I responded, my tone guarded. His presence always seemed to bring an air of unpredictability.

"Are you busy?" His inquiry was straightforward, yet it carried an undercurrent of urgency that piqued my curiosity.

"Right now, Sir?" I asked, a flicker of uncertainty in my voice. His approach was unusual, and it set my mind racing with possibilities.

"Yes, right now, Detective," he confirmed, his tone firm, leaving no room for ambiguity.

"No, Sir," I answered cautiously, my mind still trying to piece together the reason behind his directness. "What do you need?"

"Have you seen Detective Jenkins yet?" Claiborne's question hung in the air, laced with an expectation of a straightforward answer. I knew that Karl, my partner, was likely still recovering from last night's indulgences, but my relationship with the Sergeant wasn't one where I felt at ease covering for him.

"No, not yet, Sir." My response was honest, albeit reluctant. Claiborne's expression morphed into a scowl, his dissatisfaction evident.

"You'll have to join me then." His words hit me unexpectedly. *Join him where?* My mind raced with questions. *An interview?* The thought seemed implausible; I had never witnessed Sergeant Claiborne conduct an interview before.

He gave me a brief, assessing look. "You've got five minutes," he stated sternly. "Then I want you to join me in interview room one."

"Yes, Sergeant," was all I could muster, my voice a mixture of surprise and apprehension. As he walked away, I stood there for a moment, trying to quell the flutter of nervous excitement in my chest. *What awaited me in interview room one?* Taking a deep breath, the prospect both intrigued and unnerved me.

Arriving at my desk, a wave of nervous anticipation washed over me. The thought of being alone with Sergeant Claiborne set my palms to sweating, an unusual reaction for me, usually so composed in the face of pressure. I rifled through the stacks of paper cluttering my desk, each file a reminder of the countless hours spent delving into the intricate details of various cases. My search was frantic, desperate for a notebook amidst the organised chaos that was my workspace.

Frustratingly, every pen or pencil I grabbed seemed to have run out of ink or was broken. Time was slipping away, and in a decision born of necessity, I reached for a pen from Karl's desk. His desk was a stark contrast to mine - meticulously clean, not a single piece of paper out of place. It was almost unnervingly orderly, reflecting his methodical approach to everything he did.

Karl, always particular about his things, would normally complain if I took something without asking. But under the circumstances, I couldn't afford the luxury of time. *Besides*, I rationalised, *he's not here to ask. He would miss out on what seemed to be an important interview, and it was his own fault for not being present.*

With the borrowed pen in hand, I walked briskly down the corridor, my steps echoing slightly in the hallway. The meeting room was down the far end, and as I approached, I saw Sergeant Claiborne already there, waiting. He stood with his hands placed perfectly behind his back, an embodiment of his typical formal style. His posture exuded authority and a no-nonsense attitude that had always defined him.

"You're late," he stated, his gaze drifting purposefully to his watch. There was a hint of reprimand in his tone, reminding me of his strict adherence to punctuality.

"Sorry, Sergeant," I apologised, feeling a twinge of annoyance at myself. *Shit*, I thought. *Seven minutes instead of five*. The realisation that I had exceeded the time he allotted added an extra layer of tension to the already daunting prospect of what lay ahead in that room.

Allowing the Sergeant to take the lead, I watched as he entered the small, windowless room first. The space felt confined, almost claustrophobic, with its bare walls and the single table that occupied the centre. I followed, closing the door behind me with a soft click that seemed to echo slightly in the silence of the room.

"Louise," Sergeant Claiborne began, his voice steady and official. "This is Detective Sarah Lahey. She is one of Hobart's finest young detectives." His introduction, while flattering, carried an undertone of formality that set the tone for the meeting.

"It's a pleasure to meet you, Sarah," Louise said. Her voice was soft, almost fragile, as she extended her hand towards me. She remained seated, her movements somewhat restrained.

"Likewise, Louise," I replied, returning the handshake with a firm grip. Her hand felt timid in mine, a stark contrast to the strength I tried to convey with my own handshake.

As I released her hand, I took a moment to observe her more closely. Louise appeared to be in her mid-forties, her light brown hair, shoulder-length and gently curling, framing her round face. There was a profound sadness etched into her features, the kind that spoke of a deep, personal pain. Her body language was equally telling; her shoulders slumped, not just with the weight of her body, but seemingly with the weight of the world. Her hands fidgeted nervously, betraying her inner turmoil.

I settled quietly into my chair, my gaze never straying far from Louise. Sergeant Claiborne, with a practiced ease, took the lead on the interview. "It's been quite a few years, Mrs. Jeffries," he began, his voice carrying a professional politeness that belied the situation's gravity. "What can we do for you this time?" he asked.

Despite the politeness of his words, I couldn't help but detect a slight tone of contempt in the Sergeant's voice. It was subtle, but there, like a thin veil barely concealing his true sentiments. I felt a twinge of curiosity mixed with caution, wondering about the history between Louise Jeffries and the Hobart police. *What had brought her here after so many years? And what lay beneath the Sergeant's barely veiled disdain?* The room seemed to shrink a little more with these unanswered questions hanging in the air.

As Louise uttered those words, "My son is missing," her voice was curt, each syllable laced with a tension that filled the room. She paused, a deliberate moment that seemed to stretch the silence, before adding, "And so is Jamie."

The mention of a second missing person piqued my interest immediately. "Who is Jamie?" I found myself asking, the question slipping out almost instinctively.

Louise's eyes met mine, a direct, unwavering gaze that seemed to bore into me. "My brother. The gay one," she replied. Her words were matter-of-fact, but there was an undercurrent, something I couldn't quite place.

I was momentarily taken aback by her response. The way she mentioned her brother's sexuality made me unsure of her stance on it. *Was it a point of contention for her, or was it simply a descriptive detail?* "Does that concern you, Mrs. Jeffries?" I asked, my curiosity getting the better of me. I needed to understand the dynamics at play to navigate this conversation effectively.

"Which bit, Detective?" Louise's reply came back sourly. "The fact that my brother is gay or the fact that I haven't been able to reach him for several days?"

Her response left me momentarily at a loss. The last thing I wanted was to appear incompetent or insensitive, especially in a situation that required a delicate balance of empathy and professionalism. I sat there, in the starkness of the small room, struggling to find the right words. I was conscious of the weight of Sergeant Claiborne's gaze on me, his presence a silent pressure in the background.

Louise's impatience was palpable as she answered her own question, her voice tinged with a mix of resignation and underlying tension. "I've known for years that he was gay," she said, "but I have never trusted his partner." The words came out with a hint of bitterness, as if the distrust she held for this partner was a burden she had carried for a long time.

"His partner? Can you give us a name?" I found myself asking, my voice steadier now as I regained my composure. It was crucial to gather as much information as possible, and every detail mattered.

"Luke. Luke Smith," Louise answered, her tone laced with clear disdain. Each word seemed to carry a weight of unspoken stories and suspicions.

"And why don't you trust this Luke Smith?" Sergeant Claiborne's question was asked with a delicacy that spoke of his experience in handling sensitive subjects. His approach was gentle, a contrast to the tension that had started to build in the room.

Louise turned to face the Sergeant directly, her gaze sharp. "You of all people should know, Charlie, that Jamie doesn't have the best track record when it comes to deciding who to trust." Her use of the Sergeant's first name in such a formal setting was unexpected and telling. It hinted at a familiarity that went beyond professional boundaries.

I glanced towards Sergeant Claiborne, my curiosity piqued. To my surprise, I saw him begin to blush, an unusual display of discomfort from a man usually so composed. He seemed momentarily at a loss for words, floundering in a way that I had never seen before.

Louise's familiarity with him, her casual use of his first name, was unheard of in these formal settings. It was clear there was some history here that I had not been made aware of. A feeling of discomfort settled over me. As a detective, I prided myself on being informed and prepared, yet here I was, in the dark about a connection that seemed significant to the case at hand. The realisation that there were layers to this situation that I didn't understand made me feel uneasy. I silently resolved to find out more, understanding that this unknown history between Louise and Sergeant Claiborne could be crucial to unraveling the mystery of her missing son and brother.

"I believe that Luke may have done harm to both of them," Louise declared, her voice steady and resolute. There was no quiver in her tone, only a matter-of-factness that suggested she had considered this possibility deeply. Her conviction was unnerving. "I want to speak with Detective Karl Jenkins."

"Are you sure that is wise, Louise?" Sergeant Claiborne's question was cautious, probing. His eyes, usually so steady and commanding, flickered with a hint of concern.

"Yes," she replied. Her face set into a look of sheer determination, a resolve that seemed to harden her features. It was a look that left no room for argument, a clear indication that she was not to be dismissed or taken lightly.

Sergeant Claiborne turned to look at me, his gaze sharp and commanding. "Find Karl," he whispered sharply.

"Of course, Sergeant," I responded, my voice steady despite the sudden rush of adrenaline. I stumbled to my feet, feeling a surge of responsibility mixed with a twinge of apprehension. Scrambling for the door, my mind raced with the implications of Louise's statement and the urgency of finding Karl.

As I stepped briskly out of the interview room, the sense of responsibility bore down on me. Finding Karl in this critical moment felt like racing against time itself. He was likely at home, trying to shake off the aftermath of last night's celebrations, unaware of the unfolding situation at the station. The urgency was amplified by Louise's allegations against Luke Smith and her adamant request to speak with Karl directly. It was a tangled web that was getting more complex by the minute.

I pulled out my mobile and pressed Karl's number, the device feeling almost slippery against my anxious grip. Holding the phone to my ear, I listened to the endless rings, each tone heightening my sense of urgency. "Come on. Pick up, you bastard," I growled into the phone, my usual composure fraying at the edges.

"Yeah?" The groggy voice that finally answered was unmistakably Karl's, thick with the remnants of sleep or maybe something more.

"Where the hell are you, Karl?" I whispered, my voice laced with a mix of frustration and panic. I needed him here, and I needed him now.

"I'm still at home. The alarm didn't go off," came his response, feeble and unconvincing. It was clear he was trying to skirt around the truth.

"Bullshit," I retorted sharply. "I know you went out with the boys last night." There was no time for niceties or to dance around the issue. Every second we wasted was a second lost in our investigation.

Karl sighed heavily, a sound that carried his resignation. "What is it, Sarah?" he asked, perhaps sensing the urgency in my tone.

"You need to get your ass down to the station right now," I demanded. The gravity of the situation was not something I could afford to downplay.

"Can't it wait until later?" Karl groaned, his voice still heavy with lethargy.

"No, Karl, it can't. This could be your big case." I stressed the importance, trying to instil in him a sense of urgency and purpose.

There was a brief pause, a few moments of silence that stretched out longer than I would have liked. Then finally, Karl spoke, "Fine. I'll be there in half an hour," he promised, albeit reluctantly, before the call ended abruptly.

"Crap!" I muttered under my breath, hastily pocketing my phone. As I turned, I found Sergeant Claiborne standing directly behind me, his presence unexpected and slightly unnerving.

"Sarah, be careful," he said quietly, his tone serious yet imbued with a hint of concern. His words hung in the air, unclear and loaded.

I turned fully to face the Sergeant, a flicker of confusion crossing my mind. His comment left me uncertain. *Was he questioning my capabilities? Was it a warning of some sort?* The ambiguity of his statement had me second-guessing.

Thankfully, the Sergeant soon clarified his intentions. "Pay very close attention to what they both say and do," he instructed. His eyes bore into mine, emphasising the importance of his directive. "I want to read and approve your notes before you do the official filing."

"Of course, Sergeant," I replied without hesitation, though a trace of apprehension lingered in my voice. "I'll have my notes on your desk within an hour after we finish up the interview," I promised, committing to a tight deadline.

"Thank you," Sergeant Claiborne said, his gratitude seeming sincere. Yet, as he walked away, I couldn't help but feel a twinge of doubt. *Had I overpromised, especially without consulting Karl first?* The thought that I might be undermining my partner gnawed at me, leaving me momentarily conflicted.

"Detective Lahey," Sergeant Claiborne called out just as he was about to disappear down the corridor.

"Yes, Sergeant?" I responded, a sense of foreboding settling over me.

"I've known the Jeffries for a long time. This case is of particular interest to me. That's all," he stated, his words carrying a weight that suggested there was more to his interest than just professional duty. He dismissed the conversation with a wave of his hand and continued towards his office.

Closing my eyes, I inhaled deeply, trying to centre myself. *It isn't really that big of a deal*, I reassured myself. Pre-reading case notes wasn't uncommon, and it made sense given the Sergeant's vested interest. He would inevitably see them after filing, anyway. He just wanted to be kept in the loop.

Just as I began to relax, Sergeant Claiborne stopped abruptly and turned. "Oh, Detective Lahey," he called back, his voice carrying down the corridor.

My heart sank, anticipating more instructions or perhaps a reprimand.

"Do let Karl know that I am very disappointed that he is late on his first day as Senior Detective."

I nodded silently, acknowledging his message. The responsibility of conveying the Sergeant's disappointment to Karl weighed heavily on me. It was an uncomfortable position to be in, caught between my duty to my superior and my loyalty to my partner.

"Hey, Glen!" I called out, my voice carrying across the office as I spotted him passing by the door in the corridor. Hesitantly, I moved away from my desk, unsure if he had heard me over the usual din of the bustling police station.

But then, his round face, unmistakably Glen's, popped back around the corner.

"You called, my dear?" Glen's voice, tinged with a mocking tone, echoed as he stepped into the room. His face, plump and smug, was lit up with an expression of feigned politeness. "How may I assist you today?" he asked, his words dripping with condescension.

I couldn't help but roll my eyes internally. Glen was the epitome of crude and obnoxious, and I usually did my best to keep my interactions with him to a bare minimum. But today was different. I needed information, and I had a strong suspicion that Glen had just mentioned Karl's name as he passed by the door.

"Detective Crosswell," I started, striving to maintain a neutral tone despite my rising irritation. "Did I just hear you say something about Karl?"

His response was typical Glen, always ready with a snide remark. "Oh, looking for your late lover already, are you?" he replied, his smirk revealing his delight in making such insinuations.

I shot him a look of disapproval, biting back the sharp retort that almost slipped out. Instead, I composed myself and chose my words carefully. "Sergeant Claiborne wants to see him immediately," I said, my voice steady. I held my breath for a moment, hoping that my statement wouldn't provide Glen with any more fodder for his taunts.

Glen, for all his faults, was not stupid. He had been the first to sniff out the secret affair between Karl and me. It had cost me more than a few week's pay to ensure his silence. The memory of that transaction still left a bitter taste in my mouth. I watched him closely, gauging his reaction, knowing full well that he was capable of using any piece of information to his advantage. The last thing I needed was for

Glen to stir up trouble, especially today when everything seemed to hang in a delicate balance.

As Glen's eyes bore into me, I could almost feel him trying to peel back the layers of my composure, searching for any sign of vulnerability he could exploit. His gaze was like a scalpel, sharp and probing. I fought hard against the urge to cringe or show any hint of weakness. Instead, I met his gaze with a stern stare of my own, my eyes locking with his in a silent battle of wills.

"I believe he was headed for the showers," Glen finally conceded, his tone still carrying an undercurrent of slyness.

"Thank you, Glen," I replied, managing to muster a short, polite smile despite the tension coiling inside me. It was a smile that didn't quite reach my eyes, but it served its purpose.

In response, Glen gave me a slight nod, a gesture that was almost respectful, or as close to respect as Glen ever seemed to manage. Then he turned and continued on his way up the corridor, his steps echoing slightly against the cold walls.

The moment Glen was out of sight, disappearing around the corner, I released a breath I hadn't realised I'd been holding. My heart was racing, a mix of relief and urgency propelling me forward. I made a mad dash for the changing room, my steps quick and determined.

As I hurried along the corridor, the sounds of the bustling police station faded into a blur. My mind was singularly focused on finding Karl. The information we needed from him was crucial, and with each passing second, the urgency grew. I could almost hear the ticking of an invisible clock, marking the time slipping away.

The corridor seemed to stretch endlessly as I neared the changing room. My thoughts raced with possibilities and concerns about the case, about Karl, and about what Sergeant Claiborne's unusual interest in the Jeffries family might mean. As I approached the door, I braced myself for the conversation ahead, knowing that every moment was critical in the unfolding investigation.

Ignoring the surprised glances from several other officers as I briskly entered the men's changing room, I made my way towards the shower cubicles. The room was filled with the familiar sounds of lockers slamming and the muffled chatter of officers, but my focus was singular. Navigating through the benches and lockers, I moved with a purpose, each step echoing slightly on the tiled floor.

Only one of the shower cubicles was occupied; its cheap, plastic curtain hung loosely, not quite managing to close fully. Through the gap, I caught a glimpse of the man inside, enough to confirm it was Karl. The sound of running water and the silhouette of his figure were unmistakable.

I positioned myself silently outside his cubicle, waiting for him to finish. Over the years, my presence in the men's changing room had become something of a non-issue. I had been in here many times before, and by now, I'd probably seen most of the male officers in various states of undress, Sergeant Claiborne included. It struck me as odd, this acceptance of my presence in what was traditionally a male space. I wasn't sure why it had become so normalised, but it had.

There was a certain irony in the thought that if any of the other female officers were to casually stroll in here unannounced, it would likely result in a swift and uncomfortable meeting with Human Resources. But for some reason, I was the exception to this unspoken rule. Maybe it was because I'd been around long enough, or perhaps it was due to the nature of my work and the necessity of urgent communication, regardless of the setting.

As I waited, my mind momentarily wandered to the complexity of workplace dynamics and the blurred lines of professionalism. However, I quickly snapped back to the present, aware that time was of the essence and this was no moment for philosophical musings. My purpose here was clear – to get Karl briefed and ready for what was coming next. The seriousness of the situation with Louise Jeffries and the urgency in Sergeant Claiborne's instructions were at the forefront of my thoughts, overshadowing the oddity of my current surroundings.

"Shit, Sarah!" Karl exclaimed, his voice a mix of surprise and irritation as he pulled back the shower curtain. "What the fuck are you doing in here?"

His reaction was understandable, yet it did little to sway my resolve. I was here on business, and Karl's shock at my presence was the least of my concerns.

Before I could respond, Glen's taunting voice cut through the steamy air of the changing room. "Looking for some action, I'd say," he sneered, a grin plastered across his face as he leaned against the doorway, clad only in a towel. I hadn't even noticed him enter, so focused was I on finding Karl. Glen's presence was like a dark cloud, his crude demeanour unwelcome yet unsurprising.

He sauntered past me, his body brushing against my arm in a deliberate, intrusive manner. The towel, barely adequate to cover his ample belly, dropped to the floor as he stepped into the cubicle next to Karl. For a moment, Glen stood there, unabashedly exposed, before finally pulling the curtain across.

"In your dreams, pal," Karl retorted, his voice echoing off the tiled walls.

"Eew, please no. Don't encourage that fat prick," I said, unable to hide my disgust. The thought of becoming a subject in one of Glen's lewd fantasies, the kind he so freely shared around the office, was revolting. It was baffling to me why Glen even bothered with such antics. There was little about him that was appealing, especially in his current state of undress.

What perplexed me even more was the fact that Glen was happily married. I had met his wife on several occasions, and she was one of the kindest, most pleasant women I had ever encountered. What she saw in Glen was beyond my comprehension. The contrast between his sleazy personality and his seemingly content domestic life was stark. And from my observations, his detective work was as sloppy as his behaviour, a reflection of his overall lack of professionalism.

"Towel," Karl gruffly asked, nodding towards his belongings which were haphazardly piled on the bench in front of the shower.

Eager to shift my focus from Glen's crude display, I quickly reached for Karl's towel, a plain white fabric that looked almost too small against the backdrop of the steam-filled changing room. "Hurry up. You'll want to hear this," I urged, thrusting the towel towards Karl. As I did so, I made sure that my fingertips brushed against his carefully buzzed, otherwise furry chest. The brief contact with his toned pectorals sent an involuntary thrill through me.

I knew I needed to leave, and quickly. Even the slightest touch of Karl's skin stirred something within me, a craving that I constantly had to keep in check. As I turned to leave, I walked briskly out of the changing room. With each step, I deliberately swayed my hips, fully aware of the effect it would have. I could feel the eyes of the men in the room on me, their gazes trailing my every move.

A wild grin spread across my face as I exited. There was a certain power in teasing them with my femininity, a buzz that came with the knowledge that they could look but would never touch. It was a small, private victory, a moment of reclaiming control in a world where I so often had to prove myself.

SECRETS

4338.209.3

Making a beeline for the interview room where I had left Louise sitting alone, my steps were quick and purposeful. However, as I neared the frosted glass door, I instinctively slowed down. From within the room, hushed voices drifted through the door, which was left slightly ajar, inviting curiosity.

"They've been watching him for years," I heard Louise whisper, her voice laced with a mixture of fear and urgency.

"Who?" Sergeant Claiborne's voice rumbled in response. He was attempting to speak softly, but his deep baritone voice failed to lower to a whisper, making his words more audible than perhaps intended.

Curiosity piqued, I leaned closer to the door, straining to catch more of the conversation. The response was muffled, frustratingly indistinct. A part of me urged to listen more, to glean whatever information I could, but a stronger sense of professionalism held me back. *I have to stop*, I told myself firmly. *Karl will be here any moment now.* It would look unprofessional, to say the least, if I were caught eavesdropping on the Sergeant.

Taking a few discreet steps back, I set my approach to appear casual, unassuming. I walked up to the door and gave a sharp knock with my knuckle, feigning surprise. "Oh, Sergeant," I said, my voice tinged with carefully calibrated astonishment as I pushed the door open and stepped into the interview room.

"Did you find Karl?" Sergeant Claiborne asked immediately. His movements were quick, almost reflexive, as he scrunched a small piece of paper in his hand, enclosing it securely in his fist. I made a conscious effort not to stare, pretending not to have noticed his sudden action. A part of me regretted not entering the room a few moments earlier, or forgoing the formality of knocking. Had I witnessed the exchange firsthand, I might have understood better. *Was the Sergeant showing something to Louise, or had she passed the paper to him?* The possibilities swirled in my mind.

"Yes," I responded, keeping my tone neutral. "He's on his way now."

Without a word, Sergeant Claiborne rose from his seat, walking past me towards the door. His departure was swift, almost abrupt, and he didn't spare Louise even the slightest backward glance.

As we both stood in the corridor, an air of uneasiness enveloped us. The tension was palpable, a silent acknowledgment of the unspoken questions hanging between us.

The Sergeant remained silent, his demeanour closed off. I, too, stayed quiet, not daring to probe further.

"She's in there," I informed Karl as he finally arrived, my voice steady but carrying an underlying current of urgency. "You ready for this?"

Karl, looking a bit worse for wear but composed, nodded in affirmation. As he moved towards the interview room door, however, Sergeant Claiborne intervened abruptly. With a swift motion, he slammed his hand hard against Karl's chest, effectively halting him. The Sergeant's eyes bore into

Karl's with an intensity that was almost palpable. I couldn't help but think, *He is totally busted.*

"I'd normally tell you to go home," Claiborne said, his voice firm and unwavering. "But she has a unique story to tell, and she's determined to tell it to you, specifically."

I watched, surprised at the Sergeant's leniency. It was unlike him to allow any officer to remain at work in such an obviously hungover state, let alone conduct an interview. The situation piqued my curiosity even further. *What was so special about this case that warranted such an exception?*

Unique? The word echoed in my mind. From what I had gathered during the initial interview with Louise, there didn't seem to be anything particularly 'unique' about her story. *What had transpired between Louise and Sergeant Claiborne while I was away?*

Entering the room, I took a seat opposite Louise, my mind still racing with questions. The sight of her filled me with a mix of empathy and intrigue. She sat there, a picture of worry and distress. Her head was hung low, a posture of defeat, and her eyes - when they occasionally met mine - revealed the depth of her pain and anxiety.

Moments later, Karl stepped into the small, windowless room, the air heavy with anticipation. His entrance was marked by a slight hesitation as he took in the scene before him. "Louise Jeffries?" he asked, his voice tinged with a note of surprise as he recognised the woman sitting at the interview desk.

Louise turned slowly to face him, her expression solemn and unreadable. She remained silent, her gaze steady and unwavering.

"Oh my god! It is you!" Karl's voice cracked with incredulity, his usual composure slipping momentarily as he grappled with the unexpected recognition.

"You two know each other?" I couldn't hide my surprise at just how familiar they appeared to be with each other.

"You could say that," Karl replied, his voice low. He then turned his attention to Louise. "How have you been?" he asked, his tone carrying a mix of concern and a hint of awkwardness.

Louise's expression remained unchanged, her face a mask that revealed nothing of her inner thoughts or feelings. "Please, Karl. Sit," she said, her voice firm yet tinged with a note of urgency.

As Karl pulled up a chair and sat down opposite Louise, the way they looked at each other suggested a deep familiarity, a connection that went beyond a mere acquaintance. I couldn't help but feel like an outsider, intruding on a personal moment.

"I've already told most of this to your colleague here," Louise said, gesturing towards me. Her eyes briefly met mine, then flicked back to Karl. "But I wanted to tell you directly."

I watched Karl closely, observing his reaction. His face turned a dark shade of serious, a look I had never seen on him before. It was clear that whatever connection they shared, it was significant. "I'm listening," he said, his voice steady but intense. He looked directly into Louise's eyes, bracing himself for whatever revelation she was about to share.

The room seemed to shrink around us, the tension palpable. I sat quietly, aware that I was witnessing a crucial piece of the puzzle about to unfold, one that could potentially change the course of the investigation, which had barely begun.

Louise's demeanour was measured, her words deliberate, as she gathered herself to speak. There was a solemn gravity in her voice that conveyed the seriousness of her situation. "My son, Kain, is missing." She paused, letting the weight of her statement sink in. "And so is my brother," she added, her voice barely more than a whisper.

"Jamie?" Karl inquired, his tone careful, as if he was treading on fragile ground.

"Yes," Louise nodded, her affirmation carrying a sense of deep worry.

"Are you sure?" Karl's question was gentle, almost hesitant, as if he was trying to grasp the full implications of her statement.

Louise's response was detailed, her voice growing slightly more anxious. "I haven't been able to contact him for several days now. He hasn't answered any of my calls or responded to any of my texts. I've driven past his house a few times and his car is still in the driveway," she explained, her face clouding with concern.

"Have you knocked on the door?" Karl's question was straightforward, his detective instincts kicking in.

Louise's eyes started to become watery, a clear sign of her emotional turmoil. "I didn't at first," she admitted, her voice tinged with regret. "Maybe if I had, Kain would still be around," she said, her voice cracking slightly as she wiped at her eyes with the back of her hand.

"I'm confused, Louise. You said you didn't knock on his door at first. But you have now?" Karl pressed for clarification.

"Yes," she confessed, her admission laced with a sense of resignation. "But he didn't answer. I only spoke to Luke."

I observed this exchange silently, noting the complex web of emotions playing across both their faces. Louise's distress was palpable, and Karl's concern for her was evident, even as he maintained his professional demeanour.

Karl's question cut through the tension in the room. "Who is Luke?" he asked, his tone indicating that he was also struggling to piece the puzzle together.

"Luke Smith," Louise replied, her voice laced with unmistakable disdain. "His partner."

"Oh. I didn't realise," Karl responded, a hint of surprise in his voice.

"It's okay," Louise said, her tone resigned, as if she had expected this lack of awareness from Karl.

I watched as Karl took a deep breath, clearly processing the new information. It was evident he was trying to connect the dots, his mind working overtime. "Louise," he began slowly, cautiously. "I'm still quite confused. Please, start again from the beginning," he requested.

"The beginning?" Louise echoed, her surprise evident.

"Just of the disappearance," Karl clarified, trying to narrow down the focus of her narrative.

Just of the disappearance? I questioned internally, my curiosity piqued. *What the hell is that supposed to mean?* The depth of their history seemed more extensive than I had initially thought. I found myself wondering about the extent of Karl's past involvement with Louise Jeffries and Jamie Greyson. In all the time Karl and I had worked together, he had never mentioned either of them. It had to be something significant, given the growing concern etched on his face.

I sat quietly, observing the exchange intently. Karl's usually unreadable expression was now clouded with concern, his brow furrowed as he listened to Louise. The situation was clearly more complex than a simple missing persons case. There were layers here, personal connections that I hadn't anticipated, which seemed to add a weight to Karl's demeanour that I hadn't seen before.

As Louise prepared to delve into her story once more, I braced myself for the revelations to come, aware that whatever she was about to share could shed light on not only the case but also on Karl's past.

As Louise recounted the events of the past few days, I could sense her growing anxiety. "It's been four days since I've been able to get in touch with Jamie, and it's unusual that he doesn't answer any of my calls. I was concerned about his relationship with Luke and so I sent Kain over to their house to check on him. But I haven't heard from Kain since," she said, her voice wavering slightly with each word.

A surge of pity washed over me as I observed Louise struggling to maintain her composure. Her lower lip trembled as she fought to keep her emotions in check, a clear indication of the turmoil that was churning inside her.

"I'm really worried that something terrible might have happened to them," Louise continued, barely managing to keep the tears at bay. Her eyes, glimmering with unshed tears, conveyed the depth of her fear and concern.

Karl, reacting with a compassion I hadn't often seen in him, reached across the small interview table. He gently took hold of Louise's trembling hands, offering a silent gesture of support. "When did you send Kain?" he asked, his voice soft yet firm.

"Two days ago. It was first thing in the morning. I've contacted his friends, but nobody has seen or heard from him since he left our house. His fiancée swears to me she hasn't heard from him either. So, after driving past Jamie's house several times, yesterday morning —" Louise's voice trailed off, her emotions finally getting the better of her.

I watched, feeling a mix of professional detachment and personal empathy. The room felt charged with Louise's distress, and I could see the impact it was having on Karl. His usual stoic demeanour was replaced with one of genuine concern. The complexity of the situation was becoming more apparent with each passing moment.

As the conversation unfolded before me, my mind began to drift, tangling itself in a web of speculation and unanswered questions. *Jamie and Luke?* My thoughts echoed inquisitively. *Had there been a past between Jamie and Karl?* I found myself eyeing Karl, my gaze sweeping over him with a newfound curiosity. He did harbour some mysteries, that much I had always sensed. But considering the passion and frequency of our intimate encounters, the thought of Karl being gay seemed far-fetched... *or was it?*

My internal musings were abruptly interrupted by Karl's voice. "And do you believe him?" he asked.

Shit! Believe what? I berated myself internally for getting lost in my thoughts and not paying full attention to the conversation.

"Well, he did seem to be pretty upset about it all. But even if it were true and Jamie had gone to Melbourne, that doesn't explain why he won't respond to any of my calls or messages," Louise was saying, her voice tinged with a mix of confusion and skepticism.

"And did Luke say anything about Kain?" Karl pressed further.

Kain... who was Kain again? I mentally scolded myself for the lapse in concentration. *Oh yes, her son.* I quickly scribbled down the details, ensuring I didn't miss any more crucial information.

It was unlike me to let my focus waver during such a critical moment in an investigation. But the potential implications of the connection between Karl and this case had thrown me off balance. I resolved to put aside my personal conjectures and concentrate on the task at hand. This case was rapidly unfolding into something more complex than I had initially anticipated, and every piece of information was vital. I needed to stay sharp and attentive, focusing on the facts and evidence, rather than getting lost in the maze of personal entanglements and possibilities.

"Not really," Louise continued, her voice laced with a mixture of uncertainty and frustration. "He just said that Kain never made it around. He said he hadn't seen him since last Christmas."

None of this was adding up in my mind. "None of this makes any sense at all," I interjected, speaking up for the first time since we had started this interview. I was partly hoping that my comment might encourage Louise to reiterate some of the details I had missed while lost in my thoughts.

"No. It doesn't," Karl agreed. He stood up, his movements deliberate and professional. He motioned for Louise to do the same. "Thank you for coming in, Louise," he said. "Detective Lahey and I will write up our notes and open an investigation immediately. We'll keep you informed of our progress. I'm sure we'll be in touch very soon."

Shit! No, Karl! I missed the important bit! I silently lamented, wishing I could communicate my frustration to him without words.

"Thank you, Karl," Louise said, her voice cracking with emotion.

"Detective Lahey will take you to a more comfortable room where you can write up your formal statement," Karl instructed.

I breathed a sigh of relief. A second chance at redemption. And, if I played my cards right, perhaps an opportunity to gently probe for more information – not just about the case, but about Karl and Jamie's history as well.

"This way, please," I said, gesturing to Louise with a professional yet empathetic demeanour, guiding her out of the interview room. As we walked, I mentally prepared myself to carefully navigate this delicate situation. I needed to be attentive and astute, ready to pick up on any subtle cues or information that Louise might share. This was not just about solving a case anymore; it was also about understanding the hidden connections and secrets that seemed to be woven into its fabric.

The small, sparsely furnished interview room was steeped in a silence that felt heavy with unspoken words and hidden truths. The only sound was the steady scratch of Louise Jeffries' pen as she scribbled her formal statement. I sat across from her, feeling the starkness of the room pressing in on us. The sterile white walls seemed to close in, creating an atmosphere that was both clinical and foreboding. A single window, high up and barred, allowed a sliver of daylight to filter in, casting long shadows across the table.

"How long have you lived at Jeffries Manor?" I inquired, my voice casual yet laced with a professional curiosity. Watching Louise hastily write down her account, I struggled to maintain focus. The monotonous rhythm of her pen was hypnotic, and I found my thoughts drifting, making me restless and bored.

"I'm only forty-seven," Louise snapped, her response abrupt, her tone sharp. She didn't even glance up from her work, her focus solely on the pages in front of her.

"Sorry. I wasn't suggesting... I was just..." I stammered, trailing off awkwardly. Realising my question might have been misinterpreted as prying or insensitive, I let a few more minutes pass in a tense silence.

Desperate to alleviate the tension and perhaps uncover something new, I ventured another question, hoping to steer the conversation back on track. "You two sound like you have a bit of a history," I commented, striving to maintain a nonchalant tone.

"What do you mean?" Louise responded quickly, her voice tinged with defensiveness.

"Oh, just the beginning of the disappearance," I replied, echoing Karl's earlier words in an attempt to lighten the mood and possibly encourage her to divulge more details.

However, Louise's reaction was not what I had anticipated. Her head shot up, and she fixed me with a stare that was a mix of confusion and annoyance. "I don't know what you are suggesting, detective, but I suggest you stay focused," she snapped, her voice edged with anger.

A flush of embarrassment crept up my cheeks. "Of course. Sorry, Mrs. Jeffries," I replied sheepishly, feeling rebuffed. My attempt at casual probing had clearly backfired, leaving me to tread more carefully around Louise's guarded demeanour. I resolved not to let my personal curiosity interfere with the professional integrity of the investigation.

"What a bitch," I muttered under my breath, the sting of Louise's parting remark still fresh as I navigated the corridor towards Sergeant Claiborne's office. The hallways of the precinct echoed with the subdued hum of daily activity, a sharp contrast to the tension-filled room I had just left.

I reached the Sergeant's office and knocked lightly, expecting the usual gruff call to enter. Instead, the door creaked open slightly under my touch, revealing an empty office. The absence of the Sergeant was unexpected, leaving me momentarily uncertain.

Without much further thought, I stepped inside, my gaze drawn to the Sergeant's desk. It was a testament to his methodical nature, every item meticulously placed, exuding a sense of order and discipline. But amidst this orderly setup, a small, scrunched-up piece of notepaper on the desk caught my eye. It seemed oddly out of place in the otherwise immaculate environment.

As I reached across the desk to place Louise's file in the in-tray, curiosity overtook me. The paper looked vaguely familiar, stirring a sense of intrigue and unease within me. A cold shiver trickled down my spine, but I tried to dismiss the feeling. *It's just an old, crumpled piece of paper after all*, I reassured myself.

Yet, the nagging question lingered in my mind: *But what if it isn't?* The paper seemed to hold a significance that went beyond mere trash. I couldn't shake the feeling that it was more than it appeared.

Cautiously, I glanced over my shoulder towards the door. It was now half open, but my position blocked a clear view of the desk. If someone were to walk in, they wouldn't immediately see what I was doing. The thought gave me a sense of daring.

Slowly, my hand reached out towards the crumpled piece of paper, my heart thumping in my chest. *Just a small peek*, I rationalised. *It wouldn't hurt, would it?* The air around me seemed to crackle with suspense, and I could feel a bead of sweat forming on my forehead, betraying my inner conflict.

"This is ridiculous," I hissed under my breath, chastising myself for this lapse in professionalism. Just as my fingertips almost brushed the paper, I retracted my hand as if it had been burned. Dropping the manila folder onto Sergeant Claiborne's desk, I made a move to head to the door.

"Ah, shit!" I exclaimed quietly, realising my mistake. I should have placed the file in the in-tray. Glancing back at the desk, the folder stood out like a sore thumb amongst the meticulously arranged belongings. It was a glaring sign of my distraction, and I knew Sergeant Claiborne would notice it immediately. The thought of appearing distracted or careless gnawed at me.

I paused, my inner turmoil intensifying as I chewed the inside of my lip, considering the enigmatic piece of paper lying just a few inches from where I had carelessly dropped the folder. I poked my head outside the room, scanning the corridor for any signs of approaching officers. It was deserted, a rare moment of solitude in the usually bustling precinct.

I let out a nervous exhale. With calculated care, I gently pushed the door closed, leaving just a small gap. It didn't need to be completely closed; just enough to shield me from the view of any potential passersby.

"Please stay closed," I whispered to the door, my hand gesturing in a stop-sign motion, as if it could comprehend my desperate plea.

I tiptoed back to the desk. I wasn't sure why. It wasn't as though anybody would hear my boots on the carpet. I picked up the file that I'd left so indiscriminately on the desk. Taking a deep breath, I shoved the file under my armpit.

The thrill of the forbidden mingled with a sense of urgency. I knew I was crossing a line, but the potential importance of the paper's contents was too compelling to ignore. With a final glance towards the slightly ajar door, I turned back to the desk, my resolve solidifying.

My heart pounded as my fingertip hesitantly touched the edge of the crumpled paper, sending an electric rush of adrenaline surging through my arm. It felt like I was defusing a bomb, not simply touching a piece of paper. I noticed my heart thumping wildly, as if trying to escape my chest, and a nervous giggle escaped my lips. What a totally ridiculous situation I had gotten myself into.

With a held breath, I quickly snatched up the paper, eager to unveil its secrets.

"What the hell are you doing?" a booming voice erupted behind me, startling me so fiercely that my knee banged against the edge of Sergeant Claiborne's desk. The manila file slipped from the loose grip of my armpit, spewing its contents across the floor in a cascade of fluttering papers.

"Shit!" I exclaimed, my heart skipping a beat. I whirled around to confront the source of the interruption. "What the hell did you do that for, Glen?" I demanded, trying to mask my agitation and buy myself some precious seconds.

Glen's dry laugh only served to heighten my irritation. "I just came to put this file on the sergeant's desk," he responded nonchalantly, holding up the file in his hands.

"Oh, you too?" I asked, trying to sound casual while my heart raced. I bent down to gather the scattered papers, my movements deliberate and controlled.

"Yeah," Glen replied, his tone dismissive as he nudged me aside with his chubby leg to make space for himself at the desk. "I heard Claiborne has asked all detectives to let him read their case files before anything is formally filed."

"Oh?" I murmured, my mind racing. While Glen was preoccupied with his task, I seized the opportunity. I quickly folded the small piece of now somewhat smoothed-out scrap-paper and discreetly slid it into my pocket. I then proceeded to collect the remaining papers, haphazardly stacking them back into the file, acutely aware that I wasn't paying any attention to their original order.

Glen, seemingly oblivious to my internal panic, casually dropped his file into the in-tray. "I think he just wants to do a little check of his own before the auditors arrive next week," he mused aloud.

"Well, that makes sense," I agreed, my voice steady despite the turmoil inside me. I placed my own file in the in-tray on top of Glen's, hoping my feigned nonchalance was convincing.

Walking with Glen out of the office, I carefully pulled the door closed behind us. Once we were out of sight, I quickly dried my sweaty palms on my trousers and tried to calm my racing heart. My mind was a whirlwind of thoughts and emotions.

Shit! I berated myself internally, the realisation of my recklessness hitting me like a wave. *What the hell did I just do?* I had taken a significant risk, and now the unknown contents of that crumpled piece of paper were burning a hole in my pocket. The gravity of my actions weighed heavily on me as I walked alongside Glen, my mind preoccupied with what the paper might reveal and the potential consequences of my impulsive decision.

LEADS

4338.209.4

As I stepped back into the main office, the bustle of police activity buzzed around me. I approached Karl, who was deep in thought, his focus laser-sharp on the task at hand. "Where do you want to start this investigation?" I asked, effectively wrenching him from his reverie.

Karl looked up, momentarily startled, then rose from his chair, which had seen better days. The fabric was worn, bearing the imprint of countless hours spent piecing together cases. He moved towards a section of the wall that had become his makeshift workspace. A single piece of butcher's paper was stuck there, an island amidst a sea of notes, pictures, and files that cluttered the wall. "I've been putting a bit of a timeline together," he said, his voice tinged with a thoughtful, almost contemplative tone.

"On that?" I couldn't help but ask as I meandered towards his desk, eyeing the paper with a mix of curiosity and skepticism. The wall looked like the chaotic mind of a detective made tangible.

Karl simply shrugged, a hint of defensiveness in his gesture. "What? I wanted to get my thoughts out before they disappeared," he explained, his voice a mix of earnestness and slight embarrassment.

"Oh, come on, Senior Detective," I replied with a grin, trying to lighten the mood. "Give yourself a little more credit," I added, amused by his uncharacteristic foray into what looked like a detective's version of arts and crafts.

"So... what have you timelined then?" I asked, genuinely curious about his approach.

Karl's gaze returned to the wall, his eyes scanning the makeshift timeline. "Not a lot," he confessed, his eyes lingering on the wall that represented our limited understanding of the case. "We know from this," he pointed to a skinny-headed, armless stick figure near the start of the timeline, "was the last time Louise heard from her brother. This second figure," he continued, indicating another stick figure further along the timeline, "is when she sent Kain to check on them."

"And the third one?" I queried, unable to resist a smile at Karl's unexpected artistic expression.

"That's Louise coming to visit us today," he answered, a touch of seriousness returning to his voice.

"Of course," I said, scrunching my nose playfully. I should have guessed that one. As I watched Karl, I couldn't help but admire his methodical approach. He might have his flaws, but there was no denying his skills as a detective. His ability to logically piece together events and observations was commendable.

"We should start by checking their bank accounts," Karl concluded decisively, his mind already shifting gears to the next phase of our investigation.

No sooner had he voiced this decision than he turned on his heels and set to work. His sudden movement and determination were characteristic of Karl; once he had a plan, he wasted no time in putting it into action. I quickly followed suit, my mind already racing with the possibilities of what we might uncover through their financial records.

Having secured access to both Jamie and Kain's financial records, despite the less-than-accommodating attitude of the bank manager, Karl and I settled into the task of combing through the accounts. Karl focused on Kain's financial activities while I pored over Jamie's bank records. The records were surprisingly sparse, offering little in the way of substantial leads. Nothing jumped out at me as particularly significant or telling.

"Well, that was a fruitless exercise," Karl sighed after a while, his voice laced with frustration.

I didn't respond immediately, still engrossed in Jamie's bank statements. The numbers and dates swam before my eyes, but they failed to paint a coherent picture or offer any meaningful insight.

Karl continued, breaking into my concentration, "Unless Kain has additional investments and finances secretly stashed elsewhere, which I highly doubt given how generous his parents seem to be, he has very simple spending habits, and, frankly, not much money. There's no indication that he purchased plane tickets or jumped on the ferry to Melbourne. But…"

My head snapped up at that. "But?" I echoed, my interest piqued. It wasn't like Karl to leave a thought unfinished.

"Looks like Kain is a fan of the game Candy Crush. There are a few small transactions from the game at around 11:00 P.M. on the night before he visited Jamie, but I don't see how that's going to help us determine what happened after he saw Jamie. If he ever did see him, that is."

I mulled over this new piece of information. "You don't think he did?" I asked, trying to gauge Karl's thoughts on the matter.

Karl shrugged slightly, his expression thoughtful. "I'm not sure yet."

His uncertainty resonated with me. The lack of details we were uncovering seemed to lead to more questions rather than answers.

"Well, I might have something," I declared, a flicker of hope igniting within me as I reached the end of my perusal of Jamie's bank statements. I grabbed the last statement with a sense of urgency and thrust it towards Karl. "There, look at the last transaction," I insisted, my finger pressing down on the page, highlighting the specific entry I wanted him to notice.

"Possibly," Karl murmured, his eyes scanning the transaction details. His reaction was cautious, a slight nod accompanying his scrutiny, but he clearly wasn't as convinced as I was.

"Possibly?" I couldn't hide my incredulity. "Only possibly? This is huge!" The discovery had set my heart racing, the implications of it unfolding in my mind like a crime novel.

"But it doesn't prove anything, nor give us any real information to go on," Karl reasoned, ever the pragmatist.

"He totally drained his bank account in a single transaction three days ago!" I countered, my voice rising with excitement. "Louise is clearly justified in suspecting some sort of foul play." I paused, taking a deep breath to steady myself. The thrill of the chase was getting to me. "I reckon that Luke Smith killed Jamie, then Kain caught him covering up the body, so Luke killed him too," I hypothesised, my mind running wild with the possible scenario. *This could be my first major breakthrough in a murder investigation*, I thought. I could feel it in my bones.

"Sarah!" Karl snapped, his voice sharp, cutting through my train of thoughts like a knife.

I went silent, stung by the abruptness of his tone. As much as I was falling for him, and I was – teetering on the edge of admitting deeper feelings – Karl's short temper was something I struggled with. It was one of those traits that made him both infuriating and endearing in equal measure. However, after my brief interaction with Louise, I couldn't help but wonder if there were deeper, darker reasons behind his often fiery temperament.

Then, there he was, lost in his thoughts again, standing in silence as his brilliant mind whirred away. He was completely absorbed, seemingly unaware of his surroundings. I watched him, waiting anxiously for the right moment to interject. I knew all too well that timing was crucial with Karl. Interrupting him at the wrong moment could be disastrous, akin to startling someone in a deep dream right on the precipice of a nightmare.

Suddenly, Karl's voice broke the silence. "Aha!" The word escaped his lips spontaneously, a rare slip that betrayed no conscious intention on his part.

"What?" I seized the opportunity, curious to know what had sparked his sudden exclamation.

Karl, however, seemed oblivious to my question, continuing his internal deliberation. I waited, watching him intently as he mentally pieced together the puzzle. Finally, he seemed to snap back to reality. "Sarah," he said, his voice now calm and focused. "If we can find Kain, he'll lead us straight to Jamie."

"Are you sure?" I questioned Karl, genuinely surprised by his sudden assertion. Keeping up with his rapid-fire thinking was often a challenge, especially when most of it remained unspoken, swirling in his head like a private whirlwind of deductions and hypotheses.

I sometimes wondered if Karl assumed I had telepathic abilities, considering how rarely he shared his thought process with me. If only he knew that I was far from possessing any secret mutant powers or sorcery. Life as a detective would certainly be a lot easier if I did.

"Jamie has all the skills to go off the grid if he wants to. That'll make him hard to pin down on our own. We need Kain. He's the one who can lead us to Jamie," Karl explained with a certainty that seemed to come from a deep well of logic and reasoning.

Go off the grid? The phrase hung in the air, and I wanted to delve deeper into that thought, but Karl was already ahead of me, his mind racing forward. I had to focus to keep pace with him, mentally noting every piece of information, every clue.

Karl's ability to weave together disparate threads into a cohesive narrative never ceased to amaze me. His insights often proved invaluable, and I respected his methods, even if they were sometimes frustratingly enigmatic.

"I don't think you're going to find anything, but if Jamie has that much cash, he could have purchased plane tickets without leaving an online record. I want you to follow up with both the Hobart and Launceston airports to check whether either Jamie or Kain have boarded any flights in the last five days," Karl instructed, his voice laced with a mixture of determination and urgency.

"Okay," I responded, a hint of uncertainty in my voice. I was still trying to fully grasp the direction Karl's plan was taking.

"And when you're done with that, given Kain's ute is missing, go and check with the ferry service. There's a chance they could have made it to the mainland."

"I'm on it," I said, nodding with enthusiasm. This was the part of detective work I loved – the thrill of chasing down leads, the adrenaline of the hunt. "And what are you going to do?" I asked, driven by curiosity.

Karl paused, his gaze distant as he contemplated his next move. "I'm going to visit Luke Smith."

I couldn't hide my surprise at his response. It was unusual for Karl to approach a key suspect alone; we always did these things as a team. "But—"

"Time is of the essence here, Sarah. If my hunch is wrong and you're closer to the mark, then Jamie and Kain are in danger, and we have to divide and conquer," he explained, his tone firm and final.

"Fine," I replied, masking my disappointment and resisting the urge to further challenge his decision. I ran my hands down my pants, feeling the edges of the folded scrap paper hidden in my pocket. A reminder of the secret I had yet to unravel. *Anyway, you've got your own investigating to do*, I reminded myself, feeling a surge of apprehension mixed with excitement.

"This is bloody ridiculous!" The words burst out of me like a dam breaking, my frustration hitting its peak as I slammed the phone's receiver back onto its cradle with more force than necessary. My ears were still ringing from the monotonous hold music that had been my only companion for what felt like an eternity, over half an hour. All that time, just waiting, waiting, waiting for my call to be transferred to someone, anyone, in airport security. The inefficiency of it all was beyond infuriating; it was maddening.

In a huff, a storm brewing inside me, I pushed myself away from the desk. My movement was a bit too forceful, more a reflex of my mounting irritation than a conscious decision. The chair I was in went careening backwards, seemingly with a mind of its own, hurtling towards the bookshelf crammed with files and faded photographs. For a split second, I saw myself causing a disastrous domino effect, but I managed to catch myself just in time, narrowly avoiding a collision. My sudden, abrupt movement drew a few curious glances from my fellow officers. I could feel their eyes on me, probably wondering what had gotten into me, but I was too wrapped up in my own bubble of irritation to care.

With my head held low, a futile attempt to mask the annoyance that I was sure was written all over my face, I marched across the room. Each step was more determined than the last. I needed to get this sorted, and wasting time on hold with a faceless entity at the other end of the line wasn't helping anyone, least of all me.

I approached Officer Ellen Lowe, the very epitome of nonchalance as she sat at her desk, seemingly engrossed in something far more interesting than work. Slumping down in the visitor's chair next to her, I could feel the weight of the day pressing down on me, making my movements heavy and tired.

"Go away, Sarah, I'm busy" Ellen's voice cut through the air, raspy and tinged with the unmistakable gravelly tone of a dedicated smoke enthusiast. Her words were blunt, yet I wasn't deterred.

"No, you're not. You're looking at Facebook." I pointed out, a hint of playful accusation in my tone. I could see the top of a cat meme just visible on her screen, *typical Ellen*.

Ellen, with an air of mock indignation, closed her browser. "What do you want?" she huffed, her eyes finally meeting mine, expressing a mix of annoyance and curiosity.

"I need you to follow up on some information from the Hobart and Launceston airports for me. You've got great relationships with them. You'll get results quicker than I will," I said, laying on the flattery a bit thick. It was an age-old tactic, but effective, especially with Ellen.

"Fine," she replied dryly, her expression unchanging, but I could tell she was mildly pleased with the compliment.

"Great." I handed Ellen the file containing all of our case notes on the Jamie Greyson investigation. "You'll find everything you need in there," I added, pointing to the first page where I had meticulously listed key information and questions. I knew Ellen preferred a succinct summary over wading through pages of notes.

Ellen glanced at the file with a blank expression, clearly hoping for more verbal guidance to avoid the task of reading through everything. I sighed inwardly but obliged.

"Essentially, all I need you to do is find out if Jamie Greyson or Kain Jeffries boarded any flights in the last few weeks," I explained, trying to keep it as simple as possible for her.

"Should be simple enough." Her response was non-committal, but I knew she would get it done.

"Thanks, Ellen. I owe you," I said, rising from the chair, feeling a small wave of relief wash over me.

"You mean you still owe me," Ellen corrected me, a slight smirk playing on her lips.

"Exactly!" I replied with a forced chuckle. As I took several steps back towards my desk, eager to escape before Ellen could change her mind or add to my already long list of debts to her, a sudden thought stopped me in my tracks.

"Oh, and Ellen," I said, twisting back to look at her.

"What?" Ellen's response was curt, her patience clearly wearing thin.

"Can you check the same with the Spirit of Tasmania, please?" I threw in the last request, knowing full well it might be pushing it, but it was necessary. Without waiting for a reply, I turned and walked away, my mind already racing ahead to the next task.

PAPER REVELATION

4338.209.5

As I walked through the front door, the familiar, somewhat comforting creak of its hinges barely registered in my mind, preoccupied as it was with the events of the day. The moment I crossed the threshold into the sanctuary of my home, I felt a slight easing of the tension that had been coiled tightly within me. Moving almost automatically, I made my way to the kitchen, the heart of my little world where chaos and order often danced a precarious tango. Without a second thought, I tossed my keys onto the bench, hearing the familiar clatter as they landed amidst the miscellany of daily life.

Turning my nose up in mild disgust, my eyes fell upon the dirty dishes that had claimed dominion over the bench tops. They sprawled out in an unruly fashion, a testament to the hurried, harried meals of the past few days. Despite the annoyance they sparked in me, I couldn't muster the energy to tackle them just yet. Instead, I found myself reaching for a glass, an action as instinctive as breathing, and filled it with water from the tap. The sound of the water hitting the glass was oddly soothing, a mundane melody in the symphony of domesticity.

I carried my glass of water with a careful, almost reverent grip, as if it were a vessel of tranquility amidst the storm of my thoughts. Entering the dining room, I was greeted by yet another familiar sight - a pile of wrinkled, unironed clothes that seemed to mock my lack of time and energy. With a sigh, I pushed them aside, the fabrics whispering their own tales of neglect as they crumpled further under my touch. I placed my glass down carefully on the table, creating a small, clear space in the chaos. For a moment, I just stood there, the weight of the day bearing down on me, my eyes resting on the still surface of the water, finding a moment of peace in its simplicity.

For the first time since I had unceremoniously stuffed it into my pocket earlier, my fingers reached for the roughly folded scrap of paper I'd surreptitiously taken from the sergeant's desk. The very act of touching it sent a flutter of butterflies dancing a waltz in my stomach, their wings fluttering in a rhythm of anticipation and anxiety. *How could such a small, insignificant piece of paper wield the power to cause me such nerves?* I wondered, my thoughts a mix of curiosity and apprehension.

With a carefulness that belied my inner turmoil, I unfolded the scrap, smoothing it out on the dining table in front of me. The paper felt fragile under my fingers, like a secret waiting to be unveiled. I leaned in, my eyes scanning the content, a frown creasing my forehead. *Is that it?* I asked myself, a tinge of disappointment colouring my thoughts. The paper bore only two words, so simple, yet their meaning was enigmatic, shrouded in mystery. *All the tension, the sneaking around for this?* I felt cheated somehow, my mind wrestling with the anticlimax.

Sighing, I pushed a small stack of case notes off my laptop with a sense of resignation and flipped it open. The sound of the case notes hitting the floor was a stark reminder of the realities of my job, but this... this was something else, something that had piqued my curiosity against my better judgement. My expectations had plummeted, but the intrigue had rooted itself too deeply to be ignored. *It wouldn't hurt to do a quick Google search*, I rationalised, trying to justify my actions.

I waited impatiently as the machine groaned and whirred through its long-winded start-up routine, the sound seemingly in sync with the slow ticking of the clock on the wall. When it was finally ready, I opened an internet browser with a mixture of skepticism and a lingering thread of hope. "Well, here goes," I muttered to myself, an attempt at encouragement.

I glanced at the two words again, their simplicity belying the complexity of emotions they stirred in me. Typing them into the search bar, I did so carefully, methodically, as if each keystroke was a commitment to uncovering whatever mystery they held. My fingers paused momentarily before hitting 'Enter', a brief moment of hesitation before diving into the unknown.

A quick browse through the first page of search results revealed only one direct match that seemed relevant. My heart rate quickened slightly as I clicked on the top link, a tiny spark of hope igniting within me. Within seconds, a webpage materialised on my laptop screen, the bold heading "Killerton Enterprises" emblazoned across the top. I leaned in, my eyes scanning the text as I read through the few short pages of content. Each word, each sentence, I absorbed with a mixture of skepticism and a faint glimmer of hope.

Killerton Enterprises appeared, at first glance, to be just another large company. Based out of California, its primary focus was on construction – solid, mundane, and seemingly unremarkable. The company's history, dating back to its founding by Francis Killerton in 1874, unfolded on the screen. It was a tale of generational leadership, passed down through the years, with the current CEO, Bill Killerton, presumably a descendant of the founder.

As I read, a part of me couldn't help but feel let down. *Had the Sergeant and Louise really only been talking about a construction company?* I wondered, a frown etching itself deeper on my brow. My instincts screamed that there had to be more to this company than what met the eye. *But what?* The question hung in the air, unanswered, the webpage offering no hints of anything beyond the ordinary.

Feeling a mix of disappointment and frustration at the lack of excitement or answers, I glanced at the time. The clock on the wall reminded me of another commitment, snapping me back to reality. It was my night to cook dinner for grandmother, and I had promised her I wouldn't bail this time. Closing the laptop with a soft click, a sense of urgency washed over me. Grandmother would be waiting, each passing minute increasing her hunger and anticipation.

TENDER

4338.209.6

"What are you doing, Sarah?" Jane's voice, unexpectedly close behind me, made me jump slightly. Her approach had been as silent as a highly trained ninja, which was frankly impressive for a woman of her age. Turning around, I saw the familiar twinkle of mischief in her eyes, a trait that had never diminished with the years.

"I'm cooking you dinner," I replied, trying to sound more confident in my culinary skills than I felt. The kitchen, usually Jane's domain, felt like unfamiliar territory under her watchful gaze.

"Looks to me like you're burning it," she answered. Jane made a grand show of peering into the pans and pots on the stove, her theatrical scrutiny making it clear that she found my cooking efforts less than satisfactory. My grandmother always had a flair for the dramatic, and it hadn't waned in the slightest.

"Go and sit in your recliner," I told her, a gentle firmness in my voice. "It won't be long now." I ushered her towards her favourite chair, the one she claimed was moulded perfectly to her form after years of use.

As I watched her amble towards the recliner, I couldn't help but feel a sense of gratitude, mixed with a touch of relief. Her interruption was timely, pulling me away from the distracting thoughts that had been impeding my already questionable cooking skills. I wasn't a great cook at the best of times, a fact that had always been a slight sore point for me. Jane had spent countless hours over the years, patiently trying to teach me the art of cooking. The warm, laughter-filled memories of those lessons floated back to me, a stark contrast to the present where I was fumbling with basic recipes.

Despite all her efforts, and my earnest attempts, it seemed like a truth I had to accept: my cooking would never equal my grandmother's. Her dishes were more than just food; they were a blend of love, tradition, and a lifetime of experience, something I was still far from achieving. Yet, as I glanced back at her settling into her recliner, I couldn't help but feel a wave of affection. Cooking for Jane, even with my limited skills, was a small way of giving back some of the love and care she had always showered upon me.

"Have you heard from Oscar lately?" Jane's voice floated in from where she now sat comfortably ensconced in her recliner. The chair was like a cozy nest, nestled in one corner of the small living room, surrounded by an array of family photos and knick-knacks that told the story of our lives.

"No, I haven't heard from him for a few months," I responded, my voice carrying over the sizzle and clatter of the kitchen. This wasn't unusual for Oscar and me; our lives often took us in different directions, leading to long stretches where we wouldn't speak. There was no underlying tension, just the simple ebb and flow of life and distance.

"Oh," was all Jane said in reply. Her voice held a note of disappointment, but she didn't press further. I heard the soft click of the radio being turned on, filling the living room with a gentle hum of music, a soothing background to the evening.

In the kitchen, I continued clanging away, my focus now entirely on finishing the meal preparations. I was determined to salvage what I could from the slightly scarred culinary attempt. The aroma of cooking, a blend of both successful and not-so-successful elements, filled the air. I stirred and tasted, adjusted seasonings, and kept a wary eye on anything that looked like it might burn.

Cooking always had a way of grounding me, pulling me back from the whirlwind of thoughts that often occupied my mind. As I moved around the kitchen, the familiar actions brought a sense of calm. There was something therapeutic about the process, a way to express care and love, even if the results were less than perfect.

The mention of Oscar lingered in the back of my mind, a reminder of the family ties that were so important, yet often stretched thin by the demands of life. I made a mental note to reach out to him, to bridge the gap that time and distance had created. For now, though, my focus was on the meal before me and the cherished company waiting in the other room.

"Come on then. Let's get you up to the table," I said, setting aside my culinary concerns for a moment. I approached my grandmother, and gently, with a care that had become more necessary over the years, I helped her out of the chair. Her movements were slower now, each one measured and deliberate, a stark contrast to the sprightly woman she once was. I guided her to the table, ensuring she was seated comfortably before I took my own seat opposite her.

"Smells good," Jane remarked, a small, encouraging smile playing on her lips.

I smiled back at her, my heart warmed by her eternal optimism. Jane always had a way of finding the silver lining, even in the most ordinary of moments. There was no doubt in my mind that her compliment was more a show of support than a culinary critique. After all, she was a woman of uncompromising honesty, and to say that the meal looked good would surely break a lifelong tradition.

"You better get to eating it then," I replied, trying to keep the atmosphere light. I shovelled a forkful of mashed potato into my mouth, only to immediately splutter. The pepper, it seemed, had been a bit too enthusiastic in its contribution to the dish.

Noticing my reaction, I quickly reached for the small jug of gravy on the table. The brown, viscous liquid seemed like the only hope to salvage the over-seasoned meal. "I think you might need some more gravy," I said, pouring a generous amount over Jane's potatoes in a valiant effort to temper the peppery assault.

Jane let out a light chuckle, a sound that was now laced with the croaks and crackles of age, each one telling a story of the years she had lived. Despite the wear in her voice, the warmth and affection it carried remained unchanged.

We ate the meal in a companionable quiet, the only sounds being the soft clinking of cutlery and the occasional murmur of appreciation. I noticed how every week, Jane was getting slower at feeding herself, the simple act requiring more effort and concentration. Keeping up a conversation while eating seemed to exhaust her, but that was alright. Our silent meals had become a time of unspoken understanding and shared contentment.

Sitting there with Jane, in the warmth of her small space, the simplicity of our meal took on a deeper significance. It was in these quiet, unassuming dinners that the true essence of our relationship revealed itself. They were less about culinary successes or failures and more about the connection we shared. It was a bond woven from years of shared history, unspoken love, and understanding. As we sat together, the importance of just being in each other's presence, surrounded by the comforting embrace of family, became crystal clear. The quality of the meal paled in comparison to the richness of our togetherness.

"They said they told you about the cancer," Jane's words sliced through the peaceful atmosphere like a bolt out of the blue.

The suddenness of her statement caused my fork to slip from my fingers, clattering loudly against the plate. The sound seemed to echo in the room, marking a stark contrast to the serene quiet that had enveloped us moments before. Startled, I watched as specks of the over-peppered potatoes scattered across the table, like little reminders of life's unexpected and often messy turns.

I looked up, my gaze meeting Jane's. Her eyes, always so gentle and understanding, now sparkled with an uncharacteristic intensity under the soft yellow light that bathed our dining table. There was a resilience in her gaze, a strength that belied her years and the weight of the news she carried.

As I sat there, absorbing the weight of Jane's words, a tumultuous surge of emotions wrestled within me. The news of her cancer was like a sledgehammer, shattering the illusion of permanence that we so often take for granted. It was a stark, unyielding reminder of life's fragility and the relentless march of change. Yet, amidst this maelstrom of feelings, a resolve took root within me. I was determined to be strong, to stand as the unwavering pillar that Jane had always been throughout my life. My heart ached with a profound desire to protect her, to somehow shield her from the cruel onslaught of illness that now threatened to engulf her.

"Oh, Jane," I whispered, the words barely escaping my lips. "What am I going to do without you?" The question hung in the air, laden with fear and vulnerability. I could feel the tears brimming in my eyes, each one a testament to the love and bond we shared. I wanted to let them fall, to release the dam of emotions welling inside me, but I held them back. I needed to be strong for Jane, to offer her the same steadfast support she had always given me.

Jane reached out and took my hand. Her grip was surprisingly strong, a grip that spoke of a life lived with determination and resilience. She held on firmly, and with her free hand, she tenderly wiped at a single tear that had managed to escape, now glistening like a crystal on the brink of my eyelid.

"Come and sit with me," she said softly, her voice imbued with warmth and an unspoken understanding of the turmoil I was experiencing. She squeezed my hand again, a gesture that conveyed so much more than words could. It was an invitation, a plea, and a comfort all at once.

Without a word, I stood and assisted Jane down from the dining table. She moved with a careful, measured grace that spoke of years carrying wisdom and experience. I couldn't help but smile gently as she shuffled over to the couch, settling herself at the far end. It was her preferred spot, a cozy corner of the world where she often retreated when her recliner wasn't the chosen throne.

I retrieved Jane's favourite small blanket from the recliner, a soft, well-worn piece that seemed to hold as many memories as it did warmth. Draping it gently over my grandmother's lap, I was struck by the simple act of care, a role reversal that was both bittersweet and heartwarming.

"Thank you, Sarah," Jane said, her voice soft yet rich with gratitude.

Kicking off my shoes, I curled up on the couch, finding a comforting sanctuary as I rested my head on Jane's lap. In that moment, lying there, I allowed myself a brief respite from the stoic front I had been maintaining. The tears I had been fighting back began to threaten once again, but the gentle stroke of Jane's wrinkled hand through my hair was a soothing balm. Her fingers were warm against my scalp, surprisingly soft for a woman who had lived through so much. Each tender touch seemed to say, "It's okay, I'm here."

I smiled, feeling a wave of affection and gratitude wash over me, as Jane carefully pushed a long strand of my fringe back behind my ears. It was a small, maternal gesture, but it held a universe of love and understanding.

"I think you need this," Jane said, with a knowing smile. She handed me a floral handkerchief, its fabric soft and familiar, a token of countless moments of comfort provided over the years.

I took the hanky, dabbing lightly at my eyes, trying to stem the tide of emotions. Lying there, looking up at my grandmother, I was enveloped in a profound sense of connection. Her presence, her touch, her understanding, they all weaved together to create a tapestry of love and support that had always been the bedrock of my life. In that moment, I realised the invaluable gift of having someone who knew me so well, someone who could offer solace without needing words to fill the silence. The room was quiet, save for the soft, comforting sounds of our shared presence, a reminder that sometimes, just being together was enough.

"So, when do I get to meet him?" Jane's question, casual yet loaded with curiosity, caught me slightly off guard. I could feel her eyes on me, twinkling with a mix of mischief and genuine interest.

"Meet who?" I feigned ignorance, although deep down, I knew exactly who she was referring to. It was a feeble attempt at deflection, but I wasn't quite ready to dive into this conversation.

"This dream man of yours that makes you moan so much." Jane's words were blunt, her tone teasing, a reminder of her knack for cutting straight to the heart of matters, no matter how personal.

"Jane!" I couldn't help but chide her, a mix of embarrassment and amusement colouring my tone. "It was only once!" I protested, feeling my cheeks warm at the memory of that unguarded moment.

"Mmm," Jane hummed, her voice laced with playful skepticism. "Only once that you remember."

My relationship with Jane had always been open and honest, but when it came to Karl, I hesitated. I was reluctant to burden her with the complexities of my work life, and Karl, unfortunately, fell squarely into that category. There was a part of me that wanted to keep that world separate, to protect her from the stress and worries that came with my job.

"His name is Karl," I finally admitted, feeling a sense of resignation mixed with a strange relief. Admitting his name felt like crossing a threshold, acknowledging that Karl was more than just a work issue. There was a small part of him, I had to concede, that had started to transcend the confines of my professional life.

"Just Karl?" Jane's inquiry was gentle, probing but not insistent. She had always had a way of asking questions that invited honesty without demanding it.

"Just Karl," I confirmed. I was still trying to figure out where Karl fit into my life, and saying his name out loud to Jane somehow made it more real, more tangible.

Jane didn't push any further. She had always known when to press and when to let things be, a skill honed through a lifetime of caring for others. In her silence, there was an understanding, an unspoken acceptance that I would share more when I was ready. Her presence, warm and comforting, was a reminder that she was there for me, no matter what or who came into my life. In that moment, the couch felt like the safest place in the world, a sanctuary where I could be myself, vulnerabilities and all, surrounded by the unwavering support of my grandmother.

"Hey, do you know the Jeffries?" I ventured, breaking the comfortable silence that had enveloped us. As I asked the question, I was acutely aware that I was bending my self-imposed no-work rule. But in this case, curiosity overcame protocol... and Jane didn't need to know that bit.

"Jeffries," Jane echoed thoughtfully, her voice a murmur of recollection. "It's not ringing any bells." She furrowed her brow slightly, a sign that she was sifting through her vast repository of memories.

"Louise Jeffries," I added, watching closely as my grandmother closed her eyes, concentrating. I could almost see the cogs turning in her mind, searching through decades of names and faces.

"Oh, do you mean Louise Greyson?" Jane suddenly asked, her eyes springing open with the clarity of recovered memories.

I was about to dismiss the connection, but then it struck me. If Louise's brother was Jamie Greyson, then it would stand to reason that Greyson was her maiden name. I couldn't help but feel a twinge of frustration at the complexities names could introduce into my investigations. Life, and particularly my job, would indeed be so much simpler if people didn't change their names out of marital tradition and notions of romance.

"Possibly," I replied, pulling myself back from my cynical reflections on the nature of marital name changes. "She has a brother called Jamie Greyson."

"Yes! That's it!" Jane exclaimed, a spark of recognition lighting up her features. "I remember her now. Your mother was good friends with Louise's mother before she died. I believe your father used to work with her father, too. I forget his name."

I paused for a moment, mulling over this new information. "I don't know it either," I admitted. This unexpected connection between my family and the Greysons was something I hadn't anticipated. It made me wonder about the myriad of untold stories and forgotten connections that lay hidden in the past, and how they intertwined with the present.

"Come to think of it, Jamie comes to visit me every few months," Jane's words drifted into the air, casual yet laden with an unforeseen significance.

"Really?" I asked, my surprise evident. The revelation that Jamie Greyson, a person of interest in my investigation, was a visitor to my own grandmother's home was both startling and intriguing. The lines between my personal and professional life seemed to blur a little more with each passing moment.

Our conversation, however, was abruptly cut short by the insistent beeping of an alarm from the kitchen. The sound was sharp, a mechanical reminder of the routines and responsibilities that structured our lives.

"Oh," Jane remarked, a note of resignation in her voice, "Time for me to take my bedtime pills."

At her words, I felt a twinge of disappointment that our conversation had been interrupted. Yet, this feeling was quickly overshadowed by a deeper sense of care and responsibility. My grandmother's health and well-being were paramount, and her nightly medication routine was not something to be taken lightly.

As I stood up, ready to assist her, a wave of reflection washed over me. In the grand scheme of things, the urgency of my investigation paled in comparison to the precious, finite moments I had with Jane. The inexorable passing of time was a constant reminder that I couldn't hold on to my grandmother forever. But for now, in this moment, I could be with her, support her, and cherish the time we shared. Jamie Greyson and the mysteries surrounding him could wait. Right now, my priority was my grandmother.

4338.210

(29 July 2018)

THE JEFFRIES

4338.210.1

Slumping in my chair, I found myself gazing dismally across the landscape of my desk. It was a chaotic jumble of paperwork, an ever-growing mountain that seemed to spill over every available surface. The sight was a stark reminder of the less glamorous aspects of my job. Each document, each case file, was a story in itself, a puzzle waiting to be solved, yet the sheer volume felt overwhelming. There it was, the not-so-glamorous reality of detective work - less about the thrilling chase and more about wading through an endless sea of paperwork. "Become a detective, they said. Action-packed, they said." The irony of those words didn't escape me as I sat surrounded by a heap of mundane, yet crucial, administrative tasks.

In desperate need of a more pleasant sight, I let my eyes drift towards Karl's desk. It stood empty, his chair unoccupied, a silent testament to his recent habitual tardiness. *He's late again*, I mused. It had become something of a norm for Karl, my partner in anti-crime, to arrive at the station at his own leisurely pace each morning. His predictable unpredictability was both an annoyance and an oddly comforting routine in the chaos of our daily lives.

Suddenly, a jolt of realisation struck me. "Ah, shit!" I exclaimed aloud, a sharp note of frustration colouring my voice. My hand, which had reflexively slipped inside my trouser pocket in search of my phone, found nothing but emptiness. Once again, I was without my phone, a vital tool in my line of work and a lifeline to the outside world. Its absence sent a ripple of irritation through me, accompanied by a begrudging acknowledgment of my own forgetfulness.

Welcoming the distraction, which only served to further encourage my tendency to procrastinate, I stood up from my desk. With a determined stride, I navigated through the maze of corridors that crisscrossed the second floor of our old, red brick building. The structure, aged and weathered, seemed to hold as many secrets as the cases we worked on. My objective was simple yet oddly comforting: locate my misplaced phone, something I had managed to do already once this week.

As I neared the alcove which housed the station's lifts, a flicker of movement in the periphery of my vision caught my attention. Instinctively, I paused and turned my gaze down the hallway. My eyes drifted through the square windows of the doors leading to the small, enclosed courtyard. There, I saw the Sergeant engaged in a conversation with a woman. His hand was gently holding her elbow, an action that spoke of familiarity and comfort. He pulled her closer and leaned in, whispering something in her ear. The intimacy of the gesture was striking, out of place in the sterile environment of the police station.

I squinted, trying in vain to make out the movement of his lips, to glean some hint of the conversation's nature. Then, recognition hit me like a bolt of lightning. *The Sergeant is talking to Louise Jeffries.*

What does he want with her? I pondered, my mind racing with possibilities. Louise's relaxed posture and the closeness she allowed with the Sergeant indicated a level of comfort and trust between them. This raised more questions than answers. *What was their relationship? Did it tie into the investigation?*

Desperate to overhear their conversation, I cautiously moved several steps down the corridor. I was mindful of each movement, ensuring it was measured and silent, so as not to draw their attention. The need to remain unseen, to eavesdrop without being discovered, felt like a dance – a careful balancing act between curiosity and discretion.

As I inched closer, straining to catch snippets of their exchange, I felt a twinge of guilt for spying on them. Yet, the detective in me knew that any piece of information could be crucial. This unexpected encounter between the Sergeant and Louise Jeffries could potentially shed light on the murky waters of the case. My heart pounded with a mix of adrenaline and anticipation as I edged closer, determined to uncover the nature of their secretive meeting.

"Sarah!" The sudden call of a raspy voice from behind startled me, jolting my entire body with surprise. My heart skipped a beat as I stood frozen, my covert surveillance interrupted. The voice's gravelly tone was unmistakable, and it made me apprehensive. I feared that my poorly concealed attempt at espionage had been discovered, potentially unraveling my discreet observation of the Sergeant and Louise Jeffries.

Slowly, with a reluctance that weighed down each movement, I turned around. The corridor, with its dull lighting and the echo of distant footsteps, suddenly felt more confining. As the old, raspy voice called out again, "Sarah!" I braced myself for the confrontation.

With a heavy sigh, I faced Ellen. She appeared even crankier than usual this morning, her displeasure evident in the tight set of her jaw and the furrow of her brow. As she hurried along the corridor towards me, she pushed her wide-framed glasses back up onto her flat nose, a habitual gesture that spoke of her impatience.

"Where have you been? Answer your damn phone! I have been trying to call you all morning," Ellen scolded, her voice sharp and tinged with irritation.

I stammered, struggling to find the right words, my mind still partially back in the courtyard with the Sergeant and Louise. This interruption was the last thing I needed. Not now. There was a frustrating sense of helplessness, knowing that any further chance of eavesdropping was slipping away. I could feel the opportunity to uncover more about their interaction evaporating with each second I spent dealing with Ellen.

"I, uh... I think I've left my phone in my car," I replied, my voice a mixture of feigned casualness and underlying urgency. Slowly, I shuffled my feet across the old tiled floor, each step deliberate. I turned my back on Ellen, a strategic manoeuvre that would force her to move and allow me to regain my visual on the courtyard. The need to observe the Sergeant and Louise Jeffries was like an itch, growing more insistent by the second.

"Again?" Ellen's voice croaked with a mix of disbelief and mild annoyance. "You may need to start strapping that phone to your arm... or perhaps your forehead."

"Um... sure," I replied distractedly, my attention divided. Ellen's less than helpful suggestions barely registered in my mind. My focus was on the courtyard, on the fading opportunity to glean something valuable from the Sergeant's interaction with Louise.

"Did you... ah... did you need something, Ellen?" I asked, a hint of impatience creeping into my voice. I was desperate to hurry her along, to return to my clandestine observation.

"Me?" Ellen responded incredulously, her tone suggesting that she found my question absurd. "I think it is you that needs something."

"Huh?" I said, my face scrunching in genuine confusion. My mind was elsewhere, and I hadn't fully processed her words. The situation was becoming increasingly frustrating, my desire to return to the courtyard clashing with the need to address Ellen's concerns.

Ellen huffed, her frustration evident in the multiple, loud exhalations that followed. I found myself involuntarily holding my breath, trying to avoid the pervasive smell of cigarettes that seemed to cling to Ellen like a second skin. The scent was reminiscent of a fifty-year-old ashtray, a harsh reminder of her lifelong habit. The stench, combined with the urgency of my curiosity about the Sergeant and Louise, made the interaction increasingly unbearable.

"Well in case you were wondering, which obviously you weren't," Ellen began, her tone laced with a mix of sarcasm and mild annoyance. She stood there, arms crossed, embodying her typical no-nonsense demeanour that was as much a part of her as her ever-present cigarette scent. "I've heard back from both the Hobart and Launceston airports."

"Oh," I responded, a bit taken aback by the sudden shift in conversation. My surprise seemed to only intensify Ellen's glare, as if she could sense that my attention had been elsewhere.

"They've no record of either Jamie Greyson or Kain Jeffries boarding any flights in the last two weeks," Ellen declared, a hint of satisfaction in her voice. It was clear she was pleased with her investigative efforts, even if the results were less than thrilling.

"Oh," I said again, this time feeling a wave of disappointment wash over me. The information was a dead end, another puzzle piece that refused to fit into the ever-complex picture of my case. "Thank you anyway, Ellen," I added, my voice tinged with gratitude but my mind still racing with thoughts of the Sergeant and Louise.

"I'm not done yet! I've also checked with the Spirit of Tasmania ferry. They have no records of either of them travelling to Melbourne. But they have promised to send down a hard drive with the last few weeks of security footage, just in case," Ellen continued, undeterred by my attempts to rush her.

"Send down?" I repeated. The idea of transporting sensitive data via a hard drive didn't sit well with me. "Well, that's hardly a secure way to transfer data."

Ellen tilted her head, giving me a wry smile. "We are in Tasmania, remember. I don't think you need to worry," she reassured me, a touch of amusement in her tone. "They've given it to Duncan to bring with him from Devonport. He should arrive sometime today. Can't wait..."

Of course, Ellen would find Duncan attractive, I thought, rolling my eyes internally. It was just like her to mix personal interests with professional matters.

"Thanks for the update, Ellen. That's great work," I told her, offering a brief, but genuine smile. Despite my impatience, Ellen's information was valuable, and her diligence deserved recognition.

"I know," Ellen replied with a hint of pride, turning to walk away. Her confidence was a hallmark of her character, one that often bordered on arrogance but was usually backed up by her solid ability to garnish information from those who would otherwise be reluctant to give it up.

It took me a moment to register that Ellen, with her usual knack for diversion, had skilfully redirected our conversation, effectively drawing my attention away from the Sergeant once again. Spinning around, a sense of urgency propelling my movement, I found myself peering through the small window of the door, only to be greeted by the sight of an empty courtyard. The opportunity to uncover whatever was happening between the Sergeant and Louise Jeffries had slipped through my fingers. "Shit," I muttered under my breath, a mix of frustration and disappointment clouding my thoughts.

Impatiently, I stood waiting for the lift, my foot tapping rhythmically against the tiled floor in a futile attempt to hasten its arrival. The sound echoed hollowly in the empty corridor, a stark reminder of the time being wasted. The wait felt interminable, each passing second stretching out endlessly, further fuelling my irritation.

Finally, the lift arrived with a soft ding, its doors sliding open with a mechanical smoothness that contrasted sharply with the turmoil of my thoughts. I stepped in, riding down to the ground floor, my mind racing with what I had missed, the potential leads that could have been gleaned from observing the Sergeant's interaction.

Once on the ground floor, I didn't waste a moment. I marched out of the building with purposeful strides, determined to retrieve my phone from my car. The crisp air outside hit me, a sharp contrast to the stifling atmosphere of the police station. My car was parked a short distance away, and with each step, I felt a growing resolve to make up for lost time.

I slumped back in my chair, a heavy sigh escaping my lips as I surveyed the relentless array of paperwork sprawled across my desk. The stacks seemed just as towering and impenetrable as when I had last looked, a testament to the never-ending nature of detective work. No matter how much effort I put in, the paperwork was like a hydra - for every file I completed, two more seemed to take its place.

My gaze shifted, almost involuntarily, towards Karl's desk. *Still empty*. I closed my eyes, seeking a momentary escape from the daunting sight of my desk and its ever-growing mountains of work. As I embraced the darkness behind my eyelids, vivid images of the Sergeant and Louise Jeffries sprang to life in a burst of technicolor. They played out like a private cinema show, their whispered conversation and subtle gestures looping in my mind, fuelling my curiosity and frustration.

Unable to resist the pull of this curiosity, I blinked away the vivid daydream and leaned forward to boot up my ageing computer. The machine groaned and whirred into life, its various lights flickering in a hesitant dance. The sound of its inner workings was worryingly loud, a reminder of the countless hours it had endured as my faithful companion in crime-solving.

Once the computer had settled into a steady hum, I opened the central database with a sense of determination. My fingers moved with purpose, typing in 'Louise Jeffries' into the search bar. I hit 'Enter' with a force that echoed my resolve.

The screen flickered briefly before displaying the disappointing message: *No results found.* A wave of frustration washed over me. It was a dead end, another brick wall in an investigation that seemed full of them. I leaned back in my chair, my mind racing with questions. *Where else could I look? What other avenues were left unexplored?*

I typed in a second name, *Kain Jeffries*, my fingers moving swiftly over the keyboard with a mix of hope and skepticism.

No results found, the computer's response flashed on the screen once more, echoing its previous unhelpfulness. A knot of frustration formed in my stomach. The lack of results left me feeling like I was grasping at straws, trying to piece together a puzzle with missing pieces.

Determined to find something – anything – I opened a web browser and entered *Jeffries Manor* into the search bar. My eyebrows raised in surprise as the screen filled with a cascade of direct hits. Multiple pages, in fact. This was more like it. I leaned forward, my curiosity piqued, as I began to sift through the results.

Jeffries Manor had a rich and long history, dating back to the early 1800s. The details of its construction captivated me. The original owner, William Jeffries, was not just a name on a plaque but a hands-on man who had physically contributed to the building of his magnificent home. There was something intriguing about reading of a man from history who had put his own sweat into his legacy.

William Jeffries' story unfolded on my screen like a novel. From young convict to successful entrepreneur, his life read like a tale of rags to riches. His marriage to Madelyn Bally, a woman nearly twice his age, added a layer of intrigue. But it was his mysterious disappearance shortly after the birth of his son, William Jeffries Jr., that really caught my attention. The dramatic turn of events seemed to be lifted straight from a crime thriller.

As I finished reading through the first page of results, the further I delved, the more outlandish the theories became. I found myself skimming over sites dedicated to an assortment of conspiracy theories about William Jeffries' disappearance. The involvement of his wife, Madelyn, was a recurring theme. But the strangest page, authored by Rita Larkin, was on another level entirely. Aliens, swirling electrical portals, and weekly extra-terrestrial visitors tied to the Jeffries family – it was the kind of stuff you'd expect in a sci-fi movie, not a historical search.

Aliens! I scoffed internally, shaking my head in disbelief. There certainly are a lot of crazy theories out there. Working in law enforcement, I'd encountered my fair share of bizarre stories and wild speculations. This was just another to add to the list. As much as I loved a good mystery, I knew the difference between fact and fiction. *And this, undoubtedly, was fiction.*

EVIDENCE

4338.210.2

"Who was that?" I asked, a hint of annoyance creeping into my voice as Karl walked back into our shared open plan office. He held a pen in his hand and his notebook was still open, his eyes scanning the notes he had scribbled during the interview I had been notably excluded from. I watched him, feeling a mixture of irritation and curiosity. It always irked me when Karl went rogue on tasks. For the most part, he was a decent communicator, someone I could rely on. But there were times, just like now, when I felt the urge to give him a good, metaphorical slap for leaving me out of the loop.

"Jenny Triffett," Karl said nonchalantly, his voice betraying nothing of the significance of the interview. He was always like this, playing his cards close to his chest, not giving away information easily.

"Who's Jenny Triffett?" I probed further, my curiosity determined despite my annoyance. I leaned slightly forward in my chair, trying to catch a glimpse of his notes.

"The wife of Nial Triffett, of course," Karl replied, as if it were the most obvious thing in the world.

I couldn't help but give him a firm, playful thump on the shoulder. It was part of our dance, this back and forth. I knew that if I wanted to extract any meaningful information from Karl, I had to play along with his irritatingly cryptic responses. It was a game of patience and persistence, one that I had become quite adept at playing.

Despite my frustration with his secretive ways, a part of me couldn't deny the effectiveness of our dynamic. Karl's method of holding back information often led to more in-depth discussions and analysis, something that was crucial in our line of work. As detectives, piecing together the puzzle was our job, and Karl, in his own maddening way, was often the one who provided the most intriguing pieces. I settled back into my chair, mentally preparing myself for the task of unraveling the mystery of Jenny Triffett and her connection to our case.

"We need to advise the officers to be on the lookout for Nial Triffett's work ute," Karl stated, his tone serious. He looked up from his notes, his expression focused and intent.

"Why? What's up? Something else related to the investigation?" I asked, leaning forward in my chair, my enthusiasm piqued by the new development.

"I'm not sure yet," Karl replied, his brow creasing with uncertainty. "His wife said he went to visit a potential new client for his struggling fencing business yesterday and has now gone missing. But…"

I didn't let him finish. "Well, that definitely sounds like it could be connected," I interjected, my mind racing with the possibilities this new lead presented. "Do we know who he went to visit?" I asked, eager for more details.

"No," Karl said, frowning deeper. "And Jenny called the police last night. While they were there talking to her, she received a text message from Nial telling her that he would be late home and not to wait up for him."

I frowned back at Karl, skepticism creasing my forehead. "That does sound a lot more like a case of infidelity rather than a missing person, and the last time I checked being a slimy cheat wasn't actually against the law," I remarked, a hint of disappointment in my voice. The prospect that this might not be another lead for our investigation was disheartening. Still, a part of me reasoned, infidelity, while painful, was probably a better outcome for Jenny than dealing with a dead body. However, given the intensity that such situations often spiralled into, I couldn't help but think darkly that there might yet be a dead body involved in this whole mess. It never ceased to amaze me how often "crimes of passion" occurred, even in a place as seemingly tranquil as our state. The lengths people go to for sex, or love, or whatever they convinced themselves it was.

"You're right," Karl agreed, his tone indicating that he was still pondering the possibilities. "But I still think it might be worth us having a little bit of a dig ourselves. I'm sure Glen won't mind us helping him out a little." He sat down at his desk, a gesture that signalled he was settling in for some serious work. He placed his small notepad in front of him, the pages filled with his concise, scrawled handwriting.

I followed suit, standing behind him and peering over his shoulder at the notebook. Despite my initial reservations, I knew that any piece of information could be crucial, and overlooking even the smallest detail could be a mistake. Karl's instinct to dig deeper resonated with me; after all, our job was to uncover the truth, no matter how convoluted or hidden it might be.

"Glen's on the case?" I quipped, unable to resist a jab at our colleague. "God help that poor woman." My tone was light, but there was a hint of genuine concern there. Glen, while competent, had a way of complicating things that sometimes left us all wondering.

Karl chuckled at my comment, a brief moment of levity before he continued working on the database, his fingers moving with practiced ease. Within seconds of initiating the search, a match appeared on the screen. Efficiently, Karl scribbled the number plate details onto a yellow post-it note.

"Here, go put out a BOLO for Nial's ute for me," he requested, passing me the note. The simplicity of the task belied its importance. A BOLO – Be On the LookOut – could be critical in locating Nial Triffett's vehicle and, by extension, Nial himself.

I took the note from Karl, glancing down at the scrawled details. I read them aloud slowly, ensuring I had correctly deciphered Karl's often hard-to-read handwriting. "Tasmania's a small place. I can't imagine his ute staying hidden for long," I commented as I walked over to my own desk. The island's size played to our advantage in cases like these. It was hard to stay lost for long in such a tight-knit community.

Sitting at my desk, I felt a sense of anticipation. *This could be a quick investigation*, I thought. With a few keystrokes, I began the process of issuing the BOLO.

"Oh, Sarah. I almost forgot," Karl suddenly interjected, drawing my attention back to him. His addendum had a note of urgency, "Make a note to get a copy of Nial's phone records. Let's see if we can find out who he may have gone to visit."

"On it," I called back, acknowledging his request. Gathering phone records was a routine task, but it often proved to be a goldmine of information. Who Nial had been in contact with could lead us to his whereabouts or at least give us a clearer picture of his recent activities.

As Karl turned back to his computer, I saw an opportunity for a little more personal interaction, something I found myself increasingly looking forward to. "Hey Karl," I said, interrupting him. I walked over and casually sat myself down on the edge of his desk. I liked being close to him; there was something comforting about his presence. It reminded me of the subtle, affectionate nudges of my grandmother's late cat, how she would gently press her small, furry head against me. I positioned myself at an angle where, if Karl just swivelled his chair slightly, our knees would touch, almost imperceptibly.

"Found something already?" Karl asked, his attention now on me, though he hadn't moved his chair to close the small distance between us.

"Yes," I replied, a hint of hesitance in my voice.

"That was quick," he noted, a slight raise of his eyebrows showing his surprise.

"Oh, no. It's not about the Triffetts," I quickly clarified. "It's about Jamie and Kain. I meant to tell you earlier," I confessed, feeling a little guilty for not sharing the information sooner.

"Shit, Sarah," Karl exclaimed, his voice tinged with irritation. He swivelled his chair with such force that it startled me. I instinctively moved to dodge his knees as they spun around, narrowly avoiding a clumsy collision that would have been less like a gentle nudge and more akin to my grandmother's cat pouncing on me with claws unsheathed.

I shrugged off Karl's frustration, understanding his reaction but not letting it rattle me. "Ellen's spoken with both the Launceston and Hobart airports. There's no record of either Jamie or Kain having boarded a plane in the last two weeks," I reported calmly, maintaining my professional demeanour despite his evident annoyance.

"Which means they must still be in the State," Karl said, his tone shifting to one of eagerness. He leaned forward, his frustration momentarily forgotten as he focused. "At least that keeps our searching area fairly narrow." His expression then clouded over again with a frown, clearly piecing together the next steps in his mind. "What about the Spirit of Tasmania? Have you checked with them yet?"

Taking a deep breath, I prepared to fill him in on the latest development. "Yes. We've heard from the Spirit too. They have no records of Jamie or Kain having boarded in the last two weeks. But Duncan is bringing down a copy of their boarding security footage. They could have used aliases. And there is always the slim chance that they snuck on board," I explained, laying out all the possibilities, however remote they might be.

"Very slim chance," Karl agreed, nodding. "But very good work, Sarah. That's gonna keep you busy for a while."

I nodded in response, though internally, I wasn't thrilled at the prospect. The idea of trawling through countless hours of security footage didn't exactly fill me with excitement. It was one of those necessary but tedious parts of the job. The painstaking examination of video footage, looking for any sign of our suspects, was a daunting task. It required patience, sharp eyes, and an attention to detail that was often mentally exhausting.

I steeled myself for the long hours ahead, sitting in a dimly lit room, eyes glued to the screen, searching for that one crucial frame that could break the case wide open.

My head jerked upwards abruptly, my eyes snapping open wide in a desperate attempt to focus on the computer screen in front of me. The words blurred together, dancing just out of reach of comprehension. The exhaustion from the last few days was finally catching up with me, making even the simple task of reading feel like an insurmountable challenge.

Closing my eyes just a fraction, I rationalised that a brief power nap wouldn't hurt. *Surely, no one would notice.* I raised my arm, creating a makeshift pillow with my hand, and gently rested my forehead against the cupped tips of my fingers. *Just a few minutes*, I told myself, feeling my consciousness already starting to ebb away into a much-needed respite.

"Sarah!" A sharp voice boomed suddenly in my ears, rudely jolting me back to reality. My head slipped through my fingers, narrowly avoiding a graceless collision with the hard surface of the desk beneath it.

"I'm awake!" I exclaimed, perhaps a bit too loudly, my voice echoing through the open plan office. Quickly, I rubbed at the crook in my neck, trying to ease the discomfort from my awkward sleeping position. I scanned the office for Karl, assuming he was the one who had so abruptly disturbed my brief slumber. To my surprise, Karl was seated at his own desk, several meters away, engrossed in his work. He appeared calm and focused, seemingly oblivious to my abrupt awakening.

But he's so far away. Is he really the one that woke me up? I questioned internally, my mind still foggy from the shock of being awoken. The idea of Karl startling me from such a distance seemed improbable. I couldn't picture him shouting across the room, then hurriedly returning to his desk as if nothing happened.

As I swivelled my chair back to face the front of the desk, the first thing that caught my eye were two long, muscular legs. My gaze involuntarily travelled upwards, tracing the thick hairs that entwined themselves along the man's legs, creating a chaotic yet mesmerising pattern across his well-defined calves and thighs. It was a sight that both unexpected and oddly captivating.

"Duncan," I said, finally lifting my eyes to meet his face. There he stood, towering over me, the epitome of physical fitness. "It's so good to see you again. And so much of you," I quipped, a hint of playful sarcasm in my tone as I gestured towards his surprisingly short shorts and tight shirt. It was an outfit that left little to the imagination and emphasised his athletic build.

Duncan responded with a wide, charming smile. "You too, Sarah," he said warmly. "It's been a while. I wasn't sure whether I should call you." His voice was friendly, but there was an undercurrent of something else – perhaps uncertainty or a gentle reproach.

I could feel my face heat up, turning a shade of scarlet that I couldn't hide. "I'm so sorry, Duncan," I quickly apologised, the memory of my broken promise to call him after the last work dinner party flooding back. "I got distracted. My grandmother is unwell." The words tumbled out in a rush, a mixture of embarrassment and genuine concern for my grandmother.

"I'm so sorry to hear that," Duncan replied, his tone shifting to one of earnest concern. "Your grandmother is a lovely woman." There was a sincerity in his voice that touched me, reminding me that there was more to Duncan than just his physical presence.

"Thank you," I responded softly to Duncan, feeling a need to recenter myself. My gaze drifted away for a moment as I took a deep breath, trying to steer the conversation back to work-related matters. "Did you bring the hard drive?" I asked.

"Oh, yes, of course," Duncan replied, his tone business-like now.

I watched as he fumbled with the bag slung over his broad, toned shoulder. His athletic build was hard to ignore, but I tried to keep my attention on the task at hand.

"Here it is," he announced, producing a slim black box from his bag. It was barely larger than a mobile phone, a compact vessel of potentially crucial information.

"Two weeks' worth?" I inquired, accepting the hard drive from Duncan's hands. The weight of it felt significant, filled with the promise of hidden details and answers.

Duncan nodded, confirming, "Two weeks' worth. All accounted for."

"Great," I said, managing a soft smile. However, I noticed that Duncan's gaze lingered a bit too long on my chest, which made me slightly uncomfortable. His behaviour, although probably unintentional, was unsettling.

"That's all, thank you, Duncan," I said, hinting that it was time for him to leave. But he didn't seem to get the message and continued to stand there.

Seizing an opportunity to gently usher him away, I mentioned Ellen. "Uh. I believe Ellen was keen to see you too," I said, recalling our earlier conversation. Internally, I was grateful to Ellen for giving me an escape route.

"Really?" Duncan perked up, a bit too eagerly for my comfort.

Doing my best to appear serious, I nodded. "Oh, yes. I definitely remember her telling me how excited she was to hear that you were going to be visiting today. But, you know, I'm sure I remember her also saying that she had to go to court today. If you hurry, I'm sure you'll be able to catch her before she leaves."

"Oh, thanks," Duncan responded, suddenly motivated. "I guess I'd best be going then. Don't want to miss her!"

"Yeah. You'd better hurry," I reaffirmed. "Like, right now."

He straightened his shoulder bag and gave a short wave. "Bye, Sarah. It was great to see you again."

"See ya," I responded to Duncan with a quick, somewhat dismissive wave of my fingers. As soon as he was out of sight, I let out a sigh and rubbed my forehead, feeling a mix of relief and annoyance. Duncan, unwittingly, was a constant reminder of one of my personal rules: never be the most drunk at a work function. Unfortunately, it seemed everyone remembered more about that particular night than I did, especially Duncan, who harboured memories of a promise I had allegedly made – a special night he wouldn't forget. The irony was, I had absolutely no recollection of making such a promise. It wasn't that Duncan was unattractive – quite the opposite, really. But my lack of interest in him went beyond physical appearances; there was simply no spark there for me.

Picking up the hard drive Duncan had delivered, its weight was surprisingly hefty for its compact size. I was about to plug it directly into my computer when a moment of professional caution kicked in. I reminded myself that I was a police officer in a police station, and plugging in external digital devices carelessly ranked high on the 'stupid things that cause trouble' list we'd been constantly warned about. Then it struck me – why should I spend countless hours trawling through endless footage when I could leverage my resources more effectively? That's when the idea hit me. James, my favourite tech guy who also happened to be my first cousin, could do it for me. Not only would he complete it in a fraction of the time, but he'd use a more secure system too.

"Smart thinking, Sarah," I congratulated myself with a smile, feeling pleased with this strategic decision. Making my way to find James, I couldn't help but reflect on the convenience of having family in useful places. *It's funny*, I thought to myself, *how work can sometimes be the only place where you really talk to some family members. But hey, got to love family, right? Especially when they can make your job a whole lot easier.*

I wandered through what could only be described as the deep, dark dungeon of the station – the tech team's lair. Located in the basement of the old building, it was a world apart from the bustling, well-lit halls above. I always found it slightly ironic that the tech team, the ones responsible for handling some of the most advanced technology in the station, worked in such a seemingly archaic setting. They seemed to thrive down here, perhaps because the dim, cave-like environment reminded them of the apocalypse-themed video games they were fond of. To them, it was a sanctuary of sorts, a place where their technical wizardry could come to life.

The basement definitely wasn't my cup of tea, with its lack of natural light and the constant hum of machinery. Yet, I had to admit, there was something about the occasional visit here that I enjoyed. The few rooms that were occupied by the tech team were connected by a labyrinth of narrow, dimly lit corridors. These passageways were alive with the tiny, multi-coloured flashes of countless LED lights. Each flickering light, each quiet beep and whirr, signified something important – a piece of data flowing, a server operating, countless unseen processes that kept the station's digital heart beating.

Walking through these corridors, surrounded by routers, relays, and a plethora of other technical equipment, the names of which were a mystery to me, I couldn't help but feel a sense of intrigue. This was a place of unseen magic, where information was dissected and pieced back together, where clues were unearthed from the digital depths. The tech team, with their quiet efficiency and unassuming brilliance, were like modern-day wizards, weaving their spells in a world of zeros and ones.

As I approached James' workspace, I felt a familiar sense of appreciation for this hidden nerve centre of the station. Here, amidst the blinking lights and whirring machines, lay the potential keys to unlock the secrets of our latest case. I readied myself to hand over the hard drive, hoping that James and his team could work their magic and bring us one step closer to solving the enigma that lay before us.

James, seated amidst a nest of screens and cables, didn't take much convincing. He agreed to make my search through the security footage his top priority. The ease with which he accepted the task was a testament to his efficiency and dedication, qualities I had always admired in him. It also helped that we shared a familial bond, one that often made our professional interactions smoother and more straightforward.

Feeling a surge of happiness and confidence from this small victory, I strutted down the last stretch of the dimly lit corridor that led to the lift back up to what I jokingly referred to as 'civilisation'.

As I walked, my steps echoed slightly against the concrete walls, a rhythmic sound that matched my uplifted mood. There was a spring in my step, a feeling of accomplishment that came from knowing the hard drive was in capable hands. James and his team were the unsung heroes of many investigations, their technical expertise often providing the crucial breakthroughs we needed.

Reaching the lift, I pressed the button and waited, my thoughts lingering on the interaction with James. It was moments like these, where the pieces of the investigation started to align, that really solidified my love for the job. The thrill of the chase, the satisfaction of making progress, and the essential teamwork all wove together into the exciting and rewarding tapestry of detective work.

While I was lost in these reflections, I decided to make use of the waiting time. I confidently dialled Ellen's number on my phone. "Ellen, I'm glad you're back," I spoke, trying to sound as professional as possible, yet I couldn't completely mask the smug undertone in my voice. I had a hunch that Ellen had been on one of her frequent, and definitely unauthorised, cigarette breaks earlier when I had tried to visit her desk only to find it deserted.

"What is it, Sarah?" Ellen's voice came through the phone, her tone as dry as ever.

I dove straight into business. "I just wanted to check that you found the note I left on your desk. I need you to put in a request for Nial Triffett's phone records and issue an alert to all patrols to be on the lookout for his ute. All the details you need are on that note," I explained succinctly.

There was a brief pause on the other end. I could faintly hear the sound of papers being shuffled, the rustling indicating Ellen was rummaging through her desk. A part of me desperately hoped she would find the note quickly. The thought of having to revisit Ellen's desk, particularly right after one of her cigarette breaks, was not appealing in the slightest. The lingering smell of smoke that always seemed to envelope her was something I preferred to avoid.

"Yeah," Ellen finally said, her voice slow, almost as if she was relishing the act of searching. "I found it."

A wave of relief washed over me. "Thanks, Ellen," I said quickly, eager to end the call before any unnecessary small talk could begin. As soon as I hung up, I felt a sense of achievement. Despite the small hiccup earlier, I had managed to get the ball rolling on another crucial aspect of the investigation.

The lift doors opened, and I stepped inside, feeling a renewed sense of purpose. Every step taken was a step closer to solving the case.

THE DRIVER

4338.210.3

"There! Look!" I exclaimed, my attention suddenly captured by a car making a hasty exit from the bottle shop. The vehicle swerved sharply, coming perilously close to clipping a small, red hatchback parked at the side of the road. My heart raced at the near-miss, the thrill of a potential chase igniting within me.

"Shit! That was a close call," Karl breathed out, his eyes widening as he watched the scene unfold. The reckless manoeuvre by the driver was a glaring red flag, and both of us knew it.

"Random?" I asked, already knowing the answer but wanting to confirm with Karl. In situations like this, a random check could turn up anything from outstanding warrants to contraband.

"It would be irresponsible of us not to," Karl agreed, his face breaking into a wide grin that mirrored my excitement.

I grinned back at him, feeling a surge of adrenaline. "Here we go then," I said, the words laced with a bit too much glee. I reached for the controls and activated the red and blue flashing lights. The siren wailed briefly, piercing the air just long enough to signal the driver ahead that they had been spotted. I imagined the driver's reaction, no doubt begrudging and filled with annoyance, as they realised they were about to be pulled over.

Karl skilfully followed the silver Honda Civic, maintaining a safe distance as we trailed it. The driver, seemingly aware of our presence, eventually pulled over to the side of the main road that snaked through Glenorchy. Karl brought our unmarked police car to a smooth halt behind the Civic.

"You want to do the honours?" Karl asked, turning towards me with a knowing look. His voice carried a hint of amusement, as if he could sense my anticipation for this part of the job.

"Sure," I replied, my eagerness barely contained. There was something about these interactions, the unpredictability and the potential for discovery, that I found exhilarating.

"I'll do a plate check," Karl stated, already reaching for the laptop to run the vehicle's registration as I stepped out of the car.

As I approached the driver's side of the Civic, the window slid down smoothly. I composed myself, trying to maintain a professional demeanour despite the rush of excitement coursing through me. This was the moment of truth, the point of contact where anything could happen. It might be a routine stop, or it could spiral into something more. Either way, I was ready.

The driver, unaware of what was coming, was about to face the consequences of their reckless driving. I had seen enough careless behaviour on the road to know that these moments mattered, that they were essential in maintaining order and safety. The thought that this driver was in for a significant fine, and deservedly so, was at the forefront of my mind as I prepared to speak with them.

"License please," I instructed, adopting my serious, police officer voice. Despite my professional demeanour, I couldn't completely hide my surprise at seeing a rather attractive, young woman sitting in the driver's seat. It wasn't what I had expected, and for a moment, it threw me off slightly.

I watched as she reached across to the passenger side, her movements fluid as she rummaged through a leather handbag that was tossed haphazardly in the footwell. There was a casual elegance about her, even in this slightly flustered state.

"Did I do something wrong?" the woman asked, her voice tinged with genuine confusion and a hint of innocence as she handed over her driver's license. She seemed to believe she hadn't committed any infraction, which made my job a little more complicated. *Was this genuine ignorance, or was she playing a role?*

"Well, you almost hit a parked car back there when you turned out of the bottle shop," I explained, striving to keep my tone even and professional. I glanced down at the license she handed me. The photo matched the woman in front of me – Gladys Cramer, the name read. A good start, indeed.

As I held her license, a flicker of recognition sparked in my mind. *Gladys Cramer... Why does that name sound familiar?* I thought, racking my brain. There was something about it that resonated, a distant connection or a mention in passing that I couldn't quite place.

"Have you had anything to drink this afternoon?" I asked Gladys.

"No," Gladys replied confidently. "That's why I was out getting these lovelies," she added, patting the brown paper bag resting on the passenger seat.

Oh, Jesus... I thought, suppressing the urge to roll my eyes at her casual attitude. Her response suggested she didn't grasp the gravity of the situation, or perhaps she was just playing it cool.

"Gladys Cramer," I said, as I prepared the small breathalyser. "I just need you to blow into this tube here until I tell you to stop, okay?" I instructed, holding the device out to her.

Gladys nodded, showing her willingness to comply. She placed her dark, plum-coloured lips around the end of the white, plastic tube protruding from the breathalyser. There was something about her manner, a certain nonchalance, that piqued my curiosity even further.

"Okay, now blow," I directed her.

Gladys took a deep breath and exhaled loudly into the breathalyser. I observed her closely, noting that she didn't seem concerned in the slightest about the possibility of being fined. Her confidence was either a sign of innocence or a well-practiced facade.

"Stop," I instructed sharply when the breathalyser beeped, signalling that it had collected a sufficient sample. The air was thick with anticipation as the device processed the results. I leaned in, studying the display closely. My head tilted in confusion as I re-read the results. *Well, this can't be right*, I thought.

"One moment please, Ms. Cramer," I said, stepping back slightly from the car, my mind racing with curiosity.

Disappointment was etched on my face as I walked over to Karl's window. The breathalyser result had thrown a curveball into what I had assumed would be a straightforward stop. "Well, that's a bit odd. She's recorded a zero blood-alcohol reading," I reported, the perplexity evident in my tone.

"She?" Karl asked, his surprise mirroring my own.

"Yeah," I confirmed, handing him Gladys Cramer's driver's license. My fingers brushed against his as I passed it to him, a small but familiar exchange in our routine.

Karl examined the license closely. "Gladys Cramer," he read aloud, his brow furrowing with thought. "I think we might have a little problem."

"What is it?" I leaned in closer to the car, my curiosity now fully piqued. Karl's tone had shifted from surprise to something more serious.

"Is Gladys the only person in the car?" Karl inquired, looking past me towards the silver Honda Civic where Gladys sat.

"Yeah. Why?" I responded, a hint of impatience in my voice. I couldn't fathom where Karl was going with this line of questioning.

"This car belongs to Jamie Greyson," Karl revealed, and the significance of his words hit me like a ton of bricks.

"Shit!" The words burst out of me as I jerked back, narrowly avoiding a collision with the car door frame. My mind raced with the implications of Karl's revelation. The fact that this car belonged to Jamie Greyson transformed the situation from a simple traffic stop into a potentially vital lead. My heart pounded with the realisation that we might be on the brink of a significant breakthrough.

"Ok, what do you want me to do? Should I get my gun out?" I asked, instinctively reaching for my holster. The adrenaline was pumping, preparing me for any potential threat.

"No! Jesus, Sarah, what is it with you and your bloody gun?" Karl retorted sharply. "You wait here. I'll deal with her."

Reluctantly, I returned to my seat in the unmarked police car. I tapped the dashboard impatiently with the breathalyser, a physical manifestation of my frustration at being sidelined. I trusted Karl's judgment, but the detective in me wanted to be part of the action, to be in the thick of the investigation.

As I sat there, waiting for Karl to handle the situation with Gladys Cramer, a thousand scenarios played out in my head. Each one was a different version of how this could connect back to Jamie Greyson and our larger case. My gaze lingered on Karl as he approached Gladys's car, his movements calm and measured, a stark contrast to the turmoil of thoughts swirling inside me.

I took a deep breath, trying to temper my impatience. This was a crucial moment, and it was essential that we handled it correctly. The importance of teamwork, of trusting your partner, was never more evident than now. As Karl spoke with Gladys, I remained alert and ready to assist if needed, the wait both agonising and necessary.

"Well?" I couldn't help but press Karl for information as soon as he slid back into the driver's seat after his conversation with Gladys. My curiosity was like a fire, impossible to contain.

Karl, methodically taking his place behind the steering wheel and buckling his seatbelt, took his time before responding. There was a deliberate slowness to his movements, as if he was weighing his words.

"Well," he began, turning to face me with a grin that was both reassuring and slightly teasing. "It seems we are about to find Jamie Greyson."

"Where's the fun in that?!" I blurted out, my words a mix of genuine curiosity and a touch of disappointment. Of course, most of me hoped it was true for Jamie and Louise's sake – that we were close to resolving their situation. Yet, there was a small, admittedly selfish part of me that relished the thrill of the investigation, the chase. The possibility that it might be nearing its end was a bittersweet pill.

Karl started the engine, his expression turning more serious. "Not everything has to end with murder and crime," he reminded me, his voice carrying a tone of mild disapproval. It was a reminder that sounded like the kind of clichéd advice a schoolteacher might give, something about not following the crowd or the dangers of jumping to conclusions.

"I know, I know," I responded, feeling a twinge of complaint in my voice. I couldn't hide my eagerness for more action, more complexity. "But I haven't investigated a murder yet. I thought maybe this could be my first."

"Well, looks like you're about to become disappointed... Officer," Karl replied, his emphasis on the word 'Officer' driving home the point that my disappointment was somewhat misplaced given our profession. It was a gentle reprimand, reminding me that our job was ultimately about justice and resolution, not the thrill of the chase.

As we pulled away, I settled back into my seat. The prospect of finding Jamie Greyson and possibly concluding the investigation was a significant achievement, yet part of me couldn't help but feel a twinge of longing for the continued excitement and challenge of the hunt. This duality, the desire for both resolution and the thrill of the pursuit, was an inherent part of being a detective, a balance I was still learning to navigate.

We trailed closely behind Gladys, our unmarked police car making its way up the steep and winding Berriedale Road. From our vantage point, I kept a vigilant eye on her car. My gaze was sharp and focused, like a hawk surveying its prey, anticipating any slip-up. I didn't have to wait long for something to happen.

"You've got to be kidding!" I exclaimed in disbelief. "Does it look like Gladys is texting to you?" We had received extensive training on recognising the tell-tale signs of such behaviour, even from a distance. It was a skill I prided myself on having nearly perfected.

Karl squinted as he observed Gladys's actions. "Yeah. It sure looks that way, doesn't it?" he concurred.

"Lights or just keep following?" I asked, weighing our options. We needed to act, but it was crucial to handle the situation appropriately.

"Shit! We'd better pull her over," Karl decided, as Gladys's vehicle suddenly veered to the left, nearly scraping against the metal barrier lining the road. Her erratic driving was escalating, and we couldn't risk letting it go unchecked.

I activated the red and blue flashing lights for the second time that day, my heart pounding with a mix of adrenaline and frustration. But to our astonishment, Gladys didn't pull over. I watched, bewildered, as she continued her reckless behaviour, her car still swerving dangerously up the hill.

Deciding to escalate our response, I switched on the siren. The piercing sound cut through the air, finally capturing Gladys's attention and forcing her to acknowledge our presence. Reluctantly, she pulled her car over to the side of the road. Karl expertly manoeuvred our vehicle to stop just behind her.

As we prepared to confront Gladys, my mind was a whirlwind of questions and theories. Her actions were not just irresponsible; they were dangerous.

Karl was just stepping out of the car when he suddenly turned back to me, his decision clear in his firm expression.

"You wait in the driver's seat," he instructed. My initial reaction was a flash of irritation, my eyes locking onto his with an intensity that could have melted steel. "Just in case she decides to do a runner," he added quickly.

My expression softened at the logic of his decision. Being in the driver's seat meant I was in the prime position to give chase should Gladys attempt to flee. A part of me, the same part that thrived on the adrenaline of the chase and the complexity of a murder investigation, almost wished for her to make a run for it. It would add another layer of excitement to the day's events.

As Karl spoke with Gladys, every second stretched out, feeling longer than the last. I found myself tapping my fingers anxiously on the steering wheel, the rhythmic drumming a poor distraction from my growing impatience. Eventually, I reverted to a childhood habit, forming makeshift binoculars with my hands, peering intently through the gap in an attempt to decipher their conversation. But it was futile; I couldn't make out anything Karl was saying.

What's taking him so long? The question gnawed at me, my curiosity and eagerness for action mounting with each passing moment. I sighed with frustration, the suspense almost unbearable, and fell back against the seat. The waiting game was always the hardest part of the job for me. I preferred being in the thick of it, directly involved, rather than on the sidelines, even if it was a strategic position.

Moments later, Karl walked briskly back to the car, his pace quick and purposeful. He slid into the passenger seat with a sense of urgency that immediately piqued my curiosity.

"Did you give her a ticket?" I asked, as he buckled himself in. My question was more than just idle curiosity; it was a need to understand the evolving situation.

"No, just drive," Karl instructed firmly.

Without asking any more questions, I started the car and began to follow Gladys. My mind was abuzz with questions, but I knew better than to press Karl when he was like this. There was a reason for his terse instructions, and I trusted his judgment.

We drove in silence until we arrived at Luke and Jamie's house. I parked the car across the street, my eyes fixed on Gladys as she pulled into the driveway. The house itself was a modern, split-level construction, its living quarters perched on the top of a hillside. Below, a second floor with glass double doors opened up into the yard. The architecture was impressive, blending style with the natural slope of the land.

From our vantage point, I watched Gladys as she exited her car and walked towards the house. The situation felt like it was teetering on the edge of a significant breakthrough, and my senses were heightened in anticipation. This house, seemingly peaceful and picturesque, might hold the answers we had been searching for.

Hesitant to leave the car, I looked to Karl, my mind buzzing with unasked questions and theories. I needed more clarity before moving forward, before stepping into a situation that seemed to be growing more complex by the minute.

"I don't think we're going to be meeting Jamie Greyson," Karl said, as if reading my mind. His words cut through the silence, dangling the promise of an explanation.

My head tilted, my gaze still fixed on him, seeking more.

"But with a bit of luck, we might be about to speak with Luke Smith," Karl explained, a grin spreading across his face. "He's cooking dinner for her."

His revelation took me by surprise, my eyes widening for the second time that day. *Luke Smith?* The pieces of the puzzle were beginning to shift, aligning themselves into a new picture that I hadn't anticipated.

"Come on," Karl said, his smile an invitation to action, a nudge to snap me out of my thoughts and into motion.

I took a deep breath, absorbing the implications of Karl's words. This was not the direction I had expected our investigation to take, but it was undeniably intriguing. Stepping out of the car, I felt a rush of excitement mixed with the weight of responsibility.

Gladys stood on the front porch, the brown bag of 'lovelies' securely tucked under one arm while she knocked on the door with her free hand. She turned, noticing our approach. Her expression was a mix of surprise and mild confusion.

"Well, that's a bit odd," Gladys commented, her voice calm but tinged with uncertainty. "There doesn't seem to be anybody home. I wasn't gone that long."

I couldn't help but let out a loud huff of disappointment. *No Jamie, and now, no Luke.* Each step in this investigation seemed to lead to more questions than answers.

"But you have a key, don't you Gladys?" Karl interjected, his eyes fixed on the set of keys in Gladys' hand. He had quickly noticed they included those to Jamie's car, a detail that didn't escape his sharp observation.

Gladys let out a nervous laugh. "Oh, yeah," she said, lifting the keys with a little jingle, as if realising their significance for the first time. "How silly of me."

I watched Gladys closely, analysing her every move and reaction. Despite the situation, her attention seemed disproportionately focused on the brown paper bag. Her nervous laugh, her distracted manner – something didn't add up.

Is wine all you have in that paper bag of yours, Gladys? I questioned silently, my suspicion growing. My eyes narrowed as I contemplated the possible contents of the bag. Gladys' behaviour was puzzling, and I couldn't shake the feeling that there was more to her, and this situation, than met the eye.

"Well, aren't you going to invite us in?" Karl asked, breaking the tension that was building.

Gladys responded with a note of reluctance, her eyes narrowing as she glanced at Karl. "Wouldn't that be a bit rude of us to enter his house if he wasn't home?" Her voice carried a hint of desperation, as if she was grasping for reasons to keep us out.

Karl, unfazed, replied with a soft smile. "I'm pretty sure he wouldn't have given you his keys if he didn't want you being here." His tone was gentle, yet there was a firmness in it that suggested he wasn't going to back down.

I couldn't help but let out a short, quiet snort at Karl's astute observation. My hand flew to my mouth in an attempt to cover my faux pas. Karl had a knack for cutting through people's defences with his straightforward logic.

Gladys's glare shifted to me, her expression hardening. The fury in her eyes was evident, yet she seemed to recognise the futility of arguing. "I guess so," she conceded with a slight shrug, the resignation in her voice indicating she had run out of excuses.

I suppressed another snort, this one threatening to break free at the sight of Karl's subtle victory. His tactics, though not always orthodox, were effective in getting us inside.

My heart began to race as Gladys finally unlocked the door, resigning herself to letting us in. As the door opened, a million thoughts raced through my mind. *Will we really find Luke Smith? Is this the pivotal moment of our investigation?*

HOUSE HUNT

4338.210.4

"Sarah!" Karl whispered sharply, drawing my attention as he stood in the living room.

I glanced over my shoulder at him while I wandered around the space, absorbing every detail of the room. The atmosphere felt tense, like a scene waiting to reveal its secrets.

"Don't touch," he mouthed clearly, his eyes scanning the room with trained precision.

Gladys had insisted we wait in the living room that shared an open space with the spacious kitchen and dining room, while she supposedly went to find Jamie. Yet, I had barely waited ten seconds before succumbing to my instinctive urge to explore, to touch. It was a quality I knew I needed to control better, a habit I was sure I would eventually outgrow.

"I don't see any dinner preparations," I whispered back to Karl, my voice low but laced with skepticism. The lack of any signs of a meal being prepared struck me as odd, considering what Gladys had said about Luke cooking dinner.

"No," Karl agreed, his gaze sharp and searching. "And I don't think that's the only thing Gladys is being untruthful about, either."

"Oh?" I raised my eyebrows, intrigued by Karl's implication. His instincts were usually spot-on, and if he suspected Gladys was hiding something, then there was likely more to this visit than met the eye.

The room felt still, almost too quiet, as if holding its breath. I scanned the living room, noting the absence of any personal items that might suggest someone actually lived here. The lack of dinner preparations, the strange calmness of the house – it all added to the growing suspicion that Gladys was not being entirely forthright.

"Jamie doesn't appear to be here," Gladys announced, sounding genuinely surprised as she re-entered the living room. She had been calling out for him in various parts of the house, her voice echoing through the large, almost too quiet spaces.

"Does Jamie live alone?" Karl asked, his voice laced with a carefully crafted curiosity. He was playing the part of an uninformed visitor, a tactic I'd seen him use effectively in the past.

"Um, no," Gladys responded, a hint of hesitation in her voice. "He has a partner."

"Oh," Karl said, feigning surprise. "Is she about?"

At Karl's question, Gladys' face turned a deep shade of red. The reaction was curious and didn't go unnoticed. It was a tell, a small crack in her facade that hinted at something more beneath the surface.

"I'm sorry if I've embarrassed you," Karl quickly added, his tone softening in an attempt to put her at ease. He was adept at navigating these delicate conversations, always finding the right balance between inquiry and empathy.

Gladys offered a small, somewhat forced smile. "His name is Luke," she corrected Karl. "But they have been having a few personal troubles lately, and Luke has gone to Melbourne for a few weeks to think things through."

"Oh, I see," Karl responded calmly.

"May I use the bathroom, please?" Karl then asked, a request that seemed casual but I knew was part of his strategy to further assess the house.

"Sure," Gladys replied, her voice still carrying a trace of unease. "It's just down the end of the hallway on the left."

As Karl disappeared down the hallway, I remained in the living room, my gaze sweeping across the space. The house's pristine orderliness struck me as unnatural, almost as if it were a façade meticulously maintained to conceal deeper truths. My detective instincts were on high alert.

I turned my attention to Gladys, who now seemed to have regained some composure, though a trace of nervous energy still clung to her. There was something about her demeanour that didn't quite add up.

"So, what was it you said that Jamie was cooking again?" I asked, probing for more information. My eyes drifted toward the kitchen, where the benches were conspicuously bare. Not a single utensil or ingredient in sight – it was as if the kitchen hadn't been used at all.

"Would you like a glass of wine?" Gladys offered, quickly diverting the conversation. She turned away, perhaps to hide her flushed face, and reached for a wine glass from a high cupboard. The glass was large and ornately decorated, a stark contrast to the blandness of the kitchen.

I frowned slightly, sensing her evasion. "No," I responded simply, declining her offer. My focus was on unravelling the situation, not on social niceties.

Gladys merely shrugged in response, pouring herself a glass of wine.

What an odd woman, I mused internally, watching her closely. My concern for Gladys – and for what she might be hiding or protecting – was growing. There was a story here, hidden beneath the surface of her calm exterior and the too-perfect setting of the house.

"You still haven't answered my question," I pressed, my tone firm as I focused my gaze intently on Gladys.

"Oh, haven't I? I'm sorry. What was your question again?" Gladys responded, a touch of feigned confusion in her voice. She raised her wine glass to her lips, taking a large gulp as if to fortify herself against the questions she seemed reluctant to answer.

"What is Jamie—" I began to rephrase my question, hoping for a straight answer this time.

"Did you hear that?" Gladys suddenly interrupted, her head turning sharply as if she'd caught a sound. She didn't wait for my response, instead hurriedly rushing out of the room and into the hallway.

Irritated by her evasion and now alerted by her sudden reaction, I quickly followed.

"Hey! What the hell are you doing in there!" Gladys's voice ricocheted down the hallway, her tone thick with accusation.

As I rounded the corner, my eyes landed on Karl, who stood frozen in front of one of the bedroom doors, his hand still resting on its handle. The look of blatant guilt on his face was illuminated starkly by the harsh glare of the hallway light. I couldn't help but wonder, *What the hell does he think he's doing, snooping into their bedrooms? Did he really think he wouldn't get caught?* A mix of incredulity and frustration swirled within me.

"I think you better leave," Gladys snarled, her face now a canvas of anger, the flush of irritation painting her cheeks a deeper shade of red.

Karl, seemingly jarred back to reality by Gladys's sharp words, stepped back into the hallway. At that moment, the lights above flickered ominously, casting unsettling shadows across his face. His radio crackled loudly, piercing the tension-filled air. A sudden, inexplicable chill coursed through me, causing the hairs on the back of my neck to stand on end.

I couldn't shake off the feeling that something was off, something more than just the awkwardness of Karl being caught snooping. The atmosphere in the house had shifted; it felt charged, almost electric.

"You bastard!" Karl's voice erupted with a fury I had never seen in him before. In one swift, determined movement, he hurled himself at the bedroom door, sending it crashing into the wall behind it with a thunderous slam.

"Karl!" I cried out, my voice a mix of shock and concern. "What the hell are you doing!?" My mind was reeling, trying to make sense of his sudden, explosive action.

"He's here!" Karl shouted back, his voice laced with urgency. "Luke is here!"

Instinctively, I drew my gun, adrenaline surging through me. I pushed past Karl, storming into the room with a sense of desperation. My heart was pounding as I turned to face the door, my back to the large, broken window. The glass lay shattered, a testament to the force of the door's impact on the small room.

"Go, I've got you covered," I called out to Karl, my voice steady despite the chaos. I was ready for anything, prepared to protect both of us if necessary.

Karl didn't hesitate. He stepped back quickly, yanking the door handle with force, slamming the door shut just as Gladys' face appeared in the doorway, her expression a mix of shock and anger.

"What the—" I started, my words trailing off as I took in the scene before me. There was no sign of Luke, no hint of anyone hiding. All that stood before me was a blank wall, its only feature a fresh, large hole from where the door had been violently pushed into it.

I stood in utter astonishment as Karl, gripped by a sudden and intense fervour, reached for the nearest garbage bag. It was one of many that littered the room, a strange sight in itself. With a swift, forceful motion, he ripped a great hole in its side. The contents spilled out, emitting a rancid smell that quickly filled the air.

Unsatisfied with the first bag, Karl moved to the next, tearing several large holes through it, sending rubbish scattering across the carpeted floor. It was a scene of chaos and desperation.

"Karl!" I yelled, my mind struggling to comprehend the scene unfolding before me. *What the hell is Karl doing? He's acting like a frenzied madman!* The Karl I knew was composed, methodical. This frantic, chaotic version of him was completely foreign.

"I know he's here!" Karl shouted back, his voice filled with a raw, almost wild determination as he continued his frenetic search through the bags.

"Karl!" I yelled again, louder this time, as I reached out and grabbed him by the shoulder. His behaviour scared me; it was so out of character. It made me question what deep-seated emotions or past experiences with Jamie were driving this unbridled outburst.

No sooner had my hand touched Karl's shoulder than he reacted with an unexpected and violent force. His arm lashed out, striking me squarely in the chest. I lost my balance, stumbling over the debris littering the floor. My head struck the wall with a sickening crack, the pain radiating sharply through my skull. As I fell, my firearm slipped from my grasp, clattering dangerously onto the floor near the bedroom door. A cry of pain escaped my lips as I slid down the wall, my left hand catching a shard of broken window glass. I winced, feeling the sting of the cut.

I looked up at Karl, my eyes wide with disbelief. *How could he have lashed out at me like that?* I knew Karl could be temperamental and easily frustrated, but this level of emotional display was unprecedented.

Karl turned slowly to face me, his expression one of dawning horror. A myriad of emotions played across his features – shock, regret, pain. "I'm sorry," he whispered, his voice barely audible. I could see the regret etched into his face, the realisation of what he had just done sinking in.

But my trust had been shaken. This wasn't something that could be easily forgiven or forgotten. My gaze remained locked with his, a mix of hurt and defiance in my eyes. A thick, heavy silence enveloped the room, a tangible tension that seemed to press down on us, testing our resolve.

Eventually, Karl broke the silence. He looked down, unable to meet my gaze any longer, and stormed out of the room. I sat there on the floor, alone, pressing my sleeve against the fresh wound on my palm. I didn't move, didn't attempt to get up until I heard the front door slam shut, signalling Karl's departure.

In that moment, sitting alone in the chaotic aftermath, I felt a complex mix of emotions. There was pain from my injuries, shock at Karl's outburst, and a deep sense of betrayal. The events had unfolded so quickly, spiralling out of control in a way I had never anticipated.

Gladys cautiously entered the room, her eyes widening slightly at the disarray and my crumpled form against the wall. "Are you okay?" she asked, her voice laced with concern. In her hand, she still held her glass of wine, which she now extended towards me.

I hesitated for a moment, my mind still reeling from the shock and the sharp pain in my hand. Then, almost instinctively, I accepted the glass and took a grateful sip. The wine was smooth and momentarily soothing, offering a brief respite from the pulsing ache in my hand.

"I think I'll have that glass of wine now," I said, trying to muster a semblance of composure as I handed Gladys back her glass.

"Sure. I'll go and get it for you," Gladys responded with a smile, seemingly relieved to have a task. "Oh, and I'll meet you in the bathroom. It's just off the hall down there," she added, pointing down the hallway.

I nodded, taking a moment longer to gather myself amidst the whirlwind of emotions and physical discomfort. The sharp pain in my hand was a constant reminder of the physical altercation with Karl, while the sting of his betrayal cut even deeper. As I slowly stood up, using the wall for support, a mix of physical pain and emotional turmoil washed over me. Karl's unexpected and uncharacteristic behaviour had left me feeling vulnerable, a sensation I wasn't used to.

"Hey, Gladys?" I called out, my voice steady despite the chaos of thoughts in my head. Gladys paused at the doorway, turning to face me with a look of inquiry.

"Yes?" she responded, her voice reflecting a hint of apprehension.

"What happened to the window in here?" I asked, my curiosity piqued by the broken glass that littered the floor. The realisation had just hit me - the door being slammed into the wall on the opposite side of the room couldn't have caused the window to break. The pieces didn't fit.

Gladys shrugged, a look of genuine confusion crossing her face. "I'm not really sure. It was like that when Luke and I arrived earlier today," she said.

"You mean you and Jamie?" I asked her gently. The slip of the tongue was peculiar and raised more questions than it answered.

"Oh, yes. I meant Jamie. Me and Jamie," Gladys corrected herself quickly, but her response did little to ease my suspicions. Something was off, and Gladys seemed to be at the centre of it.

I watched as Gladys hurried out of the room, her departure leaving me alone with my thoughts. The inconsistency in her story, the broken window, and Karl's explosive reaction – everything was tangled in a web of half-truths and hidden motives. As I stood there, the pain in my hand a dull throb, I knew that unravelling this mystery was going to be more complicated than I had imagined.

Slowly, I made my way down the narrow hallway, each step a careful negotiation with the pain in my hand and the emotional turmoil swirling within. The house felt eerily silent, the walls almost echoing the tumult of the afternoon. Reaching the bathroom, I gently eased myself down onto the edge of the bathtub, cradling my injured hand in my lap, my gaze drifting around the unfamiliar space.

The moment Gladys entered and flicked on the light, the bathroom was bathed in a bright, revealing illumination. She held out a glass of deep, red shiraz towards me. "Here," she said, her voice oddly calm.

"Sorry about the blood," I apologised, accepting the wine with my good hand. It was only then that I noticed the small trail of blood I had inadvertently left behind me in the hallway. It was a grim contrast to the pristine cleanliness of the rest of the house.

"That's okay," Gladys replied, taking another sip from her own glass of wine. Her tone was sympathetic, albeit a bit distant. "It wasn't your fault." She then set her glass atop the vanity unit and began rummaging through the drawers and cupboards, searching for medical supplies.

As I watched her, I couldn't help but feel a sense of disconnect. Gladys's actions and demeanour were a puzzle, her responses and behaviour not quite adding up. The mystery surrounding her, Jamie, and now the broken window loomed large in my mind.

Holding the glass of shiraz, I felt a strange blend of gratitude and suspicion. The wine was a small comfort, but it couldn't numb the nagging questions that danced at the edge of my consciousness. *What was Gladys's true connection to all this? Was she merely a bystander caught up in events beyond her control, or was there more to her story?*

Getting to my feet, I approached the vanity, my movements cautious due to the pain and uncertainty of the afternoon. I turned the taps on, letting the water flow until it warmed to a comforting temperature. My fingers, tentative at first, tested the water before I began to carefully wash away the blood that had oozed from the cut on my palm and streaked down my arm. The sensation of the water was both soothing and jarring as it seeped into the wound, eliciting involuntary winces from me.

I was so focused on cleaning the wound that I almost forgot about Gladys' presence in the room. Holding out my injured hand towards her, I took another sip of the shiraz.

Gladys, with a gentle touch, dabbed my palm dry, her movements deft and careful. She then applied several butterfly bandages across the cut. There was a practiced ease to her actions, suggesting she was no stranger to caring for injuries.

"Thanks," I said, offering her a grateful nod. Despite the oddities surrounding Gladys and her involvement in the afternoon's events, there was an undeniable likability about her. She had a certain warmth, a kind of understated kindness that was hard to ignore. *Or maybe that is just the wine talking,* I mused silently, taking another sip. The wine, with its deep flavour, seemed to add a layer of complexity to my thoughts, blurring the lines between suspicion and gratitude.

Gladys gestured for me to follow her back into the living room. We each found a spot on the sleek black, leather couch, settling into the opposite ends. The room felt starkly different from the chaos of just moments ago, now filled with an uneasy calm.

"So..." I started, choosing my words carefully, "What do you know about Jamie and Karl?"

"Karl? Nothing," Gladys responded with a blunt tone, her words quick and to the point. She shifted slightly, her posture open yet guarded. "But Jamie and I have been close friends for many years."

"Really? Karl seemed like he knew rather a lot about Louise yesterday," I countered gently, probing further.

"Jamie's sister, Louise?" Gladys asked, a hint of surprise in her voice.

"Yes," I confirmed, maintaining a steady gaze on her. "She came into the station to report Jamie as a missing person. She reckons she hasn't seen Jamie or her son Kain for several days." I observed Gladys intently as I spoke, looking for any subtle change in her expression or posture. It was crucial not to let Karl's earlier outburst overshadow the importance of this conversation.

"Well, that's a bit odd. I haven't seen Kain recently, but Jamie is definitely safe and well," Gladys replied, her voice steady but with an undertone that suggested she was holding something back.

I mulled over her words, trying to piece together the puzzle. The disparity in Gladys' story and what we had learned from Louise was striking. It was clear there were missing pieces in this narrative, gaps that needed filling.

"And Luke?" I ventured cautiously, my toes involuntarily curling inside my shoes as I braced for her response. I hoped my question wouldn't push Gladys to retreat behind a wall of silence. *Although it wouldn't be the first line crossed in this house*, I mused, glancing down at my hands – one bandaged from the cut, and the other cradling the wine glass. *Shit!*

A sudden shiver ran through me as the hairs on my arms stood on end, a response to the odd sensation that had been nagging at me since Karl's departure. The living room lights flickered overhead, casting strange shadows around us. "You better have an electrician look into that," I remarked, eyeing the ceiling light with concern.

Gladys offered a warm, albeit somewhat forced, smile. "Luke is definitely safe," she said with an air of confidence.

I eyed Gladys curiously, her assurance about Luke sending an unnerving chill down my spine. "Well, cheers to that," I said, leaning across the couch and extending my glass towards her in a gesture of camaraderie.

"Cheers," Gladys replied, her glass meeting mine with a soft clink.

I finished the wine in three big gulps, the rich liquid a stark contrast to the complexity of the situation. "I had better be off then," I announced, standing up. "I'm not supposed to be drinking while on duty."

"My lips are sealed," Gladys responded, her fingers playfully mimicking the action of zipping her lips shut.

I chuckled softly to myself as I made my way out of the house. Despite the day's strange events, Gladys' cooperation, whether fully sincere or not, might prove beneficial in the long run. *Perhaps Gladys will be of some use, after all*, I contemplated, stepping back into the cooling late afternoon air and heading towards the car. As I walked, my mind worked overtime, piecing together the snippets of information, the odd behaviours, and the tangible sense of secrets just beneath the surface. This investigation was far from over, and I felt a renewed determination to uncover the truth, no matter how deep I had to dig.

As I drove down the street, my eyes caught a familiar figure. Karl, walking at a brisk pace, his posture rigid with tension. The sight of him stirred a whirlwind of emotions within me. Despite the calming effect of the glass of wine I had shared with Gladys, anger still simmered beneath the surface. The betrayal and shock of his earlier actions lingered, making it impossible for me to simply brush aside what had happened.

I slowed down momentarily, contemplating whether to stop and confront him. Part of me wanted to yell, to demand answers for his irrational behaviour back at the house. But the stronger part, the part still reeling from his physical outburst, decided against it. The wound on my hand throbbed as a physical reminder of his actions.

So, I didn't stop. I kept driving, leaving Karl to his own turbulent thoughts. The decision felt both empowering and unsettling. On one hand, it was a stand against his unacceptable behaviour; on the other, it was an acknowledgment of a rift that had formed between us, a partnership strained to its limits.

4338.211

(30 July 2018)

NATURAL TENSION

4338.211.1

As I glanced out of the side window, the contrast between the earlier sunny morning and the dark storm clouds now rolling in was stark and foreboding. They loomed ominously, a tangible symbol of the mounting tension and unresolved mysteries surrounding our investigation.

"We'd better make quick work of this investigation," Karl's voice broke the silence that had settled between us, his gaze shifting towards me. "I don't think we have much time before it hits."

I simply nodded, my response minimal. The silence that had enveloped us during the drive was a product of the unresolved tension from yesterday's incident. His outburst had left a palpable strain on our working relationship, and I found myself struggling to reconcile the Karl I knew with the man who had acted so irrationally.

Earlier, a call had come in from a distressed neighbour about Karen and Chris Owen, who hadn't been seen for a few days. Under normal circumstances, it might not have warranted our immediate attention. However, given the recent spate of disappearances, our instructions had been clear – to respond and investigate.

From the quick research I had managed to do, the Owens seemed like an integral part of the Tasmanian community, known for their unwavering commitment to environmental causes. Their dedication to the preservation of Tasmania's natural beauty was widely recognised. Given their line of work, it wasn't unusual for Karen and Chris Owen to be away from home for extended periods, travelling across the state for conservation projects. This knowledge made me skeptical about our assignment to investigate their absence. It seemed unlikely that their disappearance was linked to our ongoing case. Yet, in the back of my mind, the recent string of missing persons kept nagging at me, suggesting that there might be more to their absence than met the eye.

"Watch out!" I instinctively yelled, my hand almost reaching for the steering wheel. Karl's reaction was immediate, his foot slamming down on the brakes as a flock of brown chickens unexpectedly scurried across the road. The car jerked to a halt, just inches away from the feathered roadblock.

For a brief moment, Karl and I exchanged glances. There was a fleeting spark of humour in the absurdity of the situation, but it quickly faded, overshadowed by the lingering tension from yesterday's events. The unspoken discord between us hung heavy in the air, dampening what might have otherwise been a light-hearted moment.

"We must be getting close," Karl said, breaking the silence as he refocused on the road ahead.

"We are," I responded, trying to shift the focus back to the task at hand. I pointed to a street sign just down the road. "That's the road to the Owens' property."

Karl beeped the horn, a clear attempt to urge the lingering hens across the road. However, the fifth one, a straggler bringing up the rear, seemed utterly unfazed. I couldn't help but let out a slight snort of amusement. The chook paused, turning to look up at us with an expression that seemed to say we were the ones causing the inconvenience. Her beady eyes met Karl's with an almost determined defiance. As Karl honked again, she merely continued her leisurely pace, bobbing her head and pecking at the road, seemingly taking even longer with each successive beep.

"This is ridiculous," I muttered under my breath, my patience wearing thin. Unfastening my seatbelt, I swung the car door open and stepped out. We were on a tight schedule, and this unexpected poultry parade was the last thing we needed.

I flapped my arms, trying my best to shoo the chickens off the road. It was a comical sight, I'm sure, but we simply didn't have the time for this delay. Finally, after some persistent herding, I managed to clear the road. Yet, as I turned to run back to the car, I realised that several of the hens had taken a liking to me and were now following me back onto the road.

"Come on, you guys," I grumbled, half amused and half exasperated. The chickens, however, seemed unfazed by my pleas, happily clucking and pecking their way back onto the asphalt.

I glanced back at Karl, who was watching the scene unfold, an expression of bemusement on his face. For a fleeting moment, the tension between us seemed to lighten, replaced by the absurdity of the situation. I shook my head, a mix of laughter and frustration bubbling inside me. This investigation had taken us down some strange paths, but chicken herding was definitely not something I had anticipated.

"You shoo, I'll drive," Karl called out, his laughter echoing through his open window.

"Fine," I responded, a hint of exasperation in my voice as I rolled my eyes. In my mind, I thought wryly, *What other choice do we have? These stubborn chooks clearly aren't going to move themselves.*

Karl proceeded cautiously, ensuring he passed all the hens safely. He drove a few car lengths ahead and stopped, waiting for me. But as I began to make my way back to the vehicle, my newfound feathered friends decided to follow. It was as if I had unintentionally become the pied piper of chickens.

"Oh, shut up!" I shouted back at Karl when he burst into laughter again upon seeing my predicament. I had to admit, despite the absurdity of the situation, the hens' determination was impressive.

"Karl! Wait!" I yelled, slightly out of breath as he teasingly began to drive the car slowly up the road without me. I quickened my pace, trying to catch up, but the faster I ran, the faster my poultry entourage followed, their clucking growing louder with each step.

Karl turned right onto the laneway leading to the Owens' property, still maintaining his slow pace. He finally stopped to let me catch up just as I reached the turn-off. Panting slightly, I glanced back and, to my relief and slight amusement, saw that the hens had finally decided to abandon their pursuit. They stood at the edge of the main road, watching as I hurried towards our car.

"I think the girls like you," Karl teased with a chuckle as I slid back into the passenger seat, trying to regain my composure.

"Not funny, Karl!" I retorted, shooting him a glare. The chicken chase had been absurd, but I was not in the mood for his jokes. "There's a reason I don't do country."

"Sarah, you were born in the outback," Karl reminded me, a smirk playing at the corner of his mouth. "That's more country than country."

"That doesn't mean I liked it," I huffed, crossing my arms. Just because I was from a rural area didn't mean I had an affinity for it. The city life had always been more appealing to me.

Karl chuckled again, clearly amused. "That's not what your brother says."

I gave him a swift punch on the shoulder, a playful yet firm response. "Just drive," I commanded, not wanting to entertain his banter any further. Oscar was indeed a great storyteller, but he often embellished the truth to the point of fiction. His stories about our childhood in the outback were mostly exaggerated tales, and I rarely took them seriously.

We continued our drive, the car's tires crunching over the uneven dirt road, navigating a patchwork of pebbles, rocks, and potholes. The vehicle rocked rhythmically, making the journey feel like an off-road adventure. As I peered through the window, the dense native forest flanking either side of the road restricted our view to just the track ahead and the path we'd left behind. The tall trees formed a natural archway overhead, their twisted and gnarled branches creating a tunnel-like effect that felt both enchanting and eerie.

"Oh my god!" I couldn't help but exclaim as we emerged into a spacious clearing. Before us stood an old stone and cedar cottage, nestled at the far end of the clearing. It was small, probably no more than three bedrooms, and rustically simple. Yet, there was an undeniable charm to it. Its modest size did nothing to detract from its allure. Instead, the undulating green shades of the native forest rising majestically behind it framed the cottage perfectly, enhancing its quaint beauty. The contrast of the wild, untamed forest against the structured simplicity of the cottage created a picturesque scene that momentarily took my breath away.

I stepped out of the car, drawn to the view before me. Standing there, I allowed myself a moment to simply gaze in awe at the cottage's unassuming splendour. For a fleeting moment, the complexities of the case and the tension with Karl faded into the background, overshadowed by the peace and beauty of the natural surroundings.

"Bringing back memories?" Karl asked, his voice laced with a hint of teasing as a wide grin spread across his face.

I responded with a light, beautiful white smile, momentarily letting go of the grudge between us. Just as I was about to answer, a movement in the periphery of my vision caught my attention. "Look!" I exclaimed, pointing towards several small potoroo busily nibbling on the long grass at the shaded side of a large barn, several car lengths to the left of the cottage.

Feeling a sudden surge of curiosity and connection with the natural world around me, I started to make my way carefully towards the potoroo. My hand was outstretched, fingers gently clicking in a soft, rhythmic pattern. My voice, soft and beckoning, floated on the wind, a gentle invitation for the creatures to let me approach.

I moved slowly, mindful of each step, captivated by the sight of the potoroo in their natural habitat. It was a rare and peaceful moment, a brief connection with nature that felt almost magical.

However, the serenity was abruptly shattered by the crackle of the dispatch radio. "CITY632. Are you there? Over," the voice of the dispatcher cut through the air, loud and jarring against the quiet of the clearing.

The sudden noise startled the potoroo, and they quickly hopped away, disappearing into the safety of the underbrush. I stood there, a mix of disappointment and frustration washing over me. The moment of peace was gone, replaced by the reality of our duty.

"Damn," I muttered under my breath, turning back towards Karl and the car. The radio's interruption was a sharp reminder of why we were here. I walked back, my mind switching gears from the brief escape back to the demands of our investigation.

As Karl leaned back into the car to grab the radio, I took a moment to survey the surrounding area more closely.

"CITY632. We're at the Owens' property now. Over," Karl responded into the radio with a professional tone.

"CITY632. The neighbour that called this morning has just called back. She is pretty shaken. Said there was a lot of activity at the property. Went quiet about thirty minutes ago," the dispatcher informed us, her voice carrying a hint of urgency.

"Copy that, Dispatch," Karl replied. "We'll proceed with caution." His voice was calm, but I could sense the alertness in his posture.

With the furry distractions gone, I took the time to absorb my immediate surroundings. The Owens' property was enveloped on all sides by thick, lush forest, providing a sense of isolation and privacy. The natural barrier was broken only occasionally by other houses, each tucked away in their own clearings. The nearest neighbour was a few hundred meters away, and the one who had reported the activity was almost twice that distance on the other side.

This seclusion added a layer of complexity to our investigation. The isolation of the property meant that any unusual activity might have gone unnoticed by the wider community. It also meant that whoever had been at the property could have operated with a degree of privacy.

The dispatcher's words had set my nerves on edge, heightening my awareness of the potential danger that might be lurking on the Owens' property. I instinctively moved closer to the car, my hand reaching for my gun. Drawing it, I felt a surge of adrenaline, my senses sharpening as I prepared for whatever might unfold.

"For once, you're actually right about the gun," Karl muttered under his breath, his tone an unusual mix of seriousness and resignation. He too unholstered his weapon, readying himself for what lay ahead. "Follow my lead," he instructed, his voice low but clear.

As we advanced toward the front verandah, every sense was heightened, every sound magnified. My steps were cautious, deliberately quiet as I veered to the left, scanning every inch of the surroundings for any signs of disturbance or danger. Meanwhile, Karl moved directly towards the steps of the verandah, his focus equally intent.

Amid the tension and focus, something peculiar on the edge of the verandah decking caught my eye. Crouching down for a closer look, I found a small bunch of white daisies, their petals fresh and vibrant. It was an unexpected sight, their simple beauty starkly contrasting the severity of our purpose there.

"Karl," I whispered sharply, drawing his attention. As he turned towards me, his foot landed heavily on the second step, breaking the stillness with a thud. I held up the daisies for him to see. "These look like they've been freshly picked," I observed quietly. The discovery was curious – the flowers seemed recently placed, as if someone had set them down momentarily and forgotten to pick them back up.

"They were lying right here on the edge of the decking," I added, pointing to the spot where I had found them.

"Daisies?" Karl questioned, his brow furrowing in thought.

"Yeah," I confirmed. "It's a bit odd. Maybe the neighbour was right. There were people here earlier. Do you think they're still around?" The possibilities churned in my mind – *could these flowers be a clue to the whereabouts of the Owens, or were they left by someone else?*

Karl paused, his gaze sweeping over the property, assessing the situation. "Not sure," he finally said. "It seems pretty quiet now. Why don't you go check out the barn?"

"Yeah, alright," I agreed, feeling a mix of apprehension and determination. The barn could hold more clues, or it could be another dead end.

"Sarah," Karl called out in a loud whisper as I began to move away from the verandah, his voice carrying a note of concern. "Be careful."

I nodded appreciatively in response, despite the tension that had been between us. A small smile graced my lips as I turned my back on Karl, stepping into the unknown. My mind was alert, ready for any sign or clue that might present itself. The barn loomed ahead, its old structure a silent witness to the events that had unfolded here.

As I neared the large barn, a sense of caution enveloped me. The structure was old and weathered, bearing the marks of time, yet there was an undeniable charm to it. The barn, constructed from Tasmanian oak, had a certain robust elegance that spoke of careful craftsmanship and attention to detail. Despite its age, it stood solid and imposing.

My gun remained in a ready position, a constant reminder of the potential danger that might lurk within. I moved through the lush, green grass, which seemed to have taken over the cobbled path leading to the barn's entrance. The overgrown vegetation was a sign of neglect, contrasting with the otherwise sturdy appearance of the barn.

My heart pounded in my chest, a mix of adrenaline and anticipation, as I reached the solid, wooden door. "Police!" I called out firmly, my voice echoing slightly in the open space. I knocked sharply on the door, the sound resonating against the old wood. I tried to pull the door open, only to find it secured by chains and a padlock. The rattling of the chains against the door added to the eerie silence surrounding the property.

Realising the front door wasn't an option, I decided to explore the perimeter of the barn for an alternate entrance. I moved cautiously along the side of the barn, every sense alert. My eyes scanned for any other points of entry, while my ears strained to pick up any sound of movement from inside.

The possibility of someone being inside, whether it was the Owens or someone else, kept me on edge.

The sense of isolation enveloping the property intensified as I tiptoed cautiously along the side of the barn. The dense forest encircling the clearing seemed to stand as a silent witness to my every step, adding to the eerie stillness of the scene.

I couldn't help but cry out in sudden pain as a long splinter embedded itself into the top of my left index finger. I had been absentmindedly running my hand along the rough, weathered wood of the barn, more focused on my surroundings than the potential hazards of the old structure. My original intention to peer around the corner was abruptly forgotten as I glared at the offending piece of wood protruding from my skin.

Refusing to let the pain distract me, I gritted my teeth and swiftly pulled the splinter out with my blunt nails. The sting was sharp, but I pushed the discomfort aside, knowing there were more pressing matters at hand.

No sooner had I dealt with the splinter than a loud clang erupted from inside the barn. The sudden noise startled me, and I instinctively retreated, spinning around to face the source of the disturbance. My gun was up and ready, my body tensing for any sign of danger.

As I cautiously moved forward, ready to confront whatever lay inside the barn, I felt an abrupt whack against the back of my head. The sound of a loud crack followed the impact, sending a wave of pain through my skull. Reacting instinctively, I swivelled around and swiped at the object that had hit me – a slender, wooden rake handle.

Closing my eyes for a brief moment, I massaged the sore spot where the rake had made contact. Realising that I must have inadvertently stepped on the tool, causing it to flick up and strike me, a series of cartoonish images flashed through my mind. The absurdity of the situation wasn't lost on me. *It's not turning out to be a good day for me*, I thought, a mix of frustration and irony colouring my thoughts.

Regaining my composure after the rake incident, I reopened my eyes, only to find a small black cat stalking something in the underbrush ahead of me. The cat's sleek body moved with a predator's grace, completely absorbed in its pursuit. "What is it?" I whispered, half-expecting the cat to respond, but it paid me no mind, its focus unbroken.

Driven by curiosity and a need to momentarily distract myself from my self-inflicted pains, I quietly followed the cat, treading softly to see what had captivated its attention. It was then I spotted the object of the cat's interest: a small, brown and grey duck, lost amidst the tall grass, evidently trying to find its way to the spring-fed dam in the distance. The duck appeared confused and vulnerable in the dense undergrowth.

Feeling a sudden surge of sympathy for the little creature, I intervened. I shooed the cat away with a gentle hiss, which it met with a disgruntled look before disappearing into the bushes. The duck, startled by the commotion, let out a panicked quack but didn't flee.

Moved by the duck's plight, I decided to help it find its way. I crept behind it, using my hands to gently guide and encourage the bird towards the dam. I was careful not to scare it, moving slowly and keeping my distance to avoid causing it any more stress.

Finally, the duck reached the edge of the water and waddled into the dam. Watching it paddle away, a sense of accomplishment washed over me. There was something heartwarming about helping a small creature in distress, a brief but meaningful respite from the intensity of our investigation.

Intently focused on helping the duck and momentarily revelling in my saint-like goodness, my attention was completely diverted from any potential threats. I was blissfully unaware of any danger until it was too late. Suddenly, I felt a sharp, forceful impact against my backside. The unexpected blow threw me off balance, and I tumbled awkwardly into the mud at the edge of the dam. I landed hard among the reeds, a sharp pain shooting through my body as I saw blood start to seep through the bandage on my left hand.

A loud clap of thunder boomed overhead, startling me into a defensive crouch. As the first drops of rain began to fall, my eyes darted around, searching for the source of my attack, bracing for another assault. Out of the corner of my eye, I caught sight of a large, grey figure rising and barreling towards me from the right. It was a goose, and not just any goose – a large one, swooping at me with a ferocity that seemed almost personal, its squawks sounding like a battle cry.

"Shit!" I cried out, trying to regain my footing in the slick mud. As I pressed my bleeding palm into the ground to push myself up, it slipped, and I tumbled backward, landing with a splash in the muddy water. The goose, undeterred, dived at me again, this time aiming straight for my face.

In that moment, primal instinct overrode all reason. I raised my right arm defensively. The gun in my hand went off almost reflexively. The shot, precise and true despite my compromised position, hit the goose squarely. The bird crashed to the ground next to me, its war cry abruptly silenced.

Gasping for breath, I watched in shock as blood began to ooze from the bullet wound in the goose's chest. My heart raced, adrenaline coursing through my veins. I had never intended to shoot, let alone kill, but the suddenness of the attack had left me with no time to think.

Sitting there in the mud, soaked from the rain, with the lifeless goose beside me, I felt a mix of relief, guilt, and disbelief. This was not how I had expected my day to unfold. The absurdity of being attacked by a goose, of all things, in the middle of a serious investigation was almost too much to comprehend.

"Sarah!" Karl's voice rang out, filled with concern as he ran toward me through the rain.

I turned my head to look back at him, my vision blurred by the tears that had welled up in my eyes. I quickly wiped them away with the back of my sleeve, trying to compose myself.

Karl's footsteps slowed as he approached, his expression changing from concern to confusion when he saw the small, motionless body of the goose lying beside me in the reeds. "Ah, shit, Sarah," he sighed, his voice laced with a mixture of disbelief and frustration.

"I didn't mean to," I stammered, my voice shaky as I wiped another tear from my eye. The guilt was overwhelming; *I never intended for this to happen.*

Karl reached out, grabbing me by the arm and gently helping me to my feet. "You just shot their goose!" he exclaimed, his tone a mix of incredulity and exasperation.

"It was an accident! She flew at me. I swear she was coming for my face," I defended myself, still reeling from the shock. My heart was racing, and my thoughts were a jumble.

Karl looked at me, his frustration clear. "Do you have any idea how much paperwork this is going to be?" he asked, his voice tinged with annoyance.

His focus on the paperwork rather than my well-being soured my mood further. "I could have been seriously injured," I retorted, feeling undervalued and overlooked in the moment.

"Well, at least you wouldn't be dead," Karl shot back, gesturing towards the lifeless goose at my feet. His words, meant to be pragmatic, only served to heighten my frustration.

"You can be a real insensitive bastard sometimes, Karl!" I yelled at him, the stress of the situation finally boiling over. Without waiting for a response, I turned and began a stormy march back to the car. Every step I took was fuelled by a mix of embarrassment, guilt, and anger. Karl's lack of empathy, combined with the absurdity of having to defend myself against a goose, was more than I could handle.

"Sarah, wait!" Karl's voice followed me, echoing with urgency through the pouring rain.

I ignored him, my strides a mix of frustration and indignation as I trudged through the tall, wet grass. My mind was a tumult of emotions, replaying the absurd scene with the goose, Karl's reaction, and the overall ridiculousness of the situation.

"There's blood in the house," Karl yelled, his voice piercing through the stormy air and halting me in my tracks.

I turned slightly, the rain running down my face. "And a body?" I called back, half-expecting to hear the worst.

Karl shook his head, dispelling that fear. "No. Just the goose," he replied. He nudged the dead bird with his foot, an unnecessary confirmation of its demise. His action only served to irritate me further.

"Bastard," I muttered under my breath, my frustration reaching a boiling point. Turning fully to face him, I announced, "I'll go call for forensics."

As I approached the car, the rain seemed to intensify, mirroring the tumultuous thoughts swirling in my head. The investigation at the Owens' property had taken unexpected turns.

Settling into the driver's seat of our unmarked car, reaching down, I picked up the dispatch radio, the familiar weight of it somewhat grounding.

"CITY632 here," I called into the radio, my voice steady despite the turmoil of emotions inside me.

"Go ahead CITY632," came the deep-voiced reply from dispatch.

"CITY632 requesting forensics analysis at the Owens' property. Trace of blood found. To be treated as suspicious," I instructed, my words concise and professional. Despite the absurd incident with the goose, the potential seriousness of our situation was not lost on me.

"Copy that CITY632. Forensics and backup patrol on their way," the dispatcher confirmed.

After returning the radio to its holder, I slumped back into the seat, shifting diagonally to find a more comfortable position. I sat there uncomfortably, staring sulkily out of the window. The rain was still falling, adding a dreary backdrop to my already sour mood.

I watched Karl making his way back to the car, his progress slow and seemingly reluctant. Despite my best efforts, my eyes couldn't help but drift over him. I noticed how the rain made his tight, dark blue pants cling to his legs, highlighting their muscular definition. His shirt, dark grey and short-sleeved, was similarly plastered to his biceps. It was a sight that, under different circumstances, might have been appealing, but at that moment, it only served to remind me of the tension between us.

Struggling with my conflicting emotions, I turned my head away from Karl, forcing my gaze elsewhere to escape the unwanted and inappropriate feelings that were bubbling up inside me. He was my partner, and these lustful thoughts had no place in our professional relationship.

Just as I was grappling with these internal struggles, the radio crackled to life, breaking the tension in the car. "Urgent call for vehicles to attend a speeding incident near Collinsvale. Apparent drag race. Available units, please respond. Over," the dispatcher's voice echoed through the cabin.

At the mention of Collinsvale, a jolt of adrenaline surged through me. *Collinsvale! That's where we are!* The realisation hit me like a lightning bolt. My head was suddenly clear of all distractions, and I was back in detective mode. I reached for the radio, my fingers wrapping around it with a newfound sense of purpose. I pressed the talk button firmly, ready to respond to the call.

"CITY632, we've got this. Over," I said, my voice steady and calm, or at least as calm as I could manage under the circumstances. It felt good to be back in control, to focus on the job.

"Copy that, CITY632," the dispatcher responded, confirming our involvement.

A sense of duty and determination replaced the earlier turmoil. This was what I was trained for, what I excelled at. The call for the drag race incident was an unexpected turn, but it was a welcome distraction from the complexities of the Owens' case and my personal feelings towards Karl.

THE CHASE

4338.211.2

"Karl, we have to go!" I called out to him with a burst of energy, feeling a rush of excitement. The sudden shift from investigation to high-speed pursuit was exhilarating. This was a part of the job I absolutely loved – the unpredictability, the adrenaline rush, the rapid response required. It invigorated me, made my mind sharper, and set my blood racing.

"What is it?" Karl yelled back, his voice carrying a hint of confusion.

"A priority call has just come over the radio, two cars are driving at high speed just off the highway near Collinsvale. We're the closest unit. Quick, let's go!" I answered, urgency colouring my voice. I waved my arms animatedly, trying to convey the immediacy of the situation and hurry him along.

"We can't just leave the crime scene," Karl began, his tone one of caution and responsibility.

I quickly waved him off, not wanting to waste any more time. "It'll be fine. I've already notified dispatch and forensics are on their way. We can swing by afterwards to check up on things, but this call is urgent." I felt confident in my decision; our presence was needed elsewhere immediately.

As I reached for the ignition, Karl quickly interjected, "Shift over, I'll drive," he ordered, gesturing for me to move to the passenger seat. His tone left no room for argument, and I knew he preferred to be in control in high-speed situations.

I clambered swiftly over to the passenger seat, making myself comfortable in one fluid motion. "Come on then!" I called out to Karl, who lingered outside the car, his right arm casually resting on the top of the open door frame. I caught his gaze briefly as I shifted seats, aware of his eyes following my movements. A part of me enjoyed the attention, the subtle acknowledgment of my presence. *But really, Karl? Right now?* With a car chase beckoning, it seemed like an inopportune moment for such distractions.

Karl seemed to snap out of his momentary daze and jumped into the driver's seat. He pulled his door shut with a decisive thud and immediately slammed his foot down on the accelerator. The patrol car responded instantly, its powerful V8 engine roaring to life, filling the air with a deep, rumbling growl. We were thrust back into our seats as Karl expertly navigated the car down the long, dirt driveway of the Owens' property.

The car slightly fishtailed, its rear wheels struggling to find traction on the slick, wet earth. Despite the wild start, Karl's skilled hands kept us steady and on course. The thrill of the chase was palpable in the air, a mix of danger and excitement. I felt my heart racing in sync with the engine's revs, every sense heightened.

My excitement for the chase was evident as I picked up the radio, unable to suppress a smile despite the seriousness of the situation. "CITY632 requesting an update on the two speeding cars sighted near Collinsvale," I relayed into the radio, my voice steady and clear.

"Copy that, CITY632. We already have a Polair chopper in the air. They're looking for the vehicles now. What is your location?" the dispatcher's voice came through, crisp and professional.

Karl had slowed the patrol car to a stop where the Owens' driveway met the main road, a critical junction that would either lead us back towards Glenorchy or further into Collinsvale. The rain was relentless, pelting the windshield, reducing visibility and adding another layer of complexity to our pursuit.

"CITY632. We're just at the edge of the Owens' property in Collinsvale," I reported to dispatch, peering through the front window, trying to discern the best route in the downpour.

"Copy that, CITY632. The chopper has sight of the vehicles. They should be coming—." The dispatcher's message was suddenly drowned out as two vehicles sped past us, heading in the direction of Collinsvale. They zoomed by with such speed and force that our car was showered in a spray of water, momentarily obscuring our view even further.

I snapped to attention, adrenaline surging through my veins. "Karl, that's them!" I exclaimed, pointing in the direction the cars had gone. The moment called for immediate action, and Karl didn't hesitate. He slammed his foot on the accelerator, the car lurching forward as we joined the pursuit.

As Karl floored the accelerator, I was thrown back against my seat, the force of the acceleration a thrilling reminder of the urgency of our pursuit. Karl's swift manoeuvre to follow the speeding cars was nothing short of impressive. He turned the wheel sharply in the direction of our targets, the car momentarily losing balance before he skilfully regained control, executing a perfect power slide onto the wet main road.

I noticed a smile flicker across Karl's face, a rare moment of unguarded enjoyment. He was in his element, handling the car with a deft touch that made it seem almost effortless.

Quickly, I activated the flashing red and blue lights, and the siren started screaming, adding to the intensity of the situation. The chase was truly on now. My heart pounded in my chest, and I could feel the rush of adrenaline coursing through my body, igniting every nerve with a burst of energy.

I grabbed the radio, which had been momentarily forgotten in the heat of the moment, and called in. "We have a visual. In pursuit now," I informed dispatch. Outside, the car's wipers worked furiously, struggling against the relentless downpour of rain that blurred our vision.

"Copy that, CITY632," the dispatcher responded promptly, their voice calm and professional over the radio.

As Karl navigated the patrol car around a sharp corner at high speed, the tyres let out a screeching protest. The intensity of the chase was palpable in the confined space of the car, every move and decision critical.

"Do we know who the drivers are?" Karl asked, his voice focused and intent over the roar of the engine and the howl of the wind and rain.

"Let's find out," I responded, eager to gather more information. I repeated Karl's question into the radio, my voice firm and clear despite the cacophony of sounds around us.

"Negative, CITY632. Are you able to get a visual on a number plate?" came the dispatcher's voice from the radio.

Leaning forward in my seat, I strained to see through the relentless downpour. Karl was concentrating intensely, his gaze fixed on the vehicles ahead. "I can't make it out. Can you?" he asked, his voice tense with focus.

I squinted, trying to see through the curtain of rain. "Me neither," I replied. "You'll have to get us a little closer, just watch out for the spray from the cars." My initial rush of excitement began to give way to a sense of caution, the reality of the danger we were in becoming increasingly apparent.

"Shit Karl!" I suddenly cried out, bracing myself with my hands against the side window as Karl accelerated once more. The car bounced over a slight rise in the road, the rear wheels losing grip for a heart-stopping moment before Karl regained control.

"Well, did you get it?" Karl asked, his voice tinged with urgency.

"Yeah," I replied, a sense of accomplishment mixing with relief. I was impressed with myself for managing to catch the number plate in such challenging conditions. "I'm running it through the system now."

The pursuit was reaching a fever pitch as the two cars we were chasing wound their way around the hillside. They zigzagged along Collinsvale Road, their reckless driving evident as they continued onto Collins Cap Road. It was a treacherous path, the road twisting and turning, demanding every bit of focus and skill from Karl and me.

Suddenly, the cars made a sharp turn onto Springdale Road. "Looks like they're looping back," Karl noted, his tone laced with surprise. Without hesitation, he slammed on the brakes, bringing our patrol car to a jarring halt.

"What are you doing?" I asked, my voice tinged with incredulity. Every fibre in my body was screaming to continue the pursuit, to stay on the heels of the speeding cars.

Karl's response was calm and calculated. "We're going back. The distance is shorter, and we can cut them off when they arrive at the intersection." Without waiting for my reaction, he shifted the car into reverse and hit the accelerator. The patrol car shot backward. Then, with a swift pull of the handbrake, Karl spun the car around in a controlled yet aggressive manoeuvre before dropping it back into drive and surging forward.

"Jeez, Karl!" I exclaimed, grasping the dashboard and door handle for stability. The sudden change in direction was disorienting, yet I trusted Karl's instincts and driving ability.

Just then, the radio crackled to life. "CITY632," came the voice from dispatch. "The chopper has you in sight. You are still in front of them. If you're quick, you'll cut them off. Other units are preparing a spike strip at the end of Glenlusk Road as a precaution."

"Copy that," I responded, my voice steady despite the intense situation. As Karl drove expertly toward the intersection with Springdale Road, I prepared myself for the next phase of our operation.

The possibility of intercepting the speeding cars before they could cause any harm was within our grasp. The coordination with the other units and the chopper overhead gave us an advantage. We had to be quick, precise, and ready for anything.

The revelation hit me like a ton of bricks, the implications running through my mind at lightning speed. "Shit!" I blurted out, a mix of surprise and realisation colouring my voice.

Karl, sensing the urgency in my tone, immediately slowed the vehicle to a stop near the middle of the intersection, his eyebrows furrowed in concern. "What is it?" he asked, his voice steady but filled with curiosity.

"The rego check found a match," I explained, my voice cracking with disbelief. "It's Gladys Cramer's!"

"Gladys!" Karl echoed. "Are you sure?"

"Positive," I confirmed, my confidence growing despite the bizarre coincidence. "I mean, I could have misread the plate, but seriously, the odds of a misread returning a person of interest like this would be insane!"

Time seemed to slow down as we sat there in the patrol car, the rain continuing its relentless assault against the windows. The light from the spinning red and blue lights danced across the raindrops, creating a surreal, almost hypnotic effect. I rotated my gaze between all the car windows, vigilantly scanning for any sign of the speeding cars. My eyes darted from one direction to another, trying to penetrate the curtain of rain that shrouded our surroundings.

Where are they? I wondered, a knot of tension forming in my stomach. *They should have arrived by now.* The situation was rapidly evolving into something far more complicated than a simple high-speed pursuit. Gladys Cramer, a name already entangled in our current investigation, now potentially linked to this dangerous chase – it was a development I hadn't expected.

Every second that ticked by only added to the suspense. My mind raced, trying to piece together the puzzle. *How did Gladys fit into all this? Was she one of the drivers? Or was her vehicle stolen?* The possibilities were numerous, and each one opened up a different avenue of investigation.

The sudden, ear-piercing noise from the radio caught us completely off guard. "Aargh!" we both shouted in unison, instinctively racing to cover our ears. The sound was sharp, invasive, and completely unexpected. "What the fuck was that!?" I couldn't help but exclaim, my heart racing from the sudden jolt.

Before we could even begin to process what had just happened, Dispatch's voice crackled loudly through the radio, breaking the brief moment of shock. "CITY632," the dispatcher announced, "The vehicles have turned down Myrtle Forest Road. The chopper has lost visual on them."

"Shit!" Karl reacted instantly, his frustration palpable. He slammed his foot down on the accelerator, propelling the patrol car into a rapid pursuit down Springdale Road towards Myrtle Forest. The urgency was clear, but the situation was becoming increasingly puzzling.

"I don't understand," I said. "Where are they? How could the chopper have lost them?" The questions whirled in my mind, each one adding to the uncertainty of the chase.

"I don't know," Karl replied, his tone echoing my confusion. He was focused on the road, his eyes scanning ahead as we sped towards our new destination.

And why the hell would they be heading toward the forest? The thought nagged at me, adding another layer of complexity to an already baffling situation. My mind raced, trying to piece together the fragments of information we had.

Moments later, Karl slammed on the brakes as we reached the end of the road. I braced myself against the dashboard, the car coming to a screeching halt that sent a jolt through my entire body.

The sudden stop left us both momentarily disoriented. I quickly regained my composure, ready to jump into action. My eyes darted around, searching for any sign of the speeding vehicles or an indication of their direction. The thick forest loomed ahead of us, its dense foliage a stark contrast to the open roads we had been navigating.

The tension in the car was palpable as Karl snatched the radio from my hand, his movements sharp and urgent. "This is CITY632. Do you have a visual on the vehicles again?" His voice was a mix of hope and determination, seeking any clue that could lead us back on track.

The response from dispatch was immediate but disheartening. "CITY632. No, there is no visual on either car."

"Fuck!" Karl's frustration erupted as he yelled and pummelled his fists against the steering wheel. His usual composure buckled under the weight of the moment, his actions a clear display of the intense pressure we were under.

Compelled by the same sense of urgency, I didn't hesitate to follow Karl out of the car, despite the relentless downpour. The heavy rain blurred my vision, but I was determined to find a clue, any sign of the cars' whereabouts. My eyes scanned the ground around us, the wet foliage, the muddy patches on the road, anything that could give us a lead.

There is no way two cars can just vanish, I thought, my mind racing with possibilities. *They have to be here somewhere.* The idea that they could disappear into thin air was inconceivable. There had to be a trail, a trace, something we were overlooking.

My gaze swept over the dense forest that surrounded us, the thick underbrush, the towering trees. The forest could hide so much, and I knew that if they had ventured into its depths, finding them would be a monumental task.

"Karl, check this out," I called to him, my voice cutting through the sound of the rain. My eyes followed him as he made his way over the slippery, wet, muddy gravel towards me. For a brief moment, I allowed myself the luxury of admiring how his now wet shirt clung to his abs, accentuating the contours of his muscles through the sodden fabric. Pushing those thoughts aside, I directed his attention to what I had found – two sets of tyre treads etched deeply into the mud.

Together, we followed the tracks, our footsteps squelching in the soft earth. The tracks led us a short distance before coming to an abrupt and bewildering end. "Well, this doesn't make sense," Karl said, examining the first set of treads closely, his brow furrowed in concentration.

I echoed his confusion, my words a mix of bewilderment and frustration. "These tyre tracks look like the vehicle didn't even stop. How can they just end here? It's as though the car just disappeared?" The implausibility of the situation was maddening. Everything about it defied logic.

Karl's gaze shifted from the ground to the large, wooden toilet block that stood ominously in front of us. "I don't know," he replied quietly, his voice tinged with uncertainty. "There wouldn't be much left of that wall if they'd driven into it."

His words hung in the air, adding to the mystery of the situation. The tracks seemed to suggest that the cars had vanished into thin air, an impossibility that left us both stumped. The wall of the toilet block stood intact, showing no signs of impact. It was a dead end in the most literal sense.

"There's still this second set of tracks," I called out to Karl, my voice raised to be heard over the rain. I gestured towards the second set of tyre treads that lay before us, distinct and separate from the first. Just as the words left my mouth, a loud clap of thunder rumbled through the sky, causing both of us to instinctively duck.

"Where do you reckon they go?" I yelled to Karl, as he drew closer, his figure blurred by the heavy downpour.

"Well, they can't go too far out here," Karl replied, his voice barely audible over the rain. "They break away from the first set of tracks down there and then veer to the right. It looks like they head to the back of the toilet block."

My curiosity piqued, and I didn't wait for any further discussion. I found myself already running beside the tracks, following their path with a sense of urgency. I waved at Karl to hurry up and join me. "It's here!" I called out, my voice tinged with excitement and anticipation.

"Shit!" Karl exclaimed, rushing to my side. The discovery was startling – the passenger side door of one of the vehicles we had been chasing was left hanging wide open. With a mix of caution and intrigue, Karl approached the car. I drew my gun, following close behind him, ready for whatever we might find.

"They must have taken off on foot," Karl called through the rain, his words almost lost in the sound of the deluge. "There's nobody here."

My heart was racing, adrenaline coursing through my veins. The chase had taken a sudden turn, the suspects abandoning their vehicle and continuing on foot.

The atmosphere was charged with tension, the thunder's rolling echoes serving as a dramatic backdrop to our current predicament. As the sound of thunder peeled away into the distance, a sharp clang resonated from the vicinity of the toilet block beside us, jolting my senses into high alert.

Instinctively, I pointed my gun towards the small building, my eyes scanning for any sign of movement or threat. The toilet block sat in a small clearing, about ten meters from the edge of the dense forest that surrounded us. I noticed two large myrtle trees growing just off to the side, their gnarled lower branches scraping against the block's tin roof as they swayed in the increasingly fierce wind.

Karl, with his own gun drawn, signalled for me to follow him. Together, we moved towards the entrance of the building, our steps careful and measured. Despite the pounding rain and howling wind, we maintained our focus, ready for whatever might confront us.

"Police!" Karl called out authoritatively as we neared the entrance. "Come out slowly with your hands up." His voice was firm, carrying through the storm.

Before we could react further, another loud clap of thunder boomed directly above us, its sound almost deafening. It was quickly followed by another clang from inside the toilet block, a sound distinctly different from the natural cacophony of the storm.

My grip tightened on my gun, and I exchanged a glance with Karl. We were both aware that whatever or whoever was inside the block was not going to come out willingly. The adrenaline coursing through my body heightened my senses; every nerve was alert, ready to respond to any threat. This was it - the moment of confrontation we had been preparing for since the chase began. The storm outside mirrored the storm within me, a mix of excitement, fear, and determination.

Karl's silent signal was clear, and I nodded in understanding, ready to back him up. He moved with a practiced ease, his gun leading the way as he rounded the corner and stealthily entered the ramshackle building.

Inside, the dim lighting barely pierced the gloom, but it was enough for me to discern the layout. The toilet block was simple: just two cubicles. Karl focused on the cubicle in the far corner, its door ominously shut. He slid along the wall with a cautious grace, his movements deliberate and silent.

I waited, my own weapon at the ready, as Karl checked the first stall. The anticipation was a heavy weight in the air, every second feeling like an eternity.

Suddenly, the wind's howling crescendoed, its whistles weaving through the rooftop. Thunder clapped violently overhead, and the frail light source in the toilet block flickered treacherously before surrendering to darkness. My heart pounded in my chest, the sound nearly as loud as the thunder.

Karl reacted instantly, pulling out his flashlight and positioning it under his gun. The beam of light sliced through the darkness, revealing the closed door of the far cubicle. As the cold, white light flooded the small space, an unexpected rainbow of colours spilled out from under the door, painting the grimy floor in surreal hues.

A shiver ran down my spine as the hairs on my arms stood on end. This was no ordinary situation – the bizarre colours, the sudden loss of light, and now, both our radios crackled with interference, a static sound that seemed almost alive.

In that moment, with the storm raging around us, Karl's decisive action cut through the tension like a knife. He delivered a swift, powerful kick to the cubicle's door. The thin plywood yielded easily, swinging open with a resounding crack that echoed through the small space. As if on cue with Karl's action, a brilliant flash of lightning briefly illuminated the toilet block, casting eerie shadows that danced on the walls. The door, having hit the wooden wall, rebounded and slammed shut, plunging us back into an oppressive darkness, broken only by the thin beam of Karl's flashlight.

Karl froze, his body tensed and motionless. Stepping past him, I nudged the door open with my foot, my gun leading the way, ready for any threat that might reveal itself. "It's empty," I announced, a mix of surprise and confusion in my voice, as I turned back to Karl.

But Karl didn't respond. He stood there, silent and still, his expression unreadable in the dim light.

"What the fuck's up with you?" I pressed, concern lacing my words as we stepped out of the toilet block into the relentless downpour. I noticed his distant look, his eyes unfocused. "You look like you've seen a ghost."

Still, Karl remained silent, his gaze distant, his mind seemingly elsewhere. It was unlike him to be so withdrawn, especially in the middle of an operation.

As we stood there in the pouring rain, a sense of unease settled over me. Karl's reaction, or lack thereof, was unsettling. It was clear that something had deeply affected him, something beyond the ordinary stress of our job. I watched him closely, trying to decipher his silence, to understand what had transpired in those few moments inside the toilet block that had rendered him so uncharacteristically mute.

The voice over the radio sliced through the heavy rainfall, pulling me back from my contemplations about Karl's odd behaviour. I watched as Karl, with newfound urgency, dashed back to our patrol car, his footing precarious on the slick ground.

"CITY632, are you there?" the voice on the radio called out again, its tone businesslike and expectant.

Karl reached the patrol car and yanked the door open with more force than necessary. He grabbed the radio, responding with a tone that was sharper than usual. "CITY632 here. Go ahead," he said, his voice rough, almost aggressive.

"CITY632. Still no sightings of either car. Patrols will remain on alert for the next few hours. Over."

Karl's reply was swift and concise. "Copy that. We have located one of the vehicles. We are here with it at the start of Myrtle Creek Forest. Looks like it has been abandoned," he reported.

"Copy that, CITY632. Patrols are on their way."

"Understood. CITY632 out."

After the exchange, Karl remained seated in the car, his gaze locked on the toilet block, a look of deep contemplation on his face.

"Come on then," Karl finally said, his voice softer now, inviting me to take shelter in the car with him. I hesitated for a moment, observing his change in demeanour. There was something about the way he was looking at the toilet block, as if trying to piece together a puzzle only he could see.

The rain was relentless, drumming a rhythmic pattern on the roof of the car as I made my way to the passenger side. My heart was pounding with a mix of excitement and apprehension, a cocktail of emotions I'd become familiar with during our investigation. But as I approached, something near the start of the walking trail snagged my attention, halting me abruptly. It was as if the universe itself had placed a clue right in our path. With a sense of urgency, I tapped on the side of the car, signalling Karl to join me outside.

"What is it?" Karl's voice cut through the sound of the rain as he stepped out, his expression a blend of confusion and irritation. He pulled his jacket tighter around himself, a futile attempt to shield from the relentless downpour. "Let's just wait in the car, this rain doesn't look like it's letting up any time soon."

A smile tugged at my lips, the thrill of discovery igniting a fire within me. "I think I've found something," I said, unable to mask the grin that now spread across my face. With careful steps, I navigated towards the entrance sign of Myrtle Forest Walk. Each jump over the growing puddles felt like a small victory, keeping me a step ahead of the soaking earth.

Karl, following my lead with a skeptical gaze, queried, "What am I supposed to be looking at?"

"This!" My voice echoed with triumph as I bent down, picking up a small, seemingly insignificant bracelet from the muddy ground. It was a tiny beacon of hope amidst the vast wilderness. "And these footprints in the mud are fresh," I added, my voice tinged with excitement. The mud had preserved the shape of the footprints perfectly, like a signature left behind in haste.

"Those footprints could belong to anyone," Karl countered.

"But I don't think this does," I retorted, holding onto my discovery like a precious gem. "G. C.," I announced, thrusting the bracelet towards Karl. The initials engraved on the inside of the band gleamed faintly, despite the gloom.

Karl's eyes widened, a mirror to the surprise I felt at my own discovery. His usually composed demeanour was shaken, a testament to the gravity of what we had just uncovered.

"I'll go call it in," I declared, my voice steady despite the churn of excitement within me.

"No," Karl's response came swiftly, his hand grasping my arm with an unexpected force that jolted me. I felt myself being pulled backwards. I turned to face him, my eyes wide with shock at the aggressiveness of his grip. It was an intensity I hadn't seen in him before, at least not in this context. "Not yet," he added, his voice firm, as he released his hold on me.

Rubbing my arm, I tried to shake off the discomfort his grip had left behind. My jacket sleeve crinkled and readjusted itself with each movement, a minor distraction from the turmoil brewing inside me. Karl's touch had been rough, unfamiliar outside the boundaries of our more adventurous sexual encounters... and then there was the incident yesterday, a memory that lingered uncomfortably in my mind.

With a mix of irritation and determination, I brushed past Karl and started walking briskly down the walking trail. My footsteps were purposeful, a physical manifestation of my effort to control the waves of unwanted emotions crashing within me. The trail was a narrow ribbon through the wilderness, and with each step, I tried to put some distance between myself and the complex swirl of feelings Karl's actions had stirred.

"Sarah," Karl called out, his voice cutting through the heavy air. "Let's wait for the other patrols to arrive first." But I didn't stop. His words floated behind me, unheeded. I was propelled forward by a need to distance myself, both physically and emotionally. There was a part of me that wanted to yell back, to express my frustration and confusion, but I held it back. Instead, I focused on the path ahead, letting the rhythm of my steps and the steady beat of the rain provide a temporary refuge from the chaos of my thoughts.

For fifteen relentless minutes, I marched along the trail, my footsteps resolute against the soft earth. The rain had turned the path into a slippery canvas, but I hardly noticed, so consumed was I by the whirlwind of emotions spinning in my head. Anger, confusion, determination – they swirled together in a frenzied dance, blurring the lines of my thoughts. For a brief, disorienting moment, I even forgot what had led me down this path, so overwhelming were the feelings coursing through me.

"Sarah!" Karl's voice pierced through my reverie, a distant echo that I consciously chose to ignore. His call, filled with a mix of worry and frustration, was a tether trying to pull me back to reality, but I resisted.

Then, I heard the hurried footsteps of Karl running after me, the urgency in his pace matching the turmoil in my heart. "Sarah, stop it! This is madness," he yelled, his voice laced with desperation. "If Gladys is out here, we're never going to find her," he continued, his words attempting to anchor me with reason.

The frustration that had been simmering within me boiled over. "Why won't we find her?" I snapped back, whirling around to face him. My voice was a sharp edge, cutting through the damp, heavy air.

Karl looked at me, his expression shifting to one of deep concern. "There's too much forest, and it's raining, wet and muddy. We're just two people out here," he reasoned, his hands gently turning me to face him, an attempt to ground me in the present.

As his eyes met mine, the dam of emotions I had been holding back broke. Tears, unbidden and unstoppable, rolled down my face, each one a silent testament to the stress and confusion I felt. Karl's face grew even more concerned, a mirror to my inner turmoil.

"What's wrong?" he asked, his voice now a soft, caring whisper amidst the chaos of my emotions. The question hung in the air, echoing the confusion and pain I felt inside. The forest around us seemed to hold its breath, the rain pausing momentarily in deference to the raw moment we were sharing.

"Nothing," I replied hastily, the word slipping out more as a reflex than a true response. My hands moved quickly, the back of my sleeves serving as an impromptu wipe for my tear-streaked face. In that moment, I was grateful Karl didn't press for an explanation, sensing perhaps that I was grappling with emotions too complex to articulate.

Then, Karl cupped his hands gently around my face, his touch a stark contrast to the earlier roughness. His gaze delved deep into my eyes, searching, understanding. It was a look that seemed to transcend the chaos of our current situation, reaching into the depths of my soul. Slowly, he pulled me in close to his chest, his arms wrapping around me in a tight, protective embrace. It was a reassurance that despite the uncertainty and fear, everything would be okay.

"Thank you, Karl," I murmured softly, my voice barely audible above the rain's symphony. I rested my head on his firm chest, a solid presence in the midst of the storm. In that embrace, amidst the relentless downpour, we stood in silence. The rain, indifferent to our plight, continued its relentless shower, drenching us both.

Slowly, as Karl held me, I could feel the tumult of emotions within me start to settle. My trust in him, which had been momentarily shaken, began to return, wrapping around me as securely as his arms. But with the return of trust came a new, unsettling sensation – fear.

For a brief, haunting moment, fear crept in, weaving its way through my thoughts. It was a fear that nothing Karl could do would ever change how I felt about him. No action, no matter how terrible, would ever diminish my love for him. It was a realisation as frightening as it was profound, a testament to the depth of my feelings for him, feelings that seemed to defy logic and reason. In that moment, held close in Karl's embrace, I was acutely aware of the vulnerability and intensity of my emotions, a reminder of how deeply intertwined our lives and hearts had become.

ABANDONED LOVE

4338.211.3

The Sergeant's words hit me like a gust of cold wind as I stumbled through the doorway of his office, immediately on Karl's heels. "Well, don't you two look like shit," he remarked, his tone a blend of sarcasm and mild concern. His eyes briefly scanned us, taking in our drenched clothes and dishevelled appearances. We must have looked like two characters straight out of a noir film, except there was nothing glamorous about our current state – soaked to the bone, mud splattered, and emotionally spent.

"Sergeant," Karl began, his voice steady despite our rough exterior. He took a step forward, assuming the lead in our impromptu debriefing. "I'd like to request an unmarked car to stake out Gladys Cramer's house. Just in case she goes home tonight." His request was direct, his tone professional, yet there was an underlying urgency that suggested this was more than just a routine ask.

I stood there, slightly behind Karl, trying to compose myself. My thoughts were still a whirlwind, the emotional turmoil from the forest lingering like a stubborn fog. The safety and dryness of the office felt surreal, a stark contrast to the relentless rain and emotional intensity we had just left behind.

I watched the Sergeant's face for a reaction, his expression always a barometer of how feasible our requests were. Part of me wanted to chime in, to add weight to Karl's request, but my voice seemed to have deserted me. Instead, I found myself quietly analysing the room, the familiar sights of the office providing a strange comfort. The walls adorned with commendations, the cluttered desk, the faint smell of coffee – all these details formed a backdrop to our current, somewhat dishevelled, situation.

"No," the Sergeant replied curtly, his eyes not leaving the stack of papers in front of him.

"No?" Karl's voice echoed through the room, tinged with a frustration that had been simmering just below the surface all day.

"That's right. No," the Sergeant repeated, his attention still firmly anchored to his work. His indifference to our drenched and dishevelled state, to our urgency, felt like a silent rebuke.

"But why the hell not?" Karl's voice rose, the volume amplifying his frustration and disbelief.

"Karl," Sergeant Claiborne finally looked up, his gaze meeting Karl's. The moment felt charged, a palpable tension hanging in the air. "We already have other patrols scheduled to pass by her house regularly. If she returns home, we'll catch her and bring her in for questioning."

The Sergeant's words were meant to be reassuring, a logical explanation in a day that had been anything but. Yet, they landed like a lead weight in the room, the implication clear – our personal involvement in this part of the investigation was over.

"For fuck's sake!" The words burst from Karl like steam from a pressure valve, his composure shattering in an instant. He stormed out of the Sergeant's office, the door slamming shut behind him with a finality that echoed through the suddenly silent space.

I stood there, momentarily frozen. The façade of respectful control Karl had maintained all day had finally fallen away, leaving behind a raw, unfiltered display of emotion. I felt a pang of empathy for him, understanding all too well the frustration of being sidelined when every instinct screamed to stay involved.

I hurried after Karl, my footsteps echoing on the hard concrete of the carpark. The cool air nipped at my skin, a stark contrast to the heated tension that had just unfolded in the Sergeant's office. "Karl. Wait! Where are you going?" My voice cut through the late afternoon air as I tried to catch up to him before he could disappear into his car.

Karl paused momentarily, his back still turned to me. "To find Gladys," he said, his voice blunt, carrying a determination that bordered on recklessness.

"Karl, don't," I warned him, finally reaching his side. "The Sergeant denied the request. You can't." My words were a plea, an attempt to tether him back to reason, to remind him of the protocols and procedures we were bound to follow.

Karl turned to face me, his expression taut with frustration. "I don't really care what the Sergeant said," he snapped, the sharpness in his voice like a slap. It was clear that the denial from the Sergeant had only fuelled his resolve, pushing him further towards a path I feared would lead to more trouble.

Without another word, Karl got into his car, the movement brisk and final. He slammed the door shut, the sound reverberating through the carpark. I stood there, watching him, feeling a mix of worry and frustration. His action, so decisive and unyielding, left me feeling helpless, a bystander in a narrative that was spiralling out of control.

Before Karl could pull away, acting on impulse, my feet carried me swiftly to the passenger side of his car. Without hesitation, I opened the door and jumped into the seat, a sense of urgency propelling my movements. "I'm coming with you," I declared, my voice firm, challenging him to argue.

As I settled into the seat, I couldn't help but acknowledge the complex emotions swirling within me. Despite Karl's recent behaviour, his sudden penchant for aggression, I knew the truth that lay in my heart – I had fallen in love with him. It was a realisation that came with its own pain, especially in moments like these. Seeing Karl so tormented, so willing to break the rules, was like watching the man I knew and loved morph into someone unrecognisable. The Karl I loved, the one I had come to know so well, was methodical, respectful of the law. He would never willingly step outside the boundaries of protocol. Never.

But then, unexpectedly, Karl's demeanour shifted. He leaned over quickly and kissed me, his lips firm against mine. It was a sudden, intense moment of connection that caught me off guard. I responded instinctively, kissing him back with a passion that surprised even me. There was a desperation in that kiss, a fervent desire to hold onto the moment, to prolong the sensation of his lips on mine. For those few seconds, nothing else mattered – not the case, not the rules, not the impending storm of consequences.

As quickly as it had begun, the kiss ended. Karl pulled away, and without uttering a single word, he started the ignition. The moment had passed, but it left a lingering warmth, a silent acknowledgement of something deeper between us.

I turned to face the window, my gaze fixed on the outside world that was blurring into motion. A slight smile crossed my face, a private, treasured reaction to the unexpected kiss. In that fleeting moment of intimacy, a thought fluttered through my mind, a hopeful whisper amidst the chaos – *maybe he does really love me back*. It was a thought both frightening and exhilarating.

The silence between us was thick, laden with unspoken thoughts and emotions, as we pulled out of the station's carpark. The car's engine hummed softly, a subtle soundtrack to our journey down the Brooker and towards Gladys' house.

Outside, the city lights blurred past, painting streaks of colour against the night sky. I found myself staring out the window, lost in the myriad reflections of our recent encounter, the kiss still lingering in my mind like a sweet aftertaste.

Suddenly, my heart leaped into my throat. "Shit, Karl!" I shouted, instinctively gripping the dashboard as the car drifted dangerously towards the left lane, flirting perilously close with adjoining traffic. My voice was sharp, a reflexive burst of fear breaking the silence.

Karl's reaction was immediate and rough. He yanked the wheel, pulling us back into our own lane with a jolt that sent a rush of adrenaline through my body. The near-miss left my heart pounding, a stark reminder of the precariousness of our current situation.

"Where are we going?" I asked, my voice still tinged with the remnants of my earlier alarm. The question hung in the air as Karl made a premature right turn, exiting the highway in a move that seemed unplanned, spontaneous.

Karl remained silent, his jaw set, his focus entirely on the road ahead. He drove the car towards the Entertainment Centre, a sprawling complex that now lay dormant and shrouded in darkness. The once vibrant hub of activity was eerily quiet, its usual bustle replaced by an almost tangible stillness.

In silence, Karl manoeuvred the car into the empty car park of the Entertainment Centre, driving us towards the farthest, darkest corner of the great concrete expanse. The car's headlights cut through the darkness, casting long, ominous shadows that seemed to dance around us. As he brought the car to a stop, I felt a sense of isolation enveloping us, the darkness acting like a shroud, separating us from the rest of the world.

As I turned to look at Karl, the dim light from the dashboard faintly illuminated his profile, casting deep shadows that only served to deepen the mystery of his current state of mind. His expression was an enigma, closed off and distant, a stark contrast to the openness we had shared just moments ago. The silence between us was almost palpable, heavy with unspoken questions and tensions.

In this secluded, shadowy corner of the Entertainment Centre's car park, the world seemed to stand still. It felt as though we had entered a different realm, far removed from our identities as detectives, from the structured world of law and order that usually defined us. Here, in this hidden space, it was just Karl and me, alone with the uncertainties and complexities of our personal and professional entanglements.

"What are you doing?" I asked, my voice breaking the silence. As I turned to face him fully, my brows furrowed in confusion, betraying the turmoil of thoughts and emotions swirling within me. The dim light cast panicked wrinkles across my youthful features, a physical manifestation of the unease that gripped me.

I watched Karl intently, searching for some clue, some indication of his thoughts. The urgency of the situation, the strange detour to this deserted place, and Karl's uncharacteristic behaviour had left me feeling unmoored, adrift in a sea of uncertainty. My heart raced, a mix of apprehension and a deep-seated need to understand what was driving him, what had led us to this moment of quiet confrontation in the darkness.

As Karl leaned in to kiss me again, his movement was swift, a sudden closing of the space between us. But the moment was interrupted, almost comically, by the restraint of his still buckled seatbelt. It jammed, halting his advance just a few inches from my face, an unforeseen barrier in an otherwise fluid motion.

He tugged at it impatiently, but the more he yanked, the more stubbornly the belt seemed to hold him in place. "Ah, shit," he muttered, teeth gritted in irritation.

In that instant, as I stared into his eyes, something unexpected stirred within me. The sight of Karl, usually so in control, now momentarily hindered by the seatbelt, sent a surprising pulse of desire through me. It was the rawness of the moment, the unintended vulnerability, that was strangely captivating. The sound of the belt clanking, the physical struggle – it was real, unscripted, and far more enticing than any of our carefully orchestrated role-plays in the bedroom.

A wave of longing washed over me, intense and undeniable. I want him so badly. The thought was clear, a silent admission that echoed loudly in the quiet of the car. This was not just a physical attraction; it was deeper, more visceral. It was a desire born from the complex tapestry of our shared experiences, the tension of the day, and the unspoken understanding that had grown between us.

As Karl continued to wrestle with the seatbelt, I was acutely aware of the close proximity of our faces, of the heat that emanated from him, and of the quickening of my own heartbeat. The car, with its dimly lit interior, felt like a cocoon, isolating us from the rest of the world. In this secluded space, the lines between duty and desire, between professionalism and passion, seemed to blur, leaving us in a limbo of heightened emotions and unspoken questions. The intensity of the moment hung in the air, a palpable force that seemed to draw us inexorably closer, even as the seatbelt held us apart.

Without warning, I shoved Karl hard, forcing him back into his seat, the belt reclaiming more of itself as it retreated behind him, tightening its grip on his body. I felt my nipples harden with excitement. My hands wanted to grip his body as tightly as the belt. Tighter, in fact.

Karl let a silent tear roll down his cheek. I could feel his vulnerability, finally unshackled. It called to me. My seatbelt unbuckled with a loud click, fighting back my intense urge to strip down and expose my nakedness to him as he continued battling with the seatbelt that held him bound.

Karl reached out to me, but I only pushed him back against his seat with an intensity I didn't realise I had. Another tear escaped and rolled its way down his stubbled cheek.

I faced him, my hands feeling their way across his rippling chest. The intensity of my emotions burned like a wildfire in my eyes as I pressed my mouth against his. My tongue felt its way along the length of his rough lips, searching for a way in. After a few moments of resistance, he opened his mouth and allowed my tongue to find his. As we kissed, Karl reached out his left hand and held me firmly behind my neck, drawing me in closer to him.

With surprising force, my hands ripped open Karl's still damp shirt, sending several buttons scattering around us. His chest felt warm and firm against my cool hands. Moving my hand along Karl's inner thigh, I massaged his taut muscles with the tips of my fingers, before making my way further along to find the centre of his passion.

Karl put his hands on my waist. They found their way under my shirt and made their way gradually up my smooth, toned stomach. My breasts rested comfortably in his large hands as he massaged them gently, causing moments of pleasure to escape my lips as we continued to kiss.

I unbuckled Karl's seatbelt, finally freeing him from his canvas position. Carefully, yet purposefully, I unzipped his trousers. My body trembled with satisfaction, listening to the gentle moans that escaped his mouth as I took his pride in my mouth. His firm dick pulsed in my hands, sending waves of electrifying sexual energy through both of us with every move I made.

I came up to kiss him again, with a hungry intensity I had never experienced before. I pulled my own trousers down to my ankles and climbed onto his lap.

Karl seat slid back as far as it would go, stopping with a harsh thud. The car rocked to the rhythm of our energetic, passionate lovemaking.

Falling back into my seat, I felt the rapid pounding of my heart gradually begin to subside, a physical reminder of the intensity of the moment we had just shared. My breathing was still uneven, each breath a testament to the raw emotions that had been unleashed. The air in the car felt charged, thick with unspoken words and the echoes of our desires.

"Still want to go and see Gladys?" I asked, unable to suppress the wide, cheeky smile that spread across my face. It was a playful question, an attempt to lighten the mood, to bridge the gap between the intensity of our encounter and the reality of our situation.

Karl closed his eyes for a moment, as if gathering his thoughts, or perhaps trying to distance himself from the rush of emotions. "No," he replied bluntly, his voice firm, signalling a shift back to the matter at hand. "I think it's time to pay Beatrix a visit."

"Beatrix?" I echoed in astonishment, my mind still swirling with a cocktail of hormones and the lingering aftershocks of sex. "Who the fuck is Beatrix?" The question came out more forcefully than I had intended.

"Beatrix Cramer. Gladys' sister," he answered, his eyes opening to meet mine. There was a sharpness in his gaze, a focus that had returned with his decision. "I've done my homework."

"What! Now?" I blurted out, my expression morphing into one of sheer bewilderment. The sudden shift in Karl's demeanour, from the heat of our intimate moment to this cold, focused resolve, swept away the lingering oxytocin haze that had enveloped me.

"Yes," Karl replied firmly, his voice slicing through the air with an unwavering certainty. He reached across to the back seat, retrieving a small duffel bag that had been lying there unnoticed. From it, he fished out a fresh grey t-shirt and swiftly pulled it over his head, his movements precise and efficient. "And I need to go alone," he added, his tone leaving no room for negotiation.

I remained frozen in my seat, staring at him with wide, furious eyes. My mind was racing, a whirlwind of confusion and hurt. That had been the most passionate sex we had ever had. I was so sure, in that brief, intense moment of connection, that Karl was on the brink of confessing his love for me. *Did I misunderstand?* The question echoed in my mind, a painful doubt that clawed at my heart. *Was it not good?*

As these thoughts swirled in my head, Karl reached across me, his body stretching towards the passenger door. His long fingers found the handle, and with a single, firm action, he pushed my door open. It swung open slightly, only to fall closed again with a dull, resigned thud.

The gesture was clear, unambiguous. I didn't need him to try again to open the door to understand his message. He wanted me to leave, and he was serious about it. The realisation hit me like a physical blow, leaving me breathless with a mixture of anger, hurt, and disbelief.

Gathering my clothes scattered around me, I peered through watery eyes that blurred the harsh lines of reality. With a surge of anger and hurt, I threw open the car door and stepped out into the cool night. "You can be such a prick sometimes, Karl," I spat the words harshly, each syllable laced with a bitterness that surprised even me. Then, channeling all the frustration and betrayal I felt, I slammed the car door with as much force as I could muster, the sound echoing through the empty carpark like a gunshot.

I hurriedly put my pants back on, my movements jerky and uncoordinated, fuelled by a mix of anger and disbelief. Watching Karl drive away through the dark, empty expanse of the carpark, his car's lights soon swallowed by the night as he turned onto the highway, left me feeling abandoned, both physically and emotionally. *Did he really feel nothing?* The question pounded in my head, a relentless drumbeat that mirrored the tumultuous emotions churning inside me.

My body was shaking, a physical manifestation of the hurt and rage that coursed through me. "If Beatrix is that important to you," I muttered to myself, my voice barely audible in the vast emptiness of the carpark.

I began to storm across the carpark, the rounded heels of my black boots hammering out a steady, furious beat on the concrete. The sound echoed around the deserted space, a solitary rhythm that seemed to punctuate my tumultuous thoughts.

"Well... screw you!" The words burst forth, a defiant yell into the inky blackness of the night. It was a release, a way to voice the pent-up frustration and hurt, but it did little to ease the pain. Tears began to roll down my cheeks, unrestrained and free-flowing, each one a silent testament to the deep well of emotions that Karl's actions had tapped into. They dripped onto the concrete below, their impact soft but significant, marking out their own rhythm of pain and sorrow.

The walk from the Entertainment Centre to my small house in the suburbs felt longer than usual, every step heavy with the weight of my thoughts. The night was quiet, the only sounds my footsteps on the pavement and the occasional distant hum of traffic. The cool air did little to soothe my tumultuous emotions; if anything, it seemed to amplify the sense of loneliness that enveloped me.

By the time I reached my house, a modest structure that had always felt like a sanctuary, my mind was a whirlpool of confusion and hurt. I mechanically undressed, the actions feeling detached, as if I were operating on autopilot. The shower was a brief respite, the hot water cascading over me, attempting to wash away the turmoil of the evening. But as the steam fogged up the bathroom, it felt like a metaphor for how clouded my heart and mind were.

Exhaustion soon overtook me, a physical and emotional weariness that seemed to seep into my very bones. I slipped into my pyjamas, the familiar fabric offering a small comfort. Climbing into bed, I wrapped the blankets tightly around my aching, trembling body. The bed felt too big, too empty, accentuating the sense of isolation that Karl's departure had left behind.

Feeling alone and lost, a profound sense of solitude enveloped me. The room was silent, save for the soft rustle of the sheets and my own uneven breaths. In the darkness of my bedroom, with the shadows playing on the walls, I quietly cried myself to sleep.

4338.212

(31 July 2018)

PAFISTIS

4338.212.1

We sat in the car, enveloped in a heavy silence as we drove to investigate another disappearance. The tension was palpable, an unspoken barrier that had formed since Karl had abandoned me the night before. I found myself staring out the window, lost in thought, deliberately avoiding any conversation with Karl. The familiar landscape blurred past, but my mind was elsewhere, still grappling with the events and emotions of the previous night.

As we pulled up to our destination, my attention was momentarily drawn away from my internal turmoil. The house was a large colonial on the outskirts of town, impressive in its stature. My eyes were immediately drawn to the four columns that supported the large balcony overhead. Their renaissance-inspired architectural design was striking, lending an air of elegance and timelessness to the building. The columns flowed harmoniously into the spacious entrance, creating an inviting yet imposing facade.

"This way please, detectives," Mrs. Pafistis's voice broke through my reverie. She appeared at the ample doorway, her presence commanding yet welcoming. As we followed her into her home, I couldn't help but admire the interior.

We walked across large, square marble tiles that felt smooth underfoot. The path led us past a glamorous kitchen that seemed to be right out of a high-end design magazine. Stone benchtops paired with stainless steel appliances gave the kitchen a modern, luxurious feel. It was clear that no expense had been spared in the design and outfitting of this home.

As we continued into the main living area, the sheer scale of the house became even more apparent. The room was spacious, with high ceilings and large windows that allowed natural light to flood the space. The decor was tasteful, a perfect blend of comfort and style. It was the kind of house that spoke of wealth and sophistication, a stark contrast to the grim reason for our visit.

"Your house is exquisite," the words tumbled out of my mouth almost involuntarily as I entered the room, a genuine reaction to the opulence that surrounded us. The grandeur of the house was overwhelming, a stark contrast to the stark functionality of my own small home.

"Thank you," Mrs. Pafistis responded, her voice tinged with a hint of pride. She accepted the compliment with a grace that seemed as refined as the surroundings. "Much of this is my husband's handiwork." Her words added another layer to my impression of the house. It wasn't just a display of wealth; it was also a testament to personal effort and creativity.

"Impressive," I replied, finding it easy to appreciate the craftsmanship that had gone into creating such a space. Karl, who had been quietly observant beside me, nodded in agreement.

Mrs. Pafistis then gestured towards a gargantuan, Italian leather sofa, inviting us to take a seat. The sofa was as luxurious as the rest of the house, its material soft and inviting to the touch. It felt somewhat surreal to be sitting on such an expensive piece of furniture, considering the usual spartan nature of our fieldwork.

She took a seat of her own across from us, maintaining a poised and elegant demeanour. As she settled in, I couldn't help but take in the entire scene. The room was tastefully decorated, with artworks that likely were as expensive as they were beautiful adorning the walls. The contrast between the high-end surroundings and the gritty reality of our detective work was striking. It was a reminder of the diverse worlds our job often brought us into contact with.

As Karl leaned forward, his demeanour shifted into professional mode, a subtle but unmistakable transformation. "Your full name for the record, please," he requested, his voice carrying the official tone of our inquiry. In his hands, he held a small notebook and pen, tools of our trade that seemed almost out of place in the luxurious setting of Mrs. Pafistis's home.

"Sharon Pafistis," she answered, her voice calm and even. There was a composure about her that spoke of someone accustomed to handling situations delicately.

While Karl continued with his questions, diligently scribbling down notes in his book, I took the opportunity to observe Sharon more closely. She presented a picture of both fragility and grace. Her frame was thin, yet there was a refined quality about her, a sense of poise that permeated her being.

My eyes were drawn to her face, which was a study in delicate features. Her nose was pointy yet well-shaped, creating a sense of symmetry and balance. It was framed perfectly by her large green eyes, which held a depth and intensity that was captivating. Beneath those eyes, her wide, luscious lips were coated in a finely applied flesh-coloured lipstick, adding a touch of sophistication to her overall appearance.

As I continued to observe her, I couldn't help but feel a certain admiration for the way she held herself. Despite the gravity of our visit, she maintained a dignified air, a testament to her character. Her facial expressions and body language were controlled, yet there was an underlying strength that became more apparent with each passing moment.

Her presence in the room was like a piece of art in itself, fitting seamlessly into the elegant surroundings of her home. However, beneath the surface of this refined exterior, I wondered what stories she held, what truths lay behind those expressive eyes. In our line of work, appearances often concealed more than they revealed, and as the questioning continued, I knew that our job was to uncover the reality behind the façade, no matter how well crafted it might be.

"And you say your husband has gone missing?" Karl's voice was steady, embodying the calm professionalism we always strived for in these situations. His pen hovered over the notebook, ready to capture every detail.

"Yes," Sharon confirmed with a nod, her voice tinged with a mixture of concern and disbelief. "Adrian."

"When was the last time you had any contact with him?" Karl continued, his manner encouraging Sharon to open up.

"I last saw him yesterday morning. He said he was going out to meet with a client about a new potential job," Sharon explained, her words deliberate, as if she was trying to recall every last detail of their last interaction.

"What time was that?" Karl's questions were methodical, designed to piece together the timeline of Adrian's disappearance.

"I'm not entirely sure. It would have been before nine."

As the questioning continued, I found myself standing up from the luxurious sofa and slowly making my way around the room. This wasn't just a physical movement; it was part of my process, my way of engaging with the environment to get a better sense of the person we were speaking to. Each step I took was measured, my eyes scanning the room, taking in every detail – the family photos that adorned the walls, the expensive decor, the personal touches that turned this house into a home.

"Have you heard from him since? Any phone calls or text messages?" My question was direct, cutting through the thickening atmosphere of concern and uncertainty.

"No, nothing at all," Sharon's reply came, and I could hear the strain in her voice. The composure she had maintained since our arrival was beginning to show cracks, the weight of her husband's disappearance starting to take its toll.

Observing Sharon, I noticed the subtle changes in her demeanour – a slight tremble in her hand, the way her eyes momentarily lost focus, as if lost in thought or overcome by emotion. It was clear that the reality of her situation was beginning to sink in, the facade of control giving way to the human reality of fear and uncertainty.

In these moments, our role as detectives transcended mere questioning; it became about understanding the human element, the stories and emotions that lay beneath the surface. As I continued to move around the room, my mind was not just on the facts of the case, but also on the emotional undercurrents that would inevitably play a role in unraveling the mystery of Adrian's disappearance.

"Did you know the person he was going to meet with?" Karl's question was direct, seeking to uncover any connections that might give us a lead. He maintained eye contact with Sharon, encouraging her to reveal more.

"No. I've never met them before," Sharon replied, her voice steady but with a hint of uncertainty.

"But you've heard of them?" Karl pressed on, his tone shifting to a more optimistic note. He looked up from his notebook, catching Sharon's gaze with his own, encouraging her to think deeper.

"Yes. I think Adrian had done a few renovation quotes for him before," Sharon said.

The mention of renovation quotes suggested a professional relationship, but I knew that even the most innocent connections could lead to unexpected revelations. I observed Sharon closely, watching for any flicker of recognition or hidden concern that might suggest there was more to her story. The way she held herself, the slight pause before answering, and her gaze that sometimes seemed to drift off into the distance – all these subtleties were crucial in understanding the situation we were delving into.

As I listened, I continued to move slowly around the room, my eyes absorbing every detail. The elegant furnishings and tasteful art hinted at a life of comfort and taste.

"Is this your husband?" I interrupted, my curiosity getting the better of me as I picked up a small photo frame from a side table. The frame held a single picture of a smiling couple, captured in a moment of joy on a beautiful beach. The image was picturesque, almost idyllic, the kind of photo that speaks volumes about the people in it. As I held the frame, I was acutely aware of Karl's glare directed at me. He had warned me on several occasions about the etiquette of not touching belongings in someone's home, especially personal items like photos. However, this morning, there was a part of me that didn't mind pushing his buttons, perhaps still lingering resentment from the night before.

Besides, I rationalised, *it wouldn't hurt for us to hear a little bit more about the couple's relationship*. In cases like this, subtleties in how someone speaks about their partner can often reveal more than the most direct questioning. It's the nuances in their tone, the fleeting expressions that cross their face, that can sometimes give us the most valuable insights.

"Yes. That was taken last year. We were on holiday in Bali. We managed to escape for a week without the kids," Sharon answered, her voice taking on a nostalgic tone as she looked at the photo. It was a response that conveyed more than just the facts; it hinted at a life shared, at memories created together.

"You both look very happy," I commented, making it a point to glance over at Karl, ensuring he was paying attention to this exchange. It was a subtle reminder that our methods might differ, but our goal was the same.

"Yes. We were," Sharon replied, a hint of past tense in her voice that she quickly corrected. "I mean we are," she amended, a touch of defensiveness creeping into her tone. "We've always had a happy marriage."

Her correction had piqued my interest. It's often these small slips, the brief hesitations, that can unravel a larger truth. As Sharon spoke of their supposedly happy marriage, I kept my gaze fixed on her, searching for any subtle cues, any flicker of emotion that might betray the true nature of their relationship.

Meanwhile, I was acutely aware of Karl's growing frustration with my approach. He was sending clear signals for me to back off and let him handle the interrogation. But I couldn't shake the feeling that there was more to be uncovered, and sometimes that meant straying from the conventional path.

"You have children, then?" I asked, deliberately steering the conversation towards her family life. It was a question that might seem innocuous, but it was part of painting a fuller picture of Sharon's world.

"We have two daughters, Sarah and Brooke," Sharon replied, and for the first time since we arrived, her face lit up with genuine pride. It was a stark contrast to the tension and concern that had marked her features up to this point.

"Are they home?" I continued, following this new thread of conversation.

"No. They're at my sister's. I didn't want them to be here while I spoke with you," Sharon explained. Her decision to keep her daughters away during our visit was understandable, but it also opened up another avenue for our investigation.

"We may need to speak with them too," I said, planting the seed that our inquiry might extend beyond this initial conversation. It was crucial to prepare her for the possibility that we would need more information.

Just then, my phone began vibrating in my pocket, breaking the flow of our conversation. "Excuse me a moment," I said, excusing myself to take the call. As I walked into the adjoining room, I felt a mix of relief and tension. The call was a brief respite from the intensity of the questioning, but it was also a reminder of the many threads we were juggling in our case.

In the adjoining room, I took a deep breath, steadying myself for whatever the call might bring. It was moments like these, away from the watchful eyes of those we were questioning, that allowed me to gather my thoughts and prepare for the next phase of the investigation. Every piece of information, every interaction, was a step closer to understanding the full picture, and it was my job to piece it all together.

"Shit!" The word escaped my lips louder than I intended as I skimmed through the two emails the text messages had directed me to check. The content of the emails sent a jolt of urgency through me, shifting the dynamic of our investigation. I quickly composed myself and walked back into the living room, where Karl and Sharon were still seated.

"Karl," I called out, my voice carrying a weight of concern that was hard to mask. My face must have mirrored my inner turmoil, etched with a seriousness that was impossible to hide. This new information was critical, and it needed Karl's immediate attention.

Karl, sensing the urgency in my tone, turned to look at Sharon. "Excuse me a moment," he said, his tone polite but firm. He rose from the sofa with a sense of purpose, aware that something significant had come up.

As Karl joined me in the room, I could see the questions in his eyes. He was ready to dive into whatever information I had just received, his mind already shifting gears to assess the situation. It was moments like these that defined our partnership – the ability to seamlessly transition into addressing new challenges, relying on each other's strengths to navigate the complexities of our job.

"I've just received Nial Triffett's phone records," I blurted out quickly, the words rushing out in a torrent as I relayed the information to Karl. The urgency of the situation was pressing, and every second felt critical.

"And?" Karl's response was prompt, his expression a mix of curiosity and anticipation.

"Ignoring all the missed calls from his wife, check out the one near the end," I urged, handing the smartphone over to him.

Karl squinted slightly to read the small font on the screen. He began reading the last few names listed out loud, "Steve Lang, Jane, Brian." His voice was methodical, but as he reached the end of the list, he paused, a hint of surprise in his tone. "There's a call from Luke Smith."

"I know," I said, my voice laced with concern. The name 'Luke Smith' reverberated in the room, heavy with implications.

"Fuck, this is bad," Karl murmured, the realisation of the situation dawning on him.

"Yeah," I agreed, feeling a knot of anxiety tighten in my stomach. "But that—" I started to say.

Karl cut me off abruptly, "Sharon was just telling me that she is pretty sure the client who her husband went to see yesterday morning was Luke Smith." His words hit me like a physical blow, the pieces of the puzzle clicking into place with a clarity that was as shocking as it was revealing.

Glaring at Karl, I felt a surge of determination, a resolve to make sure my point was heard without interruption. The urgency of the situation lent an edge to my voice. "But that's not all," I said firmly, shoving another image right under his nose. I needed him to understand the full extent of what we were dealing with.

"What's this?" Karl's tone shifted to one of curiosity as he examined the image I presented.

"It's the security footage from the ATM where the withdrawals from Jamie's account took place," I explained, watching his reaction closely.

"Are you sure?" he questioned, bringing the image closer to his face in scrutiny. "But that doesn't look like Jamie."

"It's not," I confirmed, my voice steady. "It's Luke Smith."

As Karl absorbed this information, I watched his countenance change at the mention of Jamie's name. There was a shift in his expression, a flicker of something that went beyond professional concern. *What had gone on between them?* The question hung in the air, unspoken yet palpable. *What isn't he telling me?* I couldn't shake the feeling that there was more to Karl's reaction, a hidden layer that he wasn't sharing.

In that moment, standing in the adjoining room with Karl, surrounded by the unseen threads of our case, I felt a mix of frustration and curiosity. It was clear that the situation was more complex than we had initially thought, and Karl's reactions added another layer of mystery. As detectives, we were trained to look for the truth, to uncover the hidden connections and secrets. But in this case, it seemed that some of those secrets might be closer to home than I had realised.

The name Luke Smith, now linked to multiple aspects of our investigation, was like a key piece in a puzzle. I knew that we needed to delve deeper, to understand his role in this intricate web. As I stood there with Karl, the image of Luke Smith at the ATM in my hand, I was acutely aware that we were on the cusp of a significant breakthrough, one that could potentially unravel the entire case.

"You take over Sharon's interview. I'll come and get you when we've got permission to obtain a warrant for Luke's arrest," Karl promised with a sense of urgency in his voice. His words were decisive, leaving no room for debate.

"Karl, wait!" I called after him, a hint of desperation in my voice as he made his way out the front door and to the car. I felt a sudden pang of unease at the thought of being left alone to handle this. But Karl, driven by the need to act swiftly on our newfound information, didn't stop. Standing there, I watched with a sense of disappointment as he reversed out of the driveway and disappeared down the road. His departure left me feeling somewhat abandoned, a lone figure in the midst of unfolding events.

"I'll put a pot of tea on," Sharon's voice called out from down the hall, bringing me back to the task at hand. Her offer was a small gesture of hospitality in a situation that was anything but ordinary.

Slowly, I closed the front door, the sound echoing slightly in the quiet of the house. I turned and walked back to the kitchen, my steps measured, my mind racing with the next steps of the interview. "Thank you, Mrs Pafistis," I replied, my voice carrying a note of gratitude. Despite the tumultuous undercurrents of our visit, her offer of tea was a welcome semblance of normalcy.

As I entered the kitchen, I braced myself to continue the interview with Sharon. The warmth of the room, the sound of the kettle boiling, and the rich aroma of brewing tea created a stark contrast to the cold, hard facts of the case. I knew I had to maintain focus, to keep probing for information while navigating the delicate balance of being an investigator in someone's personal space. With each question, I hoped to peel back another layer of this complex situation, aware that every detail mattered. In the back of my mind, I couldn't help but wonder about Karl's next steps and the impending warrant for Luke's arrest.

I placed the teacup back onto the saucer with a small, delicate clink, the sound punctuating the silence of the room. Rubbing at my brow, I realised this was already my second cup of tea. The warm liquid had done little to ease the tension that knotted my muscles, a physical manifestation of the mental strain I was under.

"I'm sure your partner won't be too much longer," Sharon said, her voice attempting to offer comfort, perhaps sensing the unease that I was trying so hard to mask.

I managed a forced smile, the gesture feeling stiff and unnatural. "Just doing his job," I replied, trying to sound reassuring, both to Sharon and to myself. My response was as much about convincing her as it was about maintaining my own composure in the midst of uncertainty.

The phone on the table then sounded a short jingle, breaking the strained atmosphere. I quickly grabbed it, hoping for good news. "Oh, for fuck's sake," I blurted out involuntarily as I read Karl's text. The frustration I felt was immediate and intense, a reaction to the unexpected setback. For a moment, I forgot the decorum required in someone else's home.

15:09 Karl: *Claiborne has refused request to obtain either an arrest warrant or search warrant. Glen is on his way to collect you. KJ.*

The message hit me like a wave of cold water. Claiborne's refusal to grant the warrants was a significant blow to our investigation. It felt like we were so close to a breakthrough, only to be hindered by bureaucratic red tape. The mention of Glen coming to collect me only added to the sense of frustration and helplessness.

I took a deep breath, trying to collect myself. My momentary lapse of professionalism was a rare slip, but it spoke volumes about the stress of the situation. I glanced at Sharon, hoping my outburst hadn't alarmed her too much. The complexities of our job often required balancing emotional responses with professional duties, and in that moment, I was acutely aware of the challenge this posed.

"Thank you, Glen," I murmured with a small nod of gratitude as we arrived back at the station. The car journey with Glen had been uncomfortable, filled with a tense silence that reflected my growing frustration. After an hour of waiting and enduring a seemingly endless stream of "I'll be there soon" messages, the relief of finally reaching the station was palpable. Karl was definitely in for an earful when I found him. His delays and lack of clear communication had only added to the day's stresses.

With a sense of purpose, I stormed through the back door of the police station, my steps echoing down the corridor. My mind was already formulating what I would say to Karl when I abruptly stopped mid-stride, feeling my phone vibrating in my pocket.

"Hello, Virginia," I answered, trying to keep my voice steady despite the turmoil of emotions inside me.

"Hi, Sarah. Look, I'm so sorry to bother you but I think you had better come down here. Your grandmother is very distressed," Virginia's voice came through the line, her tone laced with concern.

"I'll be there in ten," I responded quickly, the urgency of the situation clear. Hanging up the phone, I felt a wave of anxiety wash over me. My grandmother's wellbeing was a priority, and hearing she was distressed added a new layer of urgency to an already challenging day.

Shoving the phone back into my pocket, I did a reluctant one-eighty and stormed straight back out the way I had come. My steps were quick, driven by a mix of concern for my grandmother and frustration at the day's events. Thankfully, the nursing home was only a short drive from the station, a small mercy in the midst of the day's chaos.

As I headed to my car, my thoughts were a whirlwind. Concern for my grandmother mingled with the frustration of the case and the irritation with Karl. It was moments like these that tested the balance between personal responsibilities and professional duties, a balance that was often precarious in the life of a detective. I braced myself for what awaited at the nursing home, mentally shifting gears to face the next challenge.

FAMILY REVELATIONS

4338.212.2

"Thank you for coming in so quickly," Virginia said as she greeted me at the door of the nursing home. Her voice carried a mix of relief and concern.

"Any time, Virginia. You know that. Where is she?" I responded immediately, my tone firm yet laced with worry. My grandmother's well-being was always a priority for me, no matter the chaos that swirled around my professional life.

"She's in her room," Virginia replied, her expression sombre. There was a brief, heavy pause before she continued, "Mr Gangley is with her," she finished, the corners of her mouth turning down in a slight cringe.

"Oh dear," I said, a sigh escaping my lips as I shook my head in slight frustration. The mention of Mr. Gangley brought a familiar annoyance. *How many times do I have to tell the old man to stop filling my grandmother's head with wild stories?* The last thing she needed was additional stress or confusion, especially given her condition.

"Tell me what happened," I urged Virginia as we moved briskly toward my grandmother's room. My steps were quick, fuelled by a mix of concern and the need to be at my grandmother's side as soon as possible.

Virginia, slightly out of breath from trying to match my pace, explained, "We believe she had a nightmare during her afternoon nap." Her voice reflected the care and attention she devoted to the residents here. "She kept saying something about Kell... Kellry... Killery—."

"Killerton?" I interjected, the name slipping out almost instinctively, and sending a ripple of unease through me.

"Yes, that's it," Virginia confirmed, her eyes briefly meeting mine. "You've heard of it before?"

I tried to play it down, to maintain a semblance of professional detachment. "Vaguely," I said, attempting nonchalance. However, my effort to appear unaffected was betrayed by the grimace that contorted my face. The name Killerton Enterprises resonated with me more than I cared to admit.

As we approached my grandmother's room, my mind was racing. The mention of Killerton wasn't just a random fragment of a nightmare; it was a name that carried significance, a piece of a puzzle that I couldn't quite place in the current context. The thought of my grandmother being tormented by such nightmares, especially given her frail health, added a layer of personal urgency to an already complicated day.

I mentally prepared myself as we reached the door to her room. I needed to be strong for her, to offer comfort and reassurance. Yet, at the back of my mind, the mention of Killerton lingered, a nagging reminder that there might be more to her distressed state than just a simple nightmare. As I stepped into the room, I was ready to put on my most comforting granddaughter facade, all the while silently grappling with the implications of what Virginia had just shared.

"Hello, Sarah," Mr. Gangley's voice, old and croaky, greeted me as I entered my grandmother's room. He looked at me with a keen eye, taking in my appearance. "You don't look so well," he commented, a note of concern underlying his observation.

"It's been a long week already, Mr. Gangley," I replied, offering a tired smile. His comment, though well-intentioned, only served as a reminder of the weariness I felt both physically and emotionally.

Jane rose gingerly from where she was seated at the table. Her movements were careful, a testament to her age and fragility. "Oh, Sarah, I am so glad you came," she said, her voice filled with relief and affection. She opened her arms wide for a hug.

As I embraced her, Mr. Gangley's voice broke the moment. "She's dreaming of Killerton again," he said, his tone serious.

"Again?" I asked, turning towards him sharply. My surprise was evident in my voice. "You mean it's happened before?" My tone unintentionally took on an edge, a reflection of my concern. The poorly concealed expression on my face mirrored my growing unease at the mention of Killerton.

Jane, sensing my discomfort, tugged at my arm firmly. "Oh, you just ignore that old man," she said dismissively. "Bob's suffering from old age. He doesn't know what he's talking about." Her words were meant to reassure, to set Mr. Gangley's comments as the ramblings of an elderly man.

"Don't I, Jane?" Bob drawled in response, his face drawn out and serious. His reaction suggested that there was more to his statement than mere confusion or forgetfulness. His serious demeanour implied a depth to his words, hinting that there might be truth to his claim about my grandmother's dreams.

I observed Bob and Jane closely, my detective instincts kicking in despite the personal nature of the visit. There was a tension between them, a silent exchange that spoke volumes. I caught the stern gaze my grandmother directed towards Bob, a clear warning not to divulge any more information. She wasn't exactly subtle about it, her eyes communicating a firm message. It was evident there was something she didn't want revealed, something about these dreams of Killerton.

A short knock at the open door pulled my attention away from the pair of conspirators.

A young girl, clearly a staff member of the nursing home, stood there, tugging nervously at the sleeve of her uniform. Her presence and question broke the tense atmosphere in the room.

"Excuse me, Virginia. Sorry to interrupt. But have you seen Jamie Greyson at all this afternoon?" she asked, her voice laced with anxiety.

I jumped in before Virginia could reply, my mind instantly connecting the dots. "Jamie Greyson?" I repeated, a sense of urgency creeping into my voice. *Was this really the same Jamie Greyson whose disappearance we were currently investigating?* The coincidence seemed too striking to ignore, and my mind raced with the implications.

"Yes," the girl confirmed, clearly unaware of how crucial her question was to me. Her innocent inquiry suddenly felt like a key turning in a lock, opening up new possibilities in the case.

"He works here, dear," said Jane, tugging at my arm, trying to gently steer me away from the door and the conversation. Her action, though well-intentioned, only served to heighten my curiosity.

"You knew?" I asked her, turning my attention back to my grandmother. My tone was one of bewilderment. *How had this connection to our case been right in front of me, yet I had been completely oblivious?*

Jane gave a gentle shrug of her frail shoulders, a simple gesture that carried so much weight. "Of course," she replied nonchalantly. "He's not assigned to me, but he and his partner come to visit me at least once a week."

Her revelation hit me like a wave. Jamie Greyson, a name that had been just a case file to me, suddenly became a real person with a connection to my own grandmother. The news that he was not only an employee here but also a regular visitor to my grandmother brought a personal dimension to the case I hadn't anticipated.

"You mean Luke Smith?" I asked, my voice taking on an edge of disbelief.

The young girl, still standing at the door, interrupted again, bringing us back to the immediate concern. "Well, have you seen Jamie?" Her question was direct, her expression one of genuine concern.

Virginia shook her head in response. "No," she said. "I haven't seen him all week."

I turned back to my grandmother, feeling a growing sense of urgency. "You know Luke Smith?" I asked again, needing confirmation, needing to understand the connection.

Jane's response was a silent, heavy pause. She closed her eyes, and when they opened again, I saw tears brimming over her eyelids, threatening to spill. Her vulnerability in that moment was palpable, a stark contrast to her usual composed demeanour.

"I'll be gone soon," she began, her voice quivering with emotion. The words hit me with a jolt of sadness. "I suppose you should know."

My face grew hot, a whirlpool concoction of anger, fear, and heartbreak swirling within me. I could feel my emotions teetering on the edge, a tumultuous mix that threatened to overwhelm my professional composure.

Virginia, standing beside us, was already wiping at her eyes, her empathy for my grandmother evident.

"Know what?" I managed to ask, my voice barely above a whisper. A part of me was afraid to hear the answer, to uncover a truth that might shake the foundations of what I thought I knew. The weight of the situation bore down on me, a heavy cloak of uncertainty and apprehension.

As I stood there, facing my grandmother, I braced myself for her revelation. The case, which had already woven its way through my professional life, was now entangling itself in my personal world in a way I had never imagined. I knew that whatever Jane was about to reveal could potentially change everything, both in terms of the investigation and in our family dynamics. The air in the room felt charged with the imminent disclosure of a long-kept secret, and I waited, heart pounding, for what was to come.

"Luke Smith is my grandson," Jane stated bluntly, her voice cutting through the tension in the room like a knife. She averted her eyes after speaking, as if the weight of her revelation was too much to bear while facing me directly.

The whirlpool of emotions inside me merged with a cyclone, sending me into a chaotic headspin. "Holy shit!" I blurted out, unable to contain my shock. The discovery of this fresh branch of the family tree was reeling in my mind, a revelation that was as unexpected as it was significant. "Please don't tell me he's my brother," I almost begged, the words escaping in a rush of anxiety and disbelief.

Jane, despite the gravity of the situation, managed a little, croaky chuckle. "No, Sarah. He's your cousin," she revealed. Her words offered a small sense of relief amidst the turmoil, but they also opened a floodgate of new questions and emotions.

"Luke's mother was my firstborn. I fell pregnant to a handsome young British fella while I was travelling in Europe. He cared for me in England until the baby was born and then we gave her up for adoption. I came straight back to Australia after that. I was broken-hearted, but I knew it was for the best," she explained, her voice laced with a mixture of sadness and nostalgia.

As I listened to Jane's story, a torrent of emotions washed over me. There was a sense of shock at the revelation, but also an undercurrent of empathy for what my grandmother had gone through. The story she shared was a window into her past, a past filled with love, loss, and tough decisions. It painted a picture of a young Jane, far from home and faced with a life-altering choice.

The revelation that Luke Smith, a person entangled in our current investigation, was actually my cousin added a new layer of complexity to the case. It was a connection that was personal and profound, and it threatened to fundamentally change the way I viewed the investigation. My mind was racing, trying to reconcile this newfound family connection with the professional role I had to play.

As I stood there, reeling from the revelations about Luke, a question nagged at me. *Why has she kept it all a secret for so long?* I wondered. The weight of years of untold stories seemed to hang in the air between us. "And how does Luke know?" I finally managed to ask, my voice a mix of curiosity and apprehension.

"Oh, he tracked me down several years ago," Jane explained, a touch of pride in her voice. "He is a rather resourceful young man. There was no denying the evidence he had collected. And now he visits me every week," she added, her face lighting up with the happiness that only family can bring.

I stared at my grandmother, my mind struggling to reconcile the image of the man we were investigating with the person she described. It pained me to see how much my grandmother cared for Luke. "No," I said defiantly, my voice rising with emotion. "Luke Smith is a monster!" I couldn't hold back the tears that began to stream down my face. The dichotomy between the Luke my grandmother knew and the one we were investigating was too much to bear.

"No, Sarah," my grandmother spoke softly, her voice filled with a calm conviction. "You have it all wrong," she said, her own tears starting to well up again.

"And does he know about me?" The question slipped out, a thought I hadn't even realised I was harbouring until that moment. I looked into my grandmother's tear-stained eyes, searching for the truth.

A grimace pulled at Jane's weary mouth. "Yes," she said, her voice barely above a whisper, her bottom lip quivering with the weight of the confession.

I looked away, feeling a mix of betrayal, confusion, and an overwhelming sense of being lost in a story far bigger than I had imagined. "I have to go," I said, the words barely audible as I turned to leave.

"Sarah!" Jane's voice echoed with desperation as I left the room, but I didn't look back. The torrent of emotions that her revelations had stirred within me was overwhelming, a maelstrom of shock, disbelief, and a sense of betrayal. Each step I took away from her was heavy, laden with the weight of this new, unexpected truth.

As I walked away, my mind was a tumult of conflicting thoughts and feelings. The case had taken on a deeply personal dimension, blurring the lines between my professional duties and my own family history. The revelation that Luke Smith was not only connected to our investigation but also a part of my family left me feeling unmoored, adrift in a sea of uncertainty. Stepping out of the room, I was acutely aware that the road ahead would be fraught with difficult decisions and revelations that could change everything I thought I knew about my family and myself.

Determined, I kept walking. *There's someone I need to find. Someone else owes me some answers.* My steps quickened as I approached the reception desk. I flashed my badge at the receptionist, a clear signal of my official capacity. "You record details of all visitors?" I demanded, my voice firm and authoritative.

"Yes, we do," replied the receptionist, her voice tinged with nervousness as she withered under my glare. Her reaction was understandable; my demeanour was that of a detective on the hunt for information, leaving little room for hesitation.

"Good. I need the contact details of Luke Smith and Jamie Greyson," I stated, my tone brooking no argument. The information was crucial, a vital piece in the puzzle that was becoming more intricate and personal by the minute.

COLLISION OF FATES

4338.212.3

As dusk began to slowly swallow the remnants of daylight, I found myself behind the wheel, driving towards Luke's house. The words of my grandmother echoed incessantly in my mind, creating a thick fog of disbelief that seemed to cloud my thoughts. *Luke has to know something about Killerton Enterprises and the missing persons. I'm certain of it.* This conviction, this certainty that Luke would provide me with answers, drove me forward, despite the turmoil churning inside me.

Pulling off the highway, I began the steady climb up Berriedale Road. The winding road, lined with its mix of shadows and the last glimmers of twilight, felt almost symbolic of the murky path the investigation had taken. My eyes were drawn to the rippling physique of a figure jogging along the road. In the dimming light, his struggle against the steep incline seemed almost metaphorical, mirroring my own battle with the complexities of the case.

I couldn't help but chuckle to myself, watching him battle with the gradient of the road. There was a certain amusement in witnessing his determination, a brief moment of levity in an otherwise tense and fraught day. However, as the car got a little closer, a startling realisation dawned on me. The man's ass became a little too familiar.

"Shit!" The word escaped my lips as I made a sharp left turn down a side street, narrowly avoiding passing the jogger who had suddenly come into clear view. My heart pounded with a mix of surprise and confusion. I slowed the car, bringing it to a halt a little further down the road, out of immediate sight.

What the hell is Karl doing out here? The question echoed in my mind. *This is nowhere near his house. Where's his car? And why is he dressed all in black?*

My mind raced with possibilities, theories forming and dissolving with each passing second. And then, an unwelcome thought crossed my distracted mind, a possibility I didn't want to entertain. "No," I whispered softly to myself, the words barely audible. "He can't be on his way to Luke's." The implication of Karl being involved in this way was unsettling. It was a connection I wasn't prepared to make, a link that could complicate everything.

With a sense of urgency, I inched the car further up the road, ensuring I remained hidden from the main road. I didn't want Karl to spot me and become alerted to my presence. The process of finding a suitably obscure parking space took what felt like an eternity, heightening my anxiety. Once the car was parked, I realised I had no choice but to jog back the way I'd driven. I had to make sure I didn't lose Karl.

As I jogged, my mind was a whirlwind of thoughts and emotions. The implications of Karl being here, in close proximity to Luke's house, were too significant to ignore. It suggested a level of involvement or knowledge that I hadn't considered before. My role as a detective demanded that I follow this lead, to uncover the truth, no matter how personal or difficult it might be. But as I followed Karl's path, a part of me dreaded what I might find, what secrets might be revealed. This investigation, already deeply intertwined with my personal life, seemed to be taking yet another unexpected turn, drawing me deeper into a web of complex relationships and hidden truths.

As I squinted up the road into the growing darkness, my eyes strained to spot any sign of Karl. But there was nothing

– he had vanished into the night. My heart began racing, pounding against my chest with a mixture of anxiety and determination. There was only one direction to go from where I had turned off, and that was up. *So, where the hell is he? Did he see me?* The questions spun in my head as I tried to make sense of his sudden disappearance. My eyes darted all around, scrutinising every shadow cast by the trees, twitching at every rustle and sound in the quiet of the evening.

Not knowing where Karl had parked his car, and without any clear idea of where he might have been heading, I took cover behind a large gum tree as a car approached from the top of the hill. My heart skipped a beat, unsure if this new vehicle had anything to do with Karl's disappearance or if it was just a local returning home.

I took a deep breath, trying to calm my racing thoughts and allow my eyes to adjust to the dimming light. I carefully stole a peek from behind the tree. The car's headlights sliced through the darkness, and for a brief moment, illuminated the outline of a tall man still jogging towards the peak. A wave of relief washed over me. *There he is.*

My relief was quickly replaced by a renewed sense of urgency. I knew I needed to keep Karl in sight, to understand why he was here and where he was heading. This was more than just following a colleague; it was about piecing together a puzzle that was becoming increasingly personal and complex. As the car passed and the darkness enveloped the road again, I prepared to move out from my hiding spot and continue tailing Karl, all the while wondering what I would discover at the end of this pursuit.

Continuing to stalk Karl as he began to disappear over the crest of the hill, I maintained a careful distance. It was becoming increasingly clear that we were headed towards what I assumed to be Luke's house. Every step felt weighted with a mix of professional duty and personal apprehension.

After some time, Karl stopped abruptly and looked around. His sudden pause sent a jolt of panic through me, forcing me to make a hasty decision. In a split second, I leapt over the small, white fence of the nearest house, grimacing as I landed in a carefully mulched flowerbed. The perfectly spaced kangaroo paws bore the brunt of my intrusion, one unfortunate plant getting flattened under my foot like a small rodent under a tire. "Sorry," I whispered apologetically to the broken plant, feeling a pang of guilt for the minor destruction in my wake.

Turning my attention back to Karl, I strained to see him in the growing evening darkness. The distance and rows of houses between us made it difficult, but I could still make out his distinctive frame. He was crouched in the bushes along the native land that sprawled across the road from what I presumed to be Luke Smith's house. *What is he doing?* The question echoed in my mind as I watched Karl shift his weight around in the bushes, seemingly trying to find a comfortable position for... whatever he was doing.

My mind was racing with possibilities. Was Karl conducting his own investigation into Luke, or was there something more to his actions? The ambiguity of the situation was frustrating. There I was, crouched in someone's garden, spying on my colleague, and still unsure of his motives or his connection to Luke Smith.

I knew I had to be patient, to wait and watch, despite the discomfort and the risk of being spotted. The answers I sought were tantalisingly close, yet shrouded in the complexities of the case and the fading light. As Karl continued to adjust his position in the bushes, I remained hidden, vigilant and ready to act on whatever unfolded. This night, with its cloak of darkness and air of mystery, felt like it held the key to understanding the tangled web of connections that had brought me here.

"Crap!" I muttered under my breath, barely audible, as a blue Holden pulled into the driveway beside me. The last thing I needed was to be caught trespassing. The front passenger side door opened with a dull click, and someone clambered out. I could only assume they would not be particularly pleased to find a stranger crouching in their flowerbeds.

Reacting swiftly, I rolled along the fence line, a sense of urgency propelling my movements. My heart raced with a mix of adrenaline and guilt as I flattened several more kangaroo paws in my hasty retreat. Finally, I found myself pushing my way behind a short wall of pittosporums, their dense foliage offering a makeshift hiding spot. I waited there, holding my breath, as the young family made their way indoors, blissfully unaware of the terrified police officer concealed in their shrubbery.

From my hiding place, I watched as lights flicked on in various rooms of the house, streams of light pouring through the as yet unclosed curtains. My position was rapidly becoming untenable. I was hidden from some angles, but alarmingly exposed to the master bedroom. If anyone looked out of the window, I would be unmistakably visible.

But how do I get out? The question echoed in my mind, a desperate search for options. If I stayed put, someone in the house was bound to see me. Yet, if I attempted to jump back over the fence, there was a good chance Karl would spot me, blowing my cover and possibly compromising the investigation.

I crouched there, weighing my options. The situation called for a quick decision, but each option seemed fraught with risk. I needed to maintain my surveillance on Karl without drawing attention to myself. The darkness of the evening was my only ally, offering some concealment as I considered my next move.

Torn between the risk of being seen by Karl or being spotted by the family, I found myself in a precarious situation. With a cautious movement, I turned my back to the house and peered out over the small fence, my heart pounding in anticipation. *Karl's gone again!* The realisation sent a wave of frustration through me. My eyes searched frantically in the ever-deepening darkness. The streetlights, few and far between, offered little assistance, casting long shadows that played tricks on my vision. *Maybe he's moved himself further into the bushes*, I considered, trying to reason out his next move.

Then, a sudden movement in the fringes of a streetlight's glare caught my attention. *There he is!* Relief mixed with renewed focus as I just about made out his hulking figure. Karl was sneaking along the property's side fence, quickly making his way towards the front driveway. Every muscle in my body tensed, ready to follow his lead while still maintaining a safe distance.

"What the hell are you doing, Karl?" I whispered into the cool, night air, more to myself than anyone else. "Did you see someone?" My whispered questions hung unanswered in the stillness of the night. The inky blackness around me gave no reply, no hint of what Karl's intentions might be or who he could be pursuing.

I continued to watch, utterly gobsmacked, as Karl approached the front door of Luke's house. The sight was surreal – my colleague, someone I had worked alongside, now a central figure in this unfolding mystery. Moments later, he disappeared from view as he headed further behind the house. My heart pounded in my chest, each beat echoing the urgency and gravity of the situation. *I have to get out of the front yard and find out what on earth is going on*, I thought, my mind racing with scenarios and possibilities.

Glancing behind me, I could see the young homeowners, whose land I was trespassing on, moving about in their bedroom. I felt a twinge of guilt for intruding in this manner, but the situation left me with little choice. Suddenly, a distraction from another room drew their attention away from the window. This was my moment.

Seizing the opportunity, I quickly launched myself back over the fence. A sharp sting of a splinter sliding into the pad of my hand was a minor inconvenience compared to the need to follow Karl. But my haste resulted in a less-than-graceful landing. I almost twisted my ankle and pain shot through my knee as it slammed hard into the concrete footpath.

Ignoring the surge of pain, I quickly gave my injuries a once-over. My knee throbbed, but fortunately, nothing was broken, and my trousers hadn't torn. Confident that I hadn't caused myself any serious injury, I made a dash for the bushes that Karl had used for cover earlier.

Forgetting about my sore knee, I crouched down behind the bushes, ignoring the brief spike of pain that shot through my leg. The discomfort was a small price to pay for maintaining surveillance. Crouched there, the evening had turned into a high-stakes game of cat and mouse, and I was right in the thick of it.

My eyes scanned the area where Karl had disappeared, trying to catch a glimpse of him or to understand his intentions. The pain in my knee was a constant reminder of the physicality of the situation, but my focus remained sharp. I was determined to uncover what Karl was doing at Luke's house, to understand how all these pieces fit together. In the shadows behind the bushes, I braced myself for what I might discover, ready to face whatever secrets the night would unveil.

Minutes dragged by with no sign of Karl, and my anxiety grew with each passing second. My eyes remained permanently trained on the house, scanning for any movement or hint of Karl's presence. Worry gnawed at the edges of my mind, creating a whirlpool of apprehension and conjecture. *He has to be heading for the broken window of the back corner room*, I surmised, recalling the one I'd hurt myself on earlier in the week. Karl's behaviour had been increasingly obsessive about this place, and I couldn't help but fear he might be on the brink of doing something regrettable.

A sudden murmur of pain from my hand drew my attention away from the house. Glancing down, I noticed a small amount of blood beginning to seep through the cloth dressing the cut I'd sustained from the broken window. *I must have aggravated the wound while jumping over the fence.* I sighed wearily, the physical pain a stark reminder of the day's tumultuous events.

The light breeze rustling the leaves of the gum trees around my hiding spot and the bright crescent moon shining in the clear night sky offered a momentary sense of calm. But the tranquility of the environment starkly contrasted with my inner turmoil. Finally, driven by a blend of professional duty and personal concern, my curiosity got the better of me. *I have to know what Karl is up to.*

With a burst of determination, I darted out from my hiding place, following the same route I'd seen Karl take a few minutes earlier. Each step was careful yet swift, my injured knee throbbing in protest as I crouched and manoeuvred up the small embankment leading to the row of houses. It wasn't long before I reached the back fence of Luke's house.

Standing at almost full height, I cautiously peered over the ageing, wooden fence. My heart pounded with anticipation and a hint of fear. *What would I find? Was Karl merely conducting his own investigation, or was there something more sinister at play?* As I looked over the fence, ready to confront whatever lay beyond, I knew that the answers I found could potentially alter the course of our investigation and have profound personal repercussions. The night, with all its secrets, seemed to hold its breath as I prepared to uncover the truth.

The fine hairs on my arms bristled to life, and my mouth dropped open in shock as the downstairs room lit up with a brief flash of colour. Just as quickly as it had burst into life, the light faded back into darkness, leaving a rather large man in its wake. A man who, I thought, had not been there before. I stared at the room in confusion, trying to make sense of what I'd just witnessed. *Maybe he had always been there*, I told myself, trying to rationalise the situation.

Either way, I knew this man was definitely not Karl. His silhouette was one I was very familiar with, and this figure did not match. I thought about calling out to warn Karl that he might be in danger, that he wasn't alone in the house, but I hesitated. Revealing my position could compromise both of us, and I wasn't sure of the right course of action.

I watched as the man headed for the stairs. *If Karl's in there, he's about to get caught.* My heart raced with the implications. I was torn between the urge to intervene and the need to maintain my cover. I knew that whatever decisions I made in the next few moments could have significant consequences.

Crouched behind the fence, I weighed my options. The situation was tense, a delicate balance of risk and necessity. I had to make a decision, and fast. The quiet of the night was deceptive, masking the high stakes of the unfolding drama.

"Answer your goddamn phone," I whispered urgently under my breath, a mix of frustration and concern colouring my tone as I attempted to call Karl. But it was to no avail. As soon as Karl's voicemail started, I hung up in an instant. The situation was too critical for voicemails; I needed to speak to him directly, and time was slipping away.

Unable to see the mystery man clearly enough to identify him from my vantage point, my mind raced with possibilities. He had to be one of the missing men, perhaps Luke himself. My fingers fumbled with the phone in a frantic rush as I searched for the contact, *Luke Smith*. If there was any chance that I could distract the man and buy Karl a few minutes to get out of the house safely, I knew I had to take it. With a sense of determination, I pressed the call button.

"Shit!" I cursed softly when the call went straight to voicemail. My heart pounded in my chest as desperation gripped me. I fought with my trembling fingers as I quickly searched for the next potential distraction, *Jamie Greyson*. Once more, I pressed the call button and held the phone to my ear, hoping for a connection this time.

After several rings, to my utter shock, the phone was answered. I recognised the voice immediately. "Karl!" I whispered sharply into the phone, my surprise momentarily overwhelming me. The unexpected sound of his voice threw me off balance. "You need to listen to me. You need to get out, right now!" I demanded, my voice trembling with fear. The realisation that Karl was potentially in immediate danger heightened my anxiety. I ended the call abruptly, knowing that every second mattered.

In that brief moment, a flurry of thoughts rushed through my mind. Karl's unexpected presence on the other end of the line raised more questions. *Was he in danger? Was he already inside the house?* The implications were dire, and I knew I had to act quickly. As I crouched there, phone in hand, the urgency of the situation bore down on me. I needed to make a move, to ensure Karl's safety while also maintaining my own cover.

Within seconds of ending the call, a confrontation erupted from upstairs in the house. The sounds were muffled, but unmistakably violent – a heavy thud, a shuffle, a clatter. My heart was pounding so fiercely I could almost hear it. Without wasting a moment, I followed the fence line, just as Karl had done, moving quickly yet stealthily towards the top of the driveway. As I neared the front door, there was one final, heavy thud, and then the house fell into an eerie silence that sent chills down my spine.

Ducking underneath the kitchen window, I paused, listening intently for any sounds from inside. The silence was almost more unnerving than the noise of the confrontation. Carefully, I peered over the window ledge, scanning the room. There was no sign of Karl or his attacker in the darkened house. Realising I needed a better vantage point, I ducked down and moved further along the wall.

Wincing in pain, I grabbed the top of the small fence, hoisting myself over to the other side. My feet landed heavier than I would have liked, sending a jolt of pain through my already battered body. The pain was a sharp reminder of the physical toll the night was taking on me.

Crouching down again, I cautiously approached the broken bedroom window. Every movement was calculated, trying to be as quiet as possible. Delicately climbing through, I was acutely aware of avoiding any further injuries. Once inside, I instinctively reached for my gun holster, only to remember, with a sinking feeling, that I had come unarmed. As my hand grasped aimlessly at the empty space where my gun should have been, a wave of vulnerability washed over me.

In the darkness of the room, my eyes slowly adjusted to my surroundings. The lack of light was disorienting, making the familiar act of navigating a room feel alien and dangerous. I stood still for a moment, allowing my senses to acclimate to the environment. I needed to be alert, ready for whatever lay ahead in the shadowy confines of the house. As I took a careful step forward, the darkness enveloped me, a stark contrast to the moonlit world outside.

Standing outside the toilet at the top of the hallway, I held my breath, straining my ears for any hint of movement. The house was engulfed in a thick, palpable silence that felt almost suffocating. *Where's Karl?* The question echoed in my head as the oppressive blackness began to worm its way into my psyche. A knot of fear tied itself in my gut, my internal organs feeling like they were dancing a jig of anxiety. As I slowly moved into the open hallway, passing the doorway of the master bedroom, my senses were on high alert.

Suddenly, two small eyes flashing in the darkness caught my attention. My heart skipped a beat. I gasped, pressing my back up against the wall. *There's no way I haven't been seen*, I thought, panic rising in my chest. Fear began to be replaced with waves of abject terror. In that moment, I desperately wished for a weapon, anything to feel less vulnerable.

Without any sort of protection, a troubling thought crossed my mind. *Would I be safer if I surrendered?* Disturbingly, I concluded that I would be. With a deep breath to steady my nerves, I turned into the master bedroom, holding my hands up to signify my intention to make peace. My sudden movement startled the eyes' owner, causing them to retreat further into the impenetrable darkness of the large room. "I'm unarmed. I come in peace," I whispered, inching my way further inside, trying to sound as non-threatening as possible.

As the eyes blinked several times, a realisation hit me, washing over me with both relief and an acute sense of foolishness. *It's just a bloody cat.* My body relaxed slightly, though I remained alert and cautious. The tension of the night had primed me for danger at every turn, and it was almost comical that a cat had caused such a spike in my anxiety.

Still, I knew I couldn't let my guard down. Karl's whereabouts and intentions were still unknown, and the house held more secrets than just a skittish feline. I continued to navigate the room carefully, aware that real danger could still be lurking in the shadows.

I took a few cautious steps towards the animal, which responded with a guttural warning growl, a sound so unlike any cat I'd ever heard. "Stupid fucking possum!" I whispered under my breath, chastising myself for the earlier mix-up. The small creature, resting on the bed, eyed me warily.

Then, heavy footsteps echoed up the hallway, instantly snapping my attention back to the immediate threat. I froze where I stood, my heart racing. *Is it Karl? Is it the other man? I can't tell*, I thought to myself, a surge of fear washing over me. My detective instincts, usually so reliable, seemed to falter in the face of the unknown.

I relaxed slightly when I saw that it was Karl. He walked straight past the bedroom door, too preoccupied with his own thoughts to even glance in my direction. A wave of relief mixed with confusion washed over me. *Why was he here? What was he looking for?*

The possum let out another low growl as Karl trod on a piece of broken glass, crushing it beneath his foot with a sharp crunch. My eyes darted around the darkness, scanning for a potential hiding spot in case Karl decided to investigate the noise. I was painfully aware of my vulnerable position, unarmed and exposed. But, thankfully, he didn't come to check. He continued on his way, oblivious to my presence.

Making my way over to the large bedroom window, I carefully extended my hand towards the heavy curtains. With a gentle touch, I created the tiniest of gaps to peer through, cautious not to reveal my presence. The brightness of the moon outside was momentarily stunning, forcing me to look away as it blinded my eyes, which had grown accustomed to the darkness of the house. *But that's not important right now,* I thought to myself. *I need to be certain that Karl leaves the property, and soon.*

Gently rubbing my eyes to help them readjust, I turned back to the small gap in the curtains. Peering through, I caught sight of Karl again. *There he is.* I watched as he jumped over the high wooden backyard fence and crossed back over the road. My eyes followed his figure as he jogged down the street, tracking him for as far as the window allowed before he disappeared beyond sight. A sense of relief washed over me, mixed with a lingering curiosity about his actions.

"Well, that was lucky," I said aloud, the words directed at the only other living soul in the room – the possum. The small creature had been an unexpected companion in this tense situation. As I released the curtain, the room was once again plunged back into darkness.

Struck by a sudden realisation as I turned back into the room, my eyes widened in fear. *There's still the unknown man.* In my haste to spy on Karl, I'd completely forgotten about the second person in the house. *How could I have been so careless?* The thought of another unknown individual potentially lurking in the shadows sent a ripple of fear through me.

Creeping towards the doorway, I cautiously turned my ear to the hallway, straining to catch any sound. The silence was oppressive, once again cloaking the house in a fog of stillness that seemed almost unnatural. *This is the perfect time to make an escape from the house,* I reasoned with myself. But something held me back, a nagging curiosity about the other man. *Was it Luke?* I wondered. *That was, after all, whom I had initially come to visit.* The whole situation was baffling – a flash of bright colour and then the man had appeared, seemingly out of nowhere.

If the glass sliding door hadn't provided such an unobstructed view of the room inside, I might have easily dismissed the occurrence as just the light from a TV. But I saw it. Whatever it was. The memory played over and over in my mind, each time hoping I'd missed something, that a logical explanation would present itself and I could simply allow myself to go home. But no such luck.

As I stood there, grappling with my thoughts, a part of me wanted to investigate further, to uncover the identity of this mysterious figure. Yet, the rational side of me knew the risks were too high, especially unarmed and in an unfamiliar environment. Despite my training and instincts as a detective, the unknown elements of the situation put me at a distinct disadvantage.

The decision weighed heavily on me. My curiosity about the unknown man battled with the very real need to ensure my own safety. After a few tense moments of indecision, I knew I had to act. Whether it was to further investigate or to make a swift exit, remaining in the doorway, indecisive and exposed, was not an option. Taking a deep breath to steady my nerves, I prepared to make my next move, knowing that the consequences of my choice could be significant.

Body tense and senses heightened, I stalked across the rest of the floor, meticulously checking each room as I went. My eyes scanned every corner, every possible hiding spot, but there was no sign of the other man. As I reached the top of the stairs, I paused to look down. The moonlight, streaming through the bare window, bathed the carpeted stairs in a pale, ghostly light, casting eerie shadows that seemed to dance with each flicker of the leaves outside.

I descended a couple of steps, my footsteps careful and measured, before something peculiar caught my eye down by my feet. Crouching down, I gently rubbed my hand over a small hole in the wall. Plaster dust fell softly, settling into the carpet. Peering further down, I realised it wasn't just one isolated hole, but rather a series of them, punctuating every few steps. The pattern was unmistakable and chilling – it was easy to picture the events that had taken place on these stairs, a scuffle, perhaps, or something more sinister. *At least now I know that Karl is unharmed,* I thought, a small relief in the midst of uncertainty.

With extreme caution, I continued descending the stairs, each step a calculated movement. As I reached the bottom, I paused before taking the final step, surveying the area for any signs of movement or any indication of the mystery man's whereabouts. My heart beat rapidly in the oppressive silence, the kind of quiet that felt too heavy, too deliberate. *It's too quiet,* I thought to myself, a shiver running down my spine. *Unnatural, almost.*

The tension was palpable, and I couldn't shake the feeling of being watched, of not being alone in the house despite the silence. My mind raced with possibilities, with scenarios of what might have transpired in this house and what might still be waiting in the shadows. With a deep breath to steady my nerves, I prepared myself for the final step, ready to confront whatever or whoever awaited me, armed only with my wits and my determination to uncover the truth.

The carpet gave a slight squelch beneath my right boot as I cautiously stepped into the doorway from the stairs. The sound was unnerving, and I instinctively looked down. At the bottom of the doorframe, there was a large patch of dark liquid, a trail of it running down to meet the carpet. In the silver light of the moon filtering through the windows, it was hard to discern the colour accurately, but my instincts told me it was a deep, scarlet red. *It has to be blood,* I realised with a sinking feeling.

I rocked my foot again, listening to the sound of the squelch, a sense of dread filling the air and seeping from my every pore. Judging by the sound of my steps and the metallic smell beginning to fill the air, a fair amount of blood had seeped into the carpet. My mind raced, trying to piece together what could have happened here.

Enough light to navigate by was coming through the floor-to-ceiling glass wall to my left. From my position in the doorway, I had a clear view of the entire room in front of me. The downstairs area was a large, single room, and it appeared the only exit was through the glass sliding door through which I had seen the technicolor lights earlier that evening. The door seemed closed from where I stood, though the dim light made it hard to be certain.

As I scanned the room, I was surprised to see that it was completely empty. There was no couch, no TV, and no man. Nothing. The emptiness of the room was almost as disconcerting as the blood-stained carpet. *Where had the man gone?*

The realisation that I was alone in a bloodstained, empty room sent chills down my spine. Every detective instinct in me was on high alert, sensing that something significant – and potentially dangerous – had transpired here. The lack of furniture or any personal effects made the space feel even more eerie, like a stage set for some unknown drama.

I stepped further into the room, every sense heightened, attuned to every sound and shadow. The strange emptiness of the space, combined with the bloodstains and the unanswered questions about Karl and the unknown man, created a pervasive sense of unease that clung to me like a second skin. As I moved slowly, surveying the room for any clue or sign of what had occurred, I felt a growing conviction that the answers were embedded in the silent walls of this mysterious house.

Turning my attention back to the large sliding door, I surmised that the unknown man must have slipped out through it. There was no evidence to suggest he was still in the house, and this seemed to be the only viable exit he could have taken. Allowing myself to let my guard down slightly, I walked over to the door, intent on making my escape and finding Karl. I needed answers, and time was of the essence.

Reaching for the door, I gave a heavy tug, fully expecting it to slide open smoothly and admit the cool night air. But to my dismay, the door was locked from the inside. My heart sank as my hand slid helplessly from the door handle, a wave of fear washing over me. *He's still in the house with me!* The realisation sent a shiver down my spine. *But where?*

I was certain I had been thorough when checking every room upstairs. The rooms were empty, or so I had believed. Doubt crept into my mind, mingling with the fear. *Had I missed something? Was there a hiding place I hadn't seen?*

My mind raced as I considered my options. The locked door meant that the unknown man, whoever he was, might still be lurking somewhere within the house. The thought of being trapped inside with a potential threat was terrifying. I knew I had to stay alert, to keep my wits about me.

Looking around fearfully, my head swinging from side to side in a frantic search for any signs of danger, I suddenly spotted something in a far corner of the room. My breath caught in my throat, and I instinctively jumped back, pressing myself flat against the glass door. There, almost at the far end of the wall, was a small door. It looks to be directly under the stairs, I realised with a jolt. *I must have walked right past it without even noticing. How had I missed it?*

My mind began to race, a whirlwind of thoughts and emotions. My gut instinct screamed at me to run, to get out of the house and find safety. Yet, my curiosity, the relentless drive of a detective, instructed my trembling legs to walk toward the door. *What secrets did it hold? Was the unknown man hiding there?*

The silver door handle gleamed in the moonlight that streamed through the glass door. It seemed almost to call to me, its metallic surface enticing me to just touch it. To open it. With every fibre of my being on high alert, I slowly reached for the handle. It felt cold and unwelcoming as I wrapped my fingers lightly around it.

Taking a deep breath to steady my nerves, I prepared myself for whatever lay behind the door. With a single, swift movement, I threw the door open, my body tense, ready to confront whatever or whoever was hiding there.

My scream tore through the silent room as the man launched himself at me. In a split second of pure terror, I stumbled backwards, tripped over my own feet in fear, and sent myself crashing down onto the carpet with a hard thump. Panic surged through me as I pressed my hands firmly into the soft, grey carpet, scrambling backwards until my back found the wall behind me. The man, however, didn't follow.

Breathing heavily, my heart pounded so hard I could feel my blood pressure rising by the second. The fear was overwhelming, and I thought absurdly that if anything else surprised me tonight, blood might start to squirt from my eyeballs. I looked at the tall, built man who lay half inside the cupboard, his upper body sprawled out, staring up at me blankly. He didn't move.

A wave of unexpected emotion washed over me as I realised the man was lifeless, his eyes empty and unseeing. A warm tear rolled down my cheek as I stared into his blank, lifeless eyes. The reality of the situation hit me hard. This was no longer just a case; it had become a life and death scenario.

Riding a wave of panic-induced adrenaline, I unsteadily got to my feet, my gaze fixated on the body. I knew I shouldn't, but against my better judgment, I gravitated towards it. I crouched down beside the man and, with a sense of grim determination, I grabbed his shoulders and pushed his torso until he sat upright. His head drooped at a freakishly abnormal angle, his snapped neck unable to support it. His eyes stared sideways at me, lifeless and accusatory. Instant regret flooded my mind as I noticed the man's right shoulder becoming damp from my own blood, seeping through the light covering on my hand.

Realising there was no turning back, I gave the body several strong shoves, trying to push it back into the cupboard under the stairs. The man's heavy frame slipped in my grip, almost falling on me again. The physical effort of moving the body, combined with the emotional toll of the situation, was overwhelming.

As I grabbed the man's jacket to give another push, a small USB device fell onto the floor. Ignoring it for the moment, I gave the body one last forceful shove into the under-stairs cupboard. With all my strength, I pushed the door closed and leaned my back against it, using my body weight to keep it from swinging back open under the weight of the body. The situation felt surreal, like a scene from a nightmare that I couldn't wake up from.

After a few moments of silence, a heavy jolt shuddered through me as the man's body slid down inside the cupboard and crashed against the door behind me with a thump.

Breathing heavily, I slid down to the floor, my back still pressing firmly against the cupboard door. The shock of the situation was overwhelming, and my mind was in overdrive, trying to piece together the chaotic events of the night. Another tear trickled down my cheek as I grappled with the gravity of what had just transpired.

What the fuck have I done? The question screamed silently in my head. *What has Karl done?* The implications were too much to bear, and yet, there was no time to dwell on them. I needed to act, to keep moving.

With a deep breath, I pushed myself away from the door, bracing myself, ready to rush back if it didn't stay closed with the weight of the dead body pushing on it from the other side. Thankfully, the door remained shut, the body securely hidden inside the cupboard.

I reached down and picked up the small USB device that had fallen from the man's pocket. Without looking at it in any detail, I hastily slid it into my jacket, understanding its potential significance. This could be a crucial piece of evidence, a lead to what was really going on in this house.

I stood up, feeling a newfound determination to leave this house of horrors behind. As I made my way towards the stairs, my every step was cautious yet decisive. I was keenly aware of the need to leave quickly but also the potential danger that could still lurk within the house.

Making my way back upstairs, a sudden thought struck me, halting me in my tracks at the start of the hallway. "Jamie's phone," I whispered to myself, the realisation dawning on me.

I turned back to face the kitchen, despite the fuzziness clouding my head and making it difficult for my eyes to focus. Pulling out my phone, I dialled Jamie's number again, a sense of urgency driving my actions. Almost instantly, a loud ringing filled the room, drawing my attention. There, on the edge of the kitchen bench, was Jamie's phone, its screen ablaze with blue light as it rang.

Without hesitation, I grabbed the phone and swiftly shoved it into my jacket, alongside the small USB device I'd found downstairs. A plan was forming in my mind. *Only hang onto it long enough to remove any trace of Karl touching it and delete the call history*, I instructed myself. *And then find a way to return it to the house.* It was crucial to ensure that no evidence linked Karl to the house or the events of tonight.

Sitting in the darkness of the car, I was fighting to control the trembling of my hands as they gripped the steering wheel with white knuckles. The tension of my grip tore at my freshly opened cut, and I could feel blood dripping onto my thigh. I closed my eyes, and took several deep breaths in an attempt to steady myself, but my body began to shake uncontrollably, shock finally setting in after the night's harrowing events.

A scream of anguish escaped my lips as tears began to pour from my eyes, falling into my lap and mixing with the blood. The reality of the situation was overwhelming. The man I thought I loved has just killed in cold blood and walked away. *And now the body has my blood on it!* The thought was unbearable, a twisting knife in an already painful wound.

For the sake of my grandmother, I pleaded with the universe, *Don't let it be Luke. Anyone but Luke.* The possibility that the dead man could be my cousin was too much to bear, adding a personal tragedy to an already devastating situation.

Sitting there alone in the car, a wave of self-loathing washed over me. *I hate what I've become. What love has made me do.* The realisation of my own actions, of how deeply I had been drawn into this nightmare, was suffocating. *What Karl has done and that now I'm complicit in his crime.* The guilt was crushing, a heavy burden that seemed to grow heavier with each passing second.

I hate this city. I hate Karl. The words echoed in my mind, a mantra of despair. *But most of all, I hate myself.* The self-reproach was intense, a reflection of how far I had strayed from who I thought I was, from the principles I had always held dear.

4338.213

(1 August 2018)

THE ARREST

4338.213.1

"Detective Lahey," Sergeant Claiborne's voice called out just as I passed by the open door to his office.

My steps halted abruptly, my fleeting hope of slipping by unnoticed dashed in an instant. My heart began to pound in my chest, each beat a hammer strike against my ribcage. I knew I shouldn't have come into work today. The emotional turmoil from the night's events left me feeling like a wreck, but I also knew staying away from work would have raised questions, questions I wasn't ready to answer.

"Lahey," Claiborne called out again, his voice firm.

I turned slowly to face him, seeing the Sergeant standing by the door. His sharp features were etched with a look of concern that seemed out of place on his usually stoic face.

"Step into my office."

My stomach responded immediately to the surge of nerves, gurgling loudly as if it were a deranged, internal blender viciously working on my breakfast. A wave of nausea washed over me, and I felt like I was going to vomit. With each step towards his office, my mind raced with possibilities. *Did he know something? Was it about Karl, or the events from last night?*

As I entered his office, I braced myself for whatever was coming. The walls of the office felt like they were closing in on me, each step heavier than the last. The sergeant's office, usually a place of discipline and order, now felt like a stage for a reckoning I wasn't prepared for.

I stood there, waiting for him to speak, my mind a tumult of thoughts and fears. The events of the previous night hung over me like a dark cloud, and I knew that whatever happened in the next few moments could change everything. My career, my future, my very sense of self – all seemed to hang in the balance as I waited for Sergeant Claiborne to break the silence.

"Have you seen Karl this morning?" Sergeant Claiborne's question pierced the heavy air in the room.

"No, Sergeant," I replied, my voice steady despite the turmoil inside me. I shook my head for emphasis. "I think he's still at home." I wasn't sure if that was true, but it was the safest answer I could give without revealing too much.

Sergeant Claiborne closed the door behind me with a decisive click. He took several quick steps towards me, encroaching on my personal space as he strode across the room. His proximity was overwhelming; he was close enough that I could smell the coffee on his breath. It was an all-too-familiar scent, reminding me painfully of Karl and our morning routines.

The memory triggered unwelcome images of the previous night's events. The dead man's snapped neck, his dark, empty eyes haunted me, forcing me to suppress a rising gag. The thought that Karl could be capable of such horrors was something I wasn't ready to accept. It was too much, too close.

"An anonymous woman called this morning to report a break-in at Luke Smith's house," the Sergeant said, his words pulling my thoughts back into the room.

The mention of Luke Smith's house sent a jolt of anxiety through me. My heart raced as I wondered about the implications. *Did someone see me? Was this about the USB and the phone?* I struggled to keep my composure, aware that any sign of panic might raise suspicions.

Holding my breath felt like the only way to ensure I didn't give away that I knew anything about the break-in at Luke Smith's house. My mind was racing, trying to maintain a facade of ignorance while internally reeling from the implications of what Sergeant Claiborne had just said.

"I've told all the other patrols to hold off. I thought you should take it," he said, giving me a sideways look that seemed to probe for a reaction.

A turmoil of thoughts whirled through my mind. *I don't want to be with Karl right now*, was my immediate thought, the idea of facing him so soon was overwhelming. *But turning down the assignment would look highly suspicious, especially given my usual eagerness for such cases.* With a careful, measured nod, I signalled my agreement, trying to mask the reluctance and fear that threatened to surface. "I'll take Glen," I managed to say, my voice steady.

The Sergeant studied me for a lingering moment from behind his desk. There was a scrutinising look in his eyes, one that made me question how much he suspected. "Fine," he finally replied, his voice giving nothing away.

As I turned to leave the office, a mix of relief and anxiety washed over me. Being assigned to the case was both a risk and an opportunity. It was a chance to control the narrative, to possibly cover any traces of what had happened. But it also meant diving back into the heart of the turmoil, back to where it all went horrible wrong.

Stepping out of Sergeant Claiborne's office, I felt the weight of the situation bearing down on me. Every step I took was towards a deeper entanglement in a web of lies and secrets.

Sitting alone in the front seat of the patrol car, I reflected on my decision to leave Glen behind. Having had no intention whatsoever to take him with me, I felt a mix of guilt and determination. This was something I needed to do alone, to piece together the events of last night without any distractions.

"Police," I called out authoritatively, knocking sharply on the front door of Luke Smith's house several times. There was no response. "I'm responding to the report of a break-in," I announced louder, aware that I was already bending the rules by not bringing Glen. But if there was anyone inside the house, they wouldn't know that.

I took a deep breath to steady my fraying nerves. *It seems that there is nobody home, again.* The thought circled in my mind. *So, who called in the break-in?* I was acutely aware of the need for caution, the memories of last night still vivid in my mind.

For the second time in as many days, I found myself jumping the small side fence, a sense of déjà vu washing over me as I approached the broken bedroom window. The scene looked very different in the daylight, the shards of glass glistening in the sunlight, casting rainbows onto the grass. The beauty of it was in stark contrast to the dark events that had transpired here.

As I stood there, taking in the scene, I knew I had to be methodical. Any evidence I might find could be crucial. But I also had to be careful not to disturb the scene any more than I already had. Balancing my duty as a detective with the personal involvement in the case was becoming increasingly challenging.

"I'm entering the house," I announced as I approached the window, my voice steady and clear. The declaration was more for the benefit of any eavesdropping, nosey neighbours than for anybody inside the house. Deep down, I was certain the house was empty, but the professional protocol had to be maintained.

Regardless of my inner certainty, I instinctively drew my gun as I climbed through the window. It was a precaution ingrained in me through years of experience. This time, I landed softly on the other side, a small victory as I managed to avoid cutting myself on the glass shards. *Progress*, I thought, a faint flicker of relief in the midst of tension.

I shivered slightly, not just from the chill in the air but from the eerie silence that enveloped the house. With my gun poised and ready, I cautiously made my way into the hallway. Every sense was heightened, every sound amplified in the quiet of the abandoned house.

The familiarity of the space did little to ease the tension that knotted my stomach. The events of the previous night hung over me like a shadow, tainting my perception of the once ordinary hallway. I moved slowly, deliberately, my eyes scanning each corner, each potential hiding spot. Despite knowing the house was likely empty, I couldn't shake off the feeling of being watched, of not being alone.

As I progressed through the hallway, I remained alert, prepared for any surprises, any hidden threats that might reveal themselves. The mystery of who called in the break-in and why weighed heavily on my mind. With each step, I was keenly aware that the answers I sought might just be a room away, hidden in the silence of this desolate house.

"Shit!" I exclaimed, my voice sharp with surprise as I walked into the living room. My heart skipped a beat at the sight before me. A lone woman sat upright on the black, leather couch, her eyes empty and expression numb. "What the fuck are you doing here, Gladys?" I demanded.

Gladys didn't reply, her gaze fixed on some distant point, lost in her own thoughts.

As I cautiously took a few steps closer, the depth of sadness in Gladys' face became more pronounced, etching lines of despair and confusion. I couldn't help but glance toward the stairs. The door at the top of the steps had been sealed closed. *Shit*, I thought, a sense of dread washing over me. *Gladys must have found the body! She must be the one who called it in.*

But as my thoughts raced, something didn't add up. *If it was Gladys, then why only report a break-in and not a murder?* The question hung in the air, thick with implications. *Was she trying to protect someone? Or was she in shock, unable to process what she had seen?*

I scrutinised Gladys, looking for any sign, any clue that might explain her presence and actions. Her vacant stare and unresponsive demeanour were unsettling. The situation was growing more complex by the second, and I knew I needed to tread carefully.

"Stand with your back to me and place your hands on your head," I instructed firmly, aiming the gun directly at Gladys' chest. The weight of the situation pressed down on me, making it difficult to breathe. I held my breath, my eyes locked on Gladys. *Will Gladys comply?* The question echoed in my mind, each second stretching into eternity as I waited for her response.

After a moment that felt like an age, Gladys slowly stood up. She fixed me with a chilling stare, her eyes piercing through me, before turning around and placing her hands on the back of her head. The tension in the room was palpable, every movement charged with uncertainty.

With Gladys now complying, I cautiously lowered my weapon and placed it tentatively back in its holster. It was a relief to holster the gun, but I remained on high alert. "Gladys Cramer," I said firmly, taking hold of Gladys' left arm and pulling it down. "I'm placing you under arrest for dangerous driving and resisting arrest. You have the right to remain silent, anything you do or say may be used against you in a court of law," I recited the familiar words with practiced ease, but they felt hollow in the context of last night's events.

With a swift, practiced motion, I snapped Gladys' right hand into the cuffs. The metallic click of the handcuffs seemed to echo in the quiet room. My heart was still racing, but there was a sense of control returning, a return to the familiar procedures and protocols of my job.

Yet, as I stood there with Gladys in cuffs, a myriad of emotions and thoughts swirled within me. The arrest, while necessary, felt like just one small piece of a much larger, more complex puzzle. I knew there was much more to this story than a simple case of dangerous driving and resisting arrest. Last night's events, the bloodied body, Karl's involvement – it all hung in the air, an unspoken question mark that loomed over us.

As I escorted Gladys out of the house, my mind was already racing ahead, piecing together the clues, trying to make sense of it all.

As I stepped away from the patrol car, where I had just secured Gladys in the backseat, I pulled out my mobile phone with a specific purpose in mind. I scrolled through my contacts, finding the number I needed. This was a delicate situation, and I needed someone I could trust implicitly.

"Hey, Benny," I greeted as the call connected. My voice was steady, but inside, I felt anything but calm. "I'm calling to cash in on that favour you owe me." My words were direct; this wasn't a casual conversation.

There was a brief pause on the other end of the line. Finally, Benny spoke, his voice casual yet attentive. "What do you need?" he asked.

"I have a smashed bedroom window I need you to fix. It's around the back of the house on the corner, you can't miss it. Make sure you also remove all the broken glass on the floor. I'll text you the address." My instructions were clear and concise.

Ending the call, I couldn't help but feel a twinge of unease. Until I knew that neither Karl nor myself could be implicated, I didn't want to leave any other reason for police to enter the property. The situation was already complicated enough, and I wasn't entirely convinced that Gladys had been the one to make the call.

As I sent Benny the address, my mind was racing with possibilities and theories. *Who made the call? What was their motive?* And most importantly, *how did all of this tie together?* Each unanswered question added to the growing knot of tension and uncertainty inside me.

Stepping back into the patrol car, I knew the next few hours were crucial. I had to tread carefully, playing my part while trying to piece together the truth behind this twisted puzzle. As I started the engine and pulled away from the curb, I was acutely aware of the delicate balancing act I was performing, walking a tightrope between my duties as a detective and the dangerous secrets that threatened to unravel everything.

"I've arranged to have your window replaced," I said to Gladys, trying to sound casual as I watched her in the rearview mirror. I needed to maintain a semblance of normalcy, despite the storm of emotions and questions swirling inside me.

Gladys remained silent, her figure a motionless silhouette in the backseat.

Minutes stretched by, the quiet only broken by the hum of the car engine. Finally, Gladys spoke, her voice low and strained. "It was you, wasn't it?" she asked.

Her question caught me off guard. "No," I replied bluntly, struggling to keep my emotions in check. My hands began to tremble against the steering wheel, betraying the calm demeanour I was desperately trying to project.

Several more minutes passed in silence, each second feeling like an eternity. "But you were there," Gladys added, a note of accusation in her voice.

I maintained my focus on the road, my mind racing. *How the fuck could Gladys possibly know that?* The question echoed in my head, setting off alarms. My instincts as a detective urged me to remain silent, to not reveal anything, but curiosity and concern got the better of me. Without thinking, I blurted out, "Did you know him?"

Gladys looked away, turning her face towards the window. I could see the pain etched on her face, a silent testament to the turmoil she was experiencing. It was a pain I recognised, one that mirrored my own internal conflict.

The question hung in the air, unanswered, adding another layer of mystery to the already complex situation. As I drove, I realised that Gladys might hold key information, not just about the man's death but also about the events leading up to it. Her reaction, her silence, and the pain on her face – all suggested a deeper knowledge about the incident.

"Why haven't you reported it?" I asked, my voice laced with genuine curiosity. It was becoming increasingly apparent that Gladys had found the man's body, and it seemed even more likely that she knew him. The pieces were starting to come together, but there were gaps, gaps that Gladys was clearly filling with her silence. She was hiding some important facts. *Maybe,* I thought, *there might be a way to strike a deal here with Gladys.*

"It's complicated," replied Gladys, her voice low and fraught with unspoken complexities.

"No shit," I agreed, my response laced with a mix of sarcasm and frustration. The situation was indeed complicated, and her vague answers were only adding to the confusion.

After allowing several more minutes to pass in silence, I made a decision. I pulled the car over to a stop at the side of the road. This was the moment to push for answers. "Here's the thing," I began, turning to look Gladys directly in the eye. It was crucial to establish a connection, to show her that this was a serious conversation. "I have to bring you in for questioning. But if you answer a few of my questions now, I'll make sure that the interview is easygoing, and you'll get released immediately." It was a gamble, but one I hoped would pay off.

Gladys glared at me, her eyes hard and unyielding. The silence stretched between us, thick with tension and unspoken thoughts. I could see the wheels turning in her head, weighing her options. Her glare was penetrating, almost as if she was trying to see through me, to understand my motives.

I held her gaze, unflinching, knowing that this was a critical moment. If Gladys chose to cooperate, she could provide the key information needed to unravel the night's events. But if she remained silent, it would only compound the mystery and leave more questions unanswered.

In a moment of desperation to get Gladys to talk, I blurted out a confession. "Fine. I was there. But I didn't kill him. He was already dead when I found him." The words came out in a rush, a gamble to break the silence and provoke a reaction.

Gladys' expression changed to one of anger in an instant. *Game over*, I thought, a sinking feeling in my stomach. *Confessing was a bad move.*

"And what the hell were you doing there?" Gladys shot back, her voice trembling with a cocktail of anger and pain. The question struck me hard, a direct challenge to my actions, my decisions.

I could feel my face turning hot, a mix of guilt and defensiveness washing over me. I turned back to the steering wheel, my grip tightening. *That's an unfair question*, I thought. *Gladys is the one who won't call in a dead body, so she doesn't get to ask the questions.* My mind was racing, trying to justify my own actions while grappling with the moral complexity of the situation.

Angry and frustrated, I indicated and pulled the car back out onto the road. There would be no more questions until we reached the station. It was a tactical retreat, a chance to regain control of the situation. If Gladys hadn't reported the dead man by now, I was certain she wouldn't raise it during the interview. And she couldn't mention my presence at the house last night without risking exposing what she was withholding now.

I hated the situation, the web of lies and half-truths I found myself entangled in. But I was confident, at least for now, that I still had the upper hand. As I drove towards the station, my mind was a whirlwind of strategy and scenarios, each turn of the road bringing us closer to an inevitable confrontation of truths and secrets.

Breaking the silence with a soft, fragile voice, Gladys said, "His name was Cody Jennings."

I glanced in the rearview mirror and watched as Gladys' eyes began to well up with tears. The sight of her pain, her vulnerability, struck a chord in me. It made the turmoil of my own emotions, which I had been fighting so hard to control, all the more difficult to keep in check. I was torn between my role as a detective and the empathy I felt for her situation.

"Thank you, Gladys," I replied gently, acknowledging the significance of her sharing that information. It was a piece of the puzzle, a name that could lead to more answers.

As we turned into the station's carpark, Gladys spoke again, her voice carrying a weight of unspoken secrets. "Another thing," she said, capturing my full attention.

"What?" I asked, my curiosity piqued.

"Luke doesn't know."

"Know what?" I pressed, unsure of what she was hinting at.

"Any of it," Gladys answered. Her words hit me like a wave. Luke was in the dark about the entire situation, the death of Cody Jennings, my presence at the house, everything.

This revelation added a new layer of complexity to the case. Luke's ignorance of the situation meant that the dynamics of what was going on were even more intricate than I had initially thought. It also meant that Luke could potentially be in danger or, conversely, that he might unknowingly hold information crucial to bringing the whole house of cards down.

"Gladys Cramer," I announced as I walked into the small, windowless interview room. The room felt even more constricting today, the walls seeming to close in with the weight of the situation. "This is Sergeant Claiborne. He'll be conducting your interview with me today." I had argued with Sergeant Claiborne, trying to convince him that I could handle the interview alone, but he had been adamant about his presence.

Sergeant Claiborne positioned himself directly opposite Gladys. I observed him carefully studying her, his eyes sharp and assessing. I tried desperately to remain calm, but the tension in the room was almost tangible.

As I dragged the only remaining vacant chair across the concrete floor, it screeched loudly, echoing in the small space. As I bent over to sit down, I reached into my front pocket to pull out a small notebook. In my haste and nervousness, I hadn't remembered to remove the strange USB device I had found on Cody Jennings last night from my clothing. To my horror, it fell out of my pocket onto the table, dragged along by the notebook. My attempt to grab the device was clumsy, and it slid across the table, landing straight in Gladys' lap.

Gladys picked up the USB device and held it out toward me, her eyes meeting mine with a mixture of curiosity and confusion.

"So sorry," I said quickly, my voice betraying my embarrassment. I took the device from Gladys, feeling my cheeks warm with a flush of awkwardness. I hastily dropped it back into my pocket, hoping that neither Gladys nor Sergeant Claiborne had noticed my unease.

As the interview was about to begin, I felt a rush of thoughts. The presence of the USB device was a reminder of the unresolved threads of the case, the secrets that were yet to be unravelled. My mind was racing, trying to stay focused on the interview with Gladys while also contemplating the significance of the device and its contents.

Sergeant Claiborne's sudden movement to stand up and head towards the door caught me off guard. "Thank you, Detective Lahey," he said as he opened the door. His tone was firm, leaving no room for argument. "I can take the rest of the interview from here," he finished, gesturing for me to leave.

A sense of dread filled me. I wasn't ready to leave; there was still so much I needed to understand from Gladys. Reluctantly, I stood up, shooting a quick, apologetic glance at Gladys. "I'm so sorry, Gladys," I mouthed silently, hoping she would understand my unspoken words.

However, Gladys' reaction was immediate and intense. She slammed her still-cuffed hands onto the table, her frustration and anger palpable. "Damn it! You promised me, Sarah!" she growled angrily and, to my dismay, not so silently.

My heart sank as I stepped out of the room, the weight of her words and the gravity of the situation pressing heavily on me. I knew the implications of what had just transpired. I had only taken a few steps when Claiborne's hand firmly grasped my right shoulder, forcing me to stop and turn around to face him. My mind raced with anxiety and guilt. I tried to bring my eyes to meet his gaze, but it was impossible. The shame and fear I felt made it difficult to look him in the eyes.

"What the hell did you promise her, Detective?" Sergeant Claiborne's question cut through the air, sharp and demanding.

I felt a wave of emotions rising within me, threatening to overwhelm my composure. I fought to keep them at bay, knowing that any sign of weakness or hesitation could be disastrous. My feet shifted slightly, grounding me as I prepared to face him. Slowly, I raised my head to meet Claiborne's intense, searching gaze. "I've got no idea," I lied calmly, my voice steady despite the chaos inside. I stared straight into his eyes, trying to project confidence and innocence.

After a few seconds, I broke the stare, allowing my eyes to drift towards the interview room door. It was a calculated move, designed to show a sense of detachment and professionalism. I pulled myself from his grip, and with an easy pivot on my left foot, I turned my back to the sergeant. I marched down the corridor as confidently as I could, each step a battle against the anxiety and guilt that threatened to surface.

As soon as I turned the corner, out of Claiborne's sight, I made a beeline for the bathroom. The moment I was alone, I leaned heavily against the closed door, letting out a breath I hadn't realised I was holding. My hands trembled slightly, and I took a moment to gather myself, to steady my racing heart and clear my head.

The bathroom felt like a temporary refuge, a place to regain control and reassess. I splashed cold water on my face, trying to wash away the stress and fear. Looking at my reflection in the mirror, I knew that the situation was spiralling, and I was walking a dangerous tightrope.

As I stood under the warm jet of water in the cramped shower cubicle, I allowed myself a moment of vulnerability, something I had been staunchly resisting. I closed my eyes, and the events of the past two days cascaded over me, each memory like a drop of water, relentless and consuming. My hands instinctively slammed into the sides of the cubicle, gripping hard for support as my legs wobbled, threatening to give way under the weight of my emotions.

Opening my eyes, I blankly stared at the tiled wall in front of me. The pointless mosaics stared back, their patterns and colours as chaotic and nonsensical as the tumultuous thoughts swirling around in my head. My mind grappled with each revelation, each decision, pulling at my every emotion and systematically dismantling my world, piece by piece.

"Fuck!" The word slipped out as a whisper, barely audible over the sound of the shower. It was a release, a small acknowledgment of the overwhelming sense of helplessness that had been plaguing me for days. This feeling had finally taken its toll, smothering my mind in a dense fog of despair and confusion.

In that solitary space, with the hot water cascading down, all I could comprehend was the sensation of my tears mingling with the shower water. They traced paths down my face, over my quaking body, and disappeared into the black abyss of the plughole below.

ACCUSATIONS

4338.213.2

"I see you got your gun back," I commented casually to Karl as I approached my desk, attempting to sound nonchalant. It was a tactical move, a way to gauge his current state of mind.

Karl didn't reply immediately. He just looked at me, his gaze intense, silently demanding an explanation for my earlier actions. The tension between us was palpable, a mixture of unspoken questions and hidden truths.

"They didn't find anything," I started, trying to sound as convincing as possible. "Nobody answered the door, and the premise was all secured." My voice was steady, but inside, I was a tumult of anxiety and doubt.

"So, you didn't go inside?" he asked, his expression puzzled, searching.

"No," I lied, sitting down in my chair and pulling myself toward the desk. The lie felt heavy on my tongue, but it was necessary. I couldn't let Karl know about my unauthorised entry or my discovery of the body.

"Oh," I added, turning to look directly at Karl. "And the broken window has been fixed." I watched his face closely for any sign of a reaction, any tell that might give away his thoughts or further involvement.

"Are you spying on me?" he asked, his question catching me off guard. He studied me carefully.

My face went white. "No," I said quickly, immediately turning back to the computer to hide any further reaction. I needed to maintain my professional façade, to keep my personal turmoil hidden.

"Sarah," Karl said gently, his voice softer now. There was a hint of concern, maybe even care, in his tone.

"I have a report to finish writing." My response was curt, a clear indication that I didn't want to continue the conversation.

Karl let several minutes pass in silence before speaking again. "Sarah," he said softly, trying to reach out to me. I didn't look up, focusing intently on my computer screen.

"Luke arrived in Adelaide this morning." His words were quiet, almost hesitant.

The mouse in my hand stopped moving at the mention of Luke. It was a significant piece of information, a new development that could change the dynamics of the entire case. But I refused to look at Karl, to show any sign of how much that news affected me. I made a mental note to remember this vital information about Luke, realising its potential significance.

Returning to my work, I pretended to review the case notes from the interview with Gladys Cramer that Sergeant Claiborne had thrown me out of. My mind, however, was elsewhere, racing through the implications of Karl's revelation and how it might fit into the larger puzzle.

It took the better part of the afternoon for me to muster enough motivation to chase up a few more potential leads. Each one, however, led to a dead end, offering nothing helpful. Feeling defeated, I closed the browser on my computer and stood up, my movements sluggish with exhaustion. With a sweep of my arm, I pushed the array of papers on my desk into a scrambled pile in the corner. The day had taken its toll on me; I felt completely shattered, emotionally and mentally spent.

"Ah, dang," Karl muttered as his phone began to ring, inadvertently catching my attention. I noticed him glance briefly in my direction before quickly looking away, a gesture that didn't go unnoticed. There was something about his reaction that piqued my curiosity.

"Detective Jenkins," he answered the phone with a formal tone.

For the next few minutes, I watched Karl closely, unable to tear my eyes away. He listened more than he spoke, his responses minimal. The lack of information was driving me insane, my mind racing to fill in the blanks with a myriad of possibilities. *Who was he talking to, and what about?*

Unable to contain my curiosity, I manoeuvred myself over to Karl's side. I saw his brow furrow in response to whatever he was hearing on the call, which only deepened my need to know more. I leaned in closer, straining my ears in hopes of catching some part of the conversation, any clue from the voice coming through on the other end of the line.

"Thank you for the update. Good night to you too, Sir," Karl finally said, concluding the call abruptly.

The sudden end of the call left me hanging, brimming with questions and speculations. Karl's demeanour had changed subtly during the conversation, a sign that whatever he had been told was significant. I found myself desperately wanting to ask him about it, to delve into the details of the call, but I was wary of overstepping.

Opting for a more subtle approach, I tried to probe Karl for information. "Well, you look grim," I commented, trying to sound casual. "Who was that?"

Karl's response was tinged with a hint of petulance. "I thought you weren't talking to me," he said, his tone reminiscent of a childish spat.

I frowned, internally wrestling between my desire to continue the silent standoff with Karl and my insatiable need to solve this crime. The gravity of the situation weighed heavily on me. *There is a corpse rotting under the stairs, and we need to know why nobody has reported it.* The thought haunted me. *Even more importantly, with no doubt in my mind that my blood will be found on that corpse, how the fuck are we going to get rid of the evidence...* The urgency of the situation pushed me to break the silence. "Just tell me," I said bluntly, my voice firm.

Karl's expression turned even more serious, his face hardening like stone. "That was Detective Santos from the Adelaide CIB," he revealed. "They called to give a courtesy update."

I stared at him intently, my eyes urging him to continue, to provide more details. His mention of Detective Santos and the Adelaide CIB was intriguing, but it was the 'courtesy update' that really caught my attention. It suggested that there was a development, something important that we needed to know.

Karl sighed before continuing. "There's not much to say, really. When they arrived at Luke's parents' house, there was nobody there. They have an officer watching the property, but there has been no sign of anybody at all. Both the family cars are still at the house. There's no sign of forced entry. They questioned the neighbours to see if they had seen anything suspicious."

"And?" I prodded, leaning forward in anticipation.

"The only piece of information that seemed remotely useful was that the elderly lady across the street said she saw a young man, matching Luke's description, arrive at the house sometime before lunch. She didn't see or hear anything unusual and hadn't noticed anybody leave the house all day."

Karl's voice was matter-of-fact, but I could sense an undercurrent of frustration.

"Well, that's great," I said, trying to sound optimistic and lift Karl's spirits.

Karl didn't look convinced. "Well, not really. All it implies is that Luke really is in Adelaide and maybe went to his parent's house. Anything beyond that is circumstantial." He frowned slightly, clearly not satisfied with the lack of solid leads.

"But?" I prodded again, sensing there was more he was holding back.

"What do you mean, 'but?'" Karl looked at me, a mix of curiosity and slight annoyance in his eyes.

"I see a 'but' on your face. You should know you can't hide your suspicions from me by now," I said, a hint of playfulness unintentionally creeping into my voice.

Karl's smile, though slight, was a rare sight through the heavy air of our conversation. "But it doesn't make any sense," he admitted. "They did a thorough search of the property, and all they found was a single drop of fresh blood on the shed door."

"Fresh?" I echoed, my interest immediately piqued. The word 'fresh' in our line of work usually indicated a recent incident, and in this case, it could be a crucial piece of evidence.

"Apparently it was still wet. They've taken a sample and sent it to the lab for priority testing. In the meantime, they're having forensics spend the next forty-eight hours examining the house and property for traces of human remains. Or anything, really," Karl elaborated.

"That is very bizarre," I agreed, my mind racing through the implications of this new information. A single drop of fresh blood could mean a number of things, and none of them were particularly reassuring.

Karl nodded in agreement. "Whatever Luke is up to, he's been very precise so far. We just need something, anything, that will give us some answers. Knowing our luck, I don't expect forensics will turn up anything new. At least nothing that will hold up in court." His voice carried a tinge of frustration and resignation.

I shrugged, feeling my short-lived playfulness dissolve into a more familiar sense of pessimistic resignation. "Perhaps you're right."

And then, as if a switch had been flipped, a sudden realisation hit me. My grandmother had been adamant that Luke was innocent, and according to Gladys, he knew nothing about... any of it. *What did she really mean by that? Is Luke running from someone? Is it his life that is in danger?*

A sense of urgency washed over me. *Fuck! I needed to be in that interview.* I needed to understand the full picture, to connect the dots between Luke's alleged innocence, the mysterious drop of blood, and the larger web of events unfolding around us.

4338.214

(2 August 2018)

DARKNESS FALLS

4338.214.1

I rubbed my hand along Karl's inner thigh, pausing just before it reached its final goal. After another heated argument at his house last night, we had found a mutually pleasing way to make peace. My hand inched slowly forwards, the tips of my fingers stretching out to gently caress his bulging crotch. Karl's hands gripped the side of his seat, his knuckles turning white. I could feel his cock engorging, his arousal intensifying by the second. Enjoying the power, I reached slowly underneath him, cupping my hands under his balls and squeezing them gently, eliciting a light gasp from him.

When Karl opened his eyes ever so slightly and glanced over at me, my tongue seductively traced the outer edges of my lips, hinting at pleasures still to come.

Finding a secluded spot, we had parked the unmarked police car, giving ourselves a brief respite from the investigation's relentless pressure. The situation with Gladys, the elusive Luke, all the bodies we couldn't find, and the one we had, had turned the case into a maddening mumbo-jumbo of confusion and secrets. Neither Karl nor I were brave enough to reveal our dark secrets from the other night to each other. And honestly, my sanity was hanging by a thread; any distraction was welcome, however fleeting.

Our moment of escape was brutally shattered by the police radio. "CITY632," it squawked. Karl and I both knew that was our call sign. He turned to me, still half dazed. "We'd better grab that," he mumbled.

"CITY632, go ahead," I announced, taking the initiative since Karl was clearly not in a state to talk to dispatch.

"CITY632, a disturbance has been reported at a property in Granton. A woman is claiming that Luke Smith is on the premises. We've been advised to notify you of any jobs that come up with the name Luke Smith," the dispatcher informed.

"Fuck me!" Karl blurted out, abruptly pushing my hand away from his leg as he started the car's engine. "This is it, tell them we've got it," he barked, his tone urgent, his daze instantly replaced by a sense of duty.

Karl revved the engine several times before turning on the red and blue lights above us. He sped down the street with the siren blaring, urgency palpable in every move he made. Meanwhile, I finished speaking with dispatch, my hands scrambling to note the job details.

Every nerve in my body was on edge as we raced toward the reported disturbance. This could be a major break in the case, a chance to finally confront Luke and untangle the web of mysteries surrounding him.

"CITY632, approaching the Jeffries property now," I spoke into the radio, my voice steady despite the tumultuous mix of adrenaline and fear coursing through my veins. I clung to the hope that Gladys was right about Luke's ignorance regarding Cody's death. It was a slim thread of hope, but it was all I had to hang onto in this chaos.

"Copy that CITY632. Proceed with extreme caution. Backup is on its way," the dispatcher's voice crackled through the radio, adding to the tension that was already building up inside me.

As we approached the property, my gaze fell upon the grand entrance. The two words, "Jeffries Manor," were etched into a metallic slab, balancing precariously between the iron arms of an aged archway. "Jeffries Manor," I repeated softly, the words leaving my mouth in a whisper. A cold shiver ran up my spine as I took in the sight of the imposing structure. The manor loomed ahead, an edifice of old secrets and untold stories, its presence somehow magnifying the gravity of our arrival.

We drove carefully up the rocky, dirt road that wound its way up the side of the hill, the tension in the car palpable as each of us prepared mentally for what might lay ahead. The road, uneven and untamed, seemed to mirror the unpredictability of our investigation. The short drive culminated at a striking sandstone building: Jeffries Manor. Its new extensions, added to both the front and back of the house, lent it an air of modern elegance and confidence, yet it stood before us like a stately home from colonial days – dignified, imposing, and laden with silent stories.

As Karl pulled up and stopped under the shade of a large gum tree, I quickly unbuckled my seatbelt. The urgency of the situation propelled me out of the car door, my hand instinctively reaching for my gun. Every sense was heightened, every instinct screamed readiness.

"No gun. Not yet," Karl cautioned me, his voice firm as he too climbed out of the patrol car. He held a hand up, a clear signal for me to follow his lead. We approached the house with caution, our steps measured and deliberate.

The grandeur of Jeffries Manor was both awe-inspiring and intimidating. Its walls, rich with history, seemed to be watching us, silently assessing our every move. The manor, with its elegant sandstone and new architectural flourishes, stood as a testament to the passage of time and changing fortunes. It felt like stepping into another era, yet the urgency of finding Luke kept me firmly grounded in the present.

As we moved closer to the entrance, I was acutely aware of the contrast between the manor's serene exterior and the potential danger that awaited us inside. The juxtaposition was unsettling, a reminder of how appearances can often be deceptive, masking the true nature of what lies beneath.

"He's in here," called out an older woman's voice, piercing the stillness just as we were about to knock on the front door of Jeffries Manor. The voice came from the direction of a shed that stood off to the side of the manor.

Both Karl and I turned toward the sound, our attention instantly redirected. There, standing outside the shed door, was Louise Jeffries. She was wielding a very large kitchen knife, her posture tense and her eyes fixed on the shed.

"Want to use those guns yet?" I asked Karl, only half-joking, as we cautiously approached Louise. My hand hovered near my gun holster, ready to act if the situation escalated.

"Louise Jeffries," Karl addressed her authoritatively, his voice calm but firm. "It's time to hand the knife over," he told her, motioning for her to hand it over to me.

"I've got the bastard trapped inside," Louise declared, a sense of triumph in her voice as she waved the large kitchen knife around with less care than the situation warranted.

As I cautiously reached forward to take the knife from her, I noticed how Louise's hands trembled uncontrollably. Her facade of control was slipping, revealing the true extent of her terror. Her hands quivered like leaves in the wind as she handed over the knife. As soon as the weapon left her grasp, she crumbled under the weight of her emotions.

"I can't find Brianne!" she cried out, her voice cracking with emotion. The name struck a chord, and I could see Karl's attention sharpen.

"Brianne?" Karl echoed, seeking clarification.

"Kain's fiancée," Louise managed to say, her voice strained with distress. "Luke came here to talk to her and now she's gone too."

"Take her back inside the house," Karl instructed me, his voice indicating the urgency of keeping Louise safe.

I gently took Louise by the arm, mindful of her fragile state. "Come inside, Louise," I prompted softly, guiding her towards the manor with a careful touch.

Reluctantly, Louise allowed herself to be led back inside the house. As we left the shed behind, her arm shook increasingly with each step we took resonating with the unease that was steadily building within me.

"Is there anybody else home?" I asked Louise as we entered the living area of the manor. I began to pull down the first of the blinds, aiming to secure the room and provide us some sense of safety.

"Yes," replied Louise, her voice trembling as much as her hands. "Thelma."

"Do you know where she is?" I asked, my eyes scanning the room for any signs of movement or other potential threats.

"Upstairs in her room," she responded.

"I'll need to check on her," I said, my mind already racing with the logistics of ensuring Thelma's safety while also keeping an eye on Louise.

Louise began to pace in circles, her movements erratic and disjointed. Her hands moved frantically in front of her as her mouth uttered incoherent sounds, reminiscent of someone in deep distress. Her state was alarming, and it was crucial to bring her some level of calmness.

Standing in front of Louise, I grabbed her hands tightly, grounding her with my firm but gentle grasp. "Louise," I said firmly, trying to cut through her panic. "Louise, look at me."

For a moment, she continued to squirm, but then her eyes met mine. There was a brief flicker of recognition, a momentary pause in her disarray.

"I need you to make sure all of these blinds are down and all the doors are locked. I need to go and make sure that Thelma is okay," I told her, my voice as calm as I could manage. It was important to give her a task, something to focus on.

Louise nodded, a semblance of understanding crossing her face.

"Can you do that for me?" I asked, needing her confirmation.

"Yes," she whispered, nodding again more assuredly this time.

"I'll be right back," I reassured her, releasing her hands.

With my gun drawn, I ascended the stairs swiftly, each step amplifying a growing sense of dread. The idea that something terrible might happen to either Luke or Karl was consuming me. Karl's recent actions, his snapping of a man's neck, whether accidental or intentional, haunted my thoughts. It was clear evidence of his volatile emotional state, rendering him unpredictable and potentially dangerous.

"Thelma," I whispered cautiously, opening the first door on the left. The room was empty, devoid of any signs of occupancy. My heart raced as I proceeded, checking each room along the long hallway. Each empty room only heightened my anxiety, the silence of the manor amplifying my fears.

Finally, I reached the last door. A sense of foreboding washed over me as my fingers wrapped around the cold doorknob. I could feel my heart pounding against my chest, its rhythm rapid and erratic. Taking a deep breath to steady my nerves, I slowly twisted the knob and pushed the door open.

"Thelma," I whispered again, my voice barely louder than a breath.

"Hello, dear," came a croaky, old voice in response.

Relief washed over me for a brief moment at the sound of Thelma's voice, but it was quickly replaced by caution. I stepped into the room, my eyes quickly scanning the surroundings, gun still in hand. The situation was still precarious, and I couldn't afford to let my guard down.

I quickly moved to the side of the old woman, who lay in a large, four-poster bed, surrounded by a fortress of cushions and pillows. Her frailty was evident, and her presence in the bed spoke of a life lived long and, perhaps, hard.

"It's so good to see you. I wasn't sure if you would come," Thelma said, her voice weak yet tinged with a sense of relief. Her frail, shaking hand reached out to take hold of mine, and I couldn't help but notice the tremble in her grasp.

I gazed into her deep hazel eyes, finding myself momentarily caught in their depths. My mind raced with the urgency of the situation. *I don't have time for this*, I thought, but I couldn't let my impatience show. "We haven't met," I told Thelma, trying to be as gentle as possible. "Are you okay?"

"No, dear," Thelma replied slowly, her voice trailing off as if caught in a distant memory.

"Are you hurt?" I asked, my concern growing. Adrenaline coursed through my veins, heightening my senses.

Thelma's shaking hand moved to pat my neck, an oddly comforting gesture. "I can't find the key," she murmured, her words seemingly disconnected from the present situation.

I fought to keep my frustration in check, mindful of Thelma's fragile state. It was clear she was confused, possibly disoriented. "I need to get back to Louise," I told her, gently disengaging her hand as I stood up. "I'm going to close the bedroom door again. Don't open it for anyone," I instructed firmly, ensuring her safety.

As I walked towards the door, ready to leave the room and return to the chaos unfolding outside, Thelma's voice suddenly pierced the air.

"Jane, dear, don't go!" she cried out desperately.

I froze, a shiver running down my spine. The name 'Jane' hung in the air, heavy with significance. Slowly, I turned back to face Thelma, whose tears were now streaming down her weathered, wrinkled face. Her expression was one of profound grief and pain. "Don't leave me again," she sobbed, her voice breaking.

A lump formed in my throat as I stood there, momentarily paralysed. *Does Thelma think that I'm my grandmother?* The realisation dawned on me, mingling with a wave of sadness. The emotional toll of the case was starting to blur the lines between my professional and personal life in ways I hadn't anticipated.

Before I could respond, the sound of a motorbike roaring to life outside snapped me back to reality.

"Karl!" I gasped, recognising the urgency of the situation. "I'm sorry. I have to go," I said to Thelma, torn between the need to comfort her and the need to act on the case. With a heavy heart, I walked briskly out of the room, pulling the door closed behind me.

As I hurried down the hallway, the weight of Thelma's mistaken identity pressed heavily on my mind. It was a poignant reminder of the human cost of our investigation, the unseen toll it took on those caught in the crossfire. But right now, I had to focus. Karl was out there, possibly in danger, and I needed to be with him. I quickened my pace, pushing aside my emotions to focus on the task at hand. The case was reaching a critical point, and every second mattered.

Get down!" I instructed Louise firmly as soon as I reentered the living area.

"It's for your own safety," I added quickly when I noticed Louise hesitate, her eyes wide with fear and confusion. My tone was urgent, leaving no room for doubt or delay.

Without waiting to see if she complied, I dashed outside. Time was of the essence, and every moment spent inside could mean missing something critical happening outside. As a detective, my instinct was to be where the action was, to respond, to protect, and to solve.

As I burst through the door and into the open air, my heart sank when I realised Louise had followed me outside. "Get back inside!" I screamed, my voice filled with a mixture of frustration and fear for her safety. Louise, in her state of panic, was putting herself in unnecessary danger.

"And lock the door," I added emphatically, gesturing towards the house.

Drawing my gun, I held it out in front of me, my eyes scanning the surroundings for any sign of the motorbike I had heard. Its absence was unsettling. The area had fallen into an eerie quiet, punctuated only by the sound of Louise securing the door behind me. I could feel the tension in the air, thick and almost tangible.

I moved towards the large, green corrugated iron shed with a sense of cautious urgency. Each step felt heavy, my awareness heightened to the potential danger that could be hiding within. The shed door was ajar, inviting yet ominous. "Karl, are you in there?" I called out, my voice echoing slightly in the open space.

Entering the shed, gun firmly in hand, I allowed my eyes a moment to adjust to the dim, murky atmosphere. The interior was startlingly barren, a stark contrast to what I had anticipated. As my gaze swept across the space, the eerie emptiness became overwhelmingly apparent. The shed, except for a sparse array of tools and items clinging to the walls, was completely devoid of content. It was as if the floor itself had been wiped clean of existence. No Karl, no Luke, no motorbike – nothing but an unsettling void where there should have been something, anything.

The sheer emptiness of the shed sent a shiver down my spine, birthing a plethora of questions in my mind. The vacant space didn't just feel abandoned; it felt unnatural, as if it defied the very essence of what a shed should contain. "What have you done now, Karl?" I whispered, my voice laced with a mix of confusion and concern. The hollowness of the shed seemed to echo back my words, amplifying the sense of mystery and tension.

I stepped back outside, my mind reeling from the bizarre scene I had just witnessed. The emptiness of the shed created a vacuum of understanding – it was as if I had stumbled upon a puzzle with missing pieces, a story with pages torn out. The sirens wailed closer now, their sound slicing through my thoughts. The blue and red lights flashed through the trees, signalling the approach of multiple police cars up the winding gravel driveway.

As I stood there, rooted to the spot, a torrent of confusion and disbelief swept over me. *How can Karl just disappear like this?* I questioned myself, my thoughts swirling chaotically. I knew he had taken a motorbike, but his ability to vanish so quickly defied logic. It felt surreal, almost like a trick of the mind, yet I knew it was all too real.

And where's Luke? The question gnawed at the edges of my consciousness, fuelling a growing sense of dread within me. A tight fear gripped my chest, constricting my breathing. The possibility that Karl might have killed Luke in a struggle and was now trying to dispose of the body loomed ominously in my mind. I hated to entertain such grim thoughts, but given what I now knew Karl was capable of, I couldn't dismiss them. The once outrageous accusations against my partner now seemed like a dire possibility, a terrifying reality that I was struggling to come to terms with.

Caught in this daze of fear and confusion, I barely registered the arrival of the patrol cars. They skidded on the gravel outside the manor, kicking up dust and stones, but it all seemed to happen at a distance, as if I were observing it through a thick, sound-dulling fog. The sergeant's arrival was nothing more than a blur to me. I saw him spring from his car and hurry over, but his actions felt disconnected, as though part of a scene in a film I was watching rather than my reality.

His footsteps approached, a faint clop in my ears, yet it sounded distant, almost inconsequential in the midst of the turmoil that engulfed my mind. The urgency of his movement, the concern likely etched on his face, none of it seemed to penetrate the bubble of shock and disbelief that enveloped me.

In that moment, time seemed to slow down, and I felt disconnected from the world around me. The reality of Karl's actions, the fear for Luke's safety, and the uncertainty of what lay ahead created a vortex of emotions that I was struggling to navigate. I knew I had to snap out of this trance, to engage with the situation at hand, but it felt like an insurmountable task, as if I were trying to swim against a powerful current that was determined to pull me under.

Sergeant Claiborne's grip on my shoulders felt both stabilising and intrusive as he jolted me from my daze. "Where the hell is Karl?" he demanded, his tone a mix of urgency and concern. The gentle shake he gave was enough to pull me back from the edge of my spiralling thoughts.

I blinked several times, trying to clear the fog that had settled over my mind. "I don't know," I admitted, my voice barely above a whisper. "I think he took off on a motorbike." The words felt hollow, even to my own ears, as if I was talking about someone else's life, not the surreal reality I was living.

"Are you sure?" Claiborne pressed, giving me another gentle shake, a clear attempt to prevent me from glazing over again. His concern was evident, but it felt distant, as if filtered through a thick veil.

My vision blurred, and I watched, almost detached, as a multitude of officers swarmed around the house. The scene before me was chaotic, officers moving swiftly, their voices a cacophony of urgency and command. "Louise and Thelma are still in there," I managed to say, pointing weakly towards Jeffries Manor. The names felt significant, anchors to the reality I was struggling to grasp.

As the chaos continued to unfold around me, my legs gave way, the muscles seemingly dissolving under the weight of the situation. I slumped down into the dirt, the coolness of the earth a stark contrast to the turmoil in my head. I rested my spinning head in my hands, feeling overwhelmed and powerless. The ground beneath me was solid, yet everything else seemed to be spinning out of control.

In that moment, sitting in the dirt, the world around me a blur of activity and noise, I felt utterly lost. The disappearance of Karl, the safety of Louise and Thelma, the unknown fate of Luke – it all converged into a maelstrom of uncertainty and fear. The responsibility of the situation weighed heavily on me, and I felt the crushing burden of not knowing what to do next.

❖

Resting my back against the cool metal of the shed, I felt utterly spent. The day's events had sapped every ounce of energy from me. Over a dozen officers had scoured every inch of the Jeffries' property and the dense wilderness beyond, but to no avail. As the sun dipped below the horizon, painting the sky in shades of gold and crimson, the search was reluctantly called off. The impending darkness made it too risky to continue in the rough, unfamiliar terrain.

"Don't worry, Sarah. We'll find Karl," Sergeant Claiborne reassured me, his voice confident as he leaned against the shed beside me. I wanted to believe him, but doubt and fatigue clouded my thoughts.

Suddenly, a young officer approached us, his face alarmingly pale against the backdrop of the setting sun. "Sergeant!" he called out breathlessly. "An anonymous caller has just reported another break-in at Luke Smith's house."

My heart plummeted at the news. Without thinking, my body reacted, propelling me towards my car with a sense of urgency.

"Sarah!" Sergeant Claiborne's voice echoed behind me. He sprinted past, reaching out to push my car door closed just as I was about to open it.

"Sarah," he said softly, his hand gripping my shoulder, causing me to jump at the unexpected contact. I turned to face him, but my vision was blurred, his features barely registering.

"Sarah," Claiborne repeated, his tone firm yet gentle. "You're exhausted. Go home. I've got it from here."

His words penetrated the haze of my exhaustion. I realised then how worn out I truly was, both physically and emotionally. Nodding in silent agreement, I climbed into the car. My body felt heavy, each movement an effort. As I started the engine, the weight of the day's events pressed down on me.

❖

Parked unobtrusively twenty meters up the road from Luke's house, the silence in my car was deafening compared to the distant wail of police sirens. The realisation hit me with the force of a tidal wave. *My blood... they're going to find my blood at the scene!* A fresh surge of panic cascaded through my weary body, exacerbating the exhaustion that already clung to me like a heavy shroud.

In a futile attempt to grasp some control over the spiralling situation, I dialled Karl's number for the fourth time since leaving Jeffries Manor. Each ring heightened my anxiety, and, as expected, it went straight to voicemail once again. The frustration and helplessness I felt were overwhelming.

"Where the fuck are you, Karl!?" I screamed into the phone, my voice a mixture of anger, fear, and desperation. My fists pounded against the steering wheel, the thuds echoing in the small confines of the car. Each strike was weaker than the last, my energy reserves nearly depleted.

I slumped back in my seat, feeling utterly defeated and alone. The weight of the events, the decisions made, the actions taken - it all seemed to converge into this one moment of despair. Staring blankly at Luke's house, the flickering blue and red lights in the distance felt like harbingers of an impending storm. My mind raced with the possibilities of what the police would find, what they would think, and how I could possibly navigate the web of lies and half-truths that had entangled me.

The sudden movement of two figures darting across the vacant corner block adjacent to Luke's house jolted me from my overwhelmed stupor. Reflexively, I leaned out of the car window, my eyes straining against the encroaching darkness of the evening. The figures were too distant, their identities shrouded in the growing shadows of twilight, rendering them unrecognisable.

In a desperate attempt to capture any clue that might unravel this ever-complicating mystery, I grabbed my phone. Leaning out the window once more, I quickly snapped a picture of the two women as they hastened across the road, making their way toward a car parked alongside the bushes.

Falling back into my seat, my eyes focused on the image as I zoomed in on the targets.

Settling back into the driver's seat, I brought the phone closer, my fingers working to zoom in on the image. The digital enhancement gradually brought their features into focus. A wave of disbelief washed over me as I recognised the faces. "Mrs. Pafistis and Mrs. Triffett," I whispered to myself, my voice a mix of shock and confusion. "What the fuck are they doing here?"

The sudden intrusion shattered the fragile calm within the car. The passenger door swung open with a force that made me jump, and before I could react, a figure slid into the seat beside me. My heart thundered in my chest, a rapid drumbeat of shock and fear. Instinctively, my hand moved towards where my gun should have been, but I realised I hadn't even had the chance to draw it.

Turning to face the intruder, I was met with a familiar face. "Gladys!" I exclaimed, my voice a mix of surprise and apprehension. The sight of her there, unexpected and uninvited, sent a surge of questions racing through my mind.

Gladys looked back at me, her face a canvas of sorrow, marked by trails of tears that glistened in the dim light of the car's interior. In her trembling hand, she held out an open bottle of red wine, an offering that seemed bizarrely out of place in the situation.

"Sarah," she said, her voice cracking with emotion. "I need your help."

DEAL

4338.214.2

In that surreal moment, my senses were torn between the chaos unfolding at Luke's house and the unexpected presence of Gladys beside me. My mind struggled to process the situation, each shout from the police operation outside clashing violently with the storm of confusion within me.

"Gladys, what the fuck!?" I finally managed to articulate, my voice a blend of bewilderment and rising panic. The silence that had enveloped us was thick, almost tangible, and my demand for answers seemed to echo in the confined space of the car.

Gladys, her expression a mask of desolation, took a long swig from the bottle of red wine, as if seeking solace in its contents before she could muster the strength to speak. Her actions felt detached, almost in slow motion.

Then, a gunshot pierced the night, shattering the fragile bubble that had formed around us in the car. It was a sound that instinctively triggered a response in me, both as a police officer and as someone who cared deeply for the people involved in this unfolding drama.

"Karl!" The name erupted from me, a reflex born of fear and concern. At that moment, the world seemed to stand still, suspended in the briefest second of horror and anticipation.

"Luke!" Gladys cried out next to me, her voice laced with a different kind of fear, one that spoke of personal connection and dread.

"Karl!" I choked out his name again, my voice strangled by a surge of emotion. It was more than a call; it was a plea, a desperate hope that he was safe.

Without thinking, I threw open the car door, my movements driven by instinct and adrenaline. I stumbled out, my knees slamming painfully into the gravel. My fall was graceless, a physical manifestation of the turmoil inside me.

My heart was a relentless drumbeat in my chest, each thud echoing the urgency and fear that propelled me forward. Blood seeped through my trousers where my knees had met the unforgiving gravel, but I paid no mind to the pain or the damage. All that mattered was getting to the house, to Karl.

As I sprinted toward Luke's house, the pulsing pain in my legs became a distant sensation, overshadowed by the adrenaline coursing through my veins. The night was fractured by the flashing red and blue lights, casting an eerie, chaotic glow over everything.

The scene was surreal, like a snapshot of chaos frozen in time. An unmarked police car was parked haphazardly across the street, its front door hanging open in a silent scream. The sight sent a jolt of alarm through me. *Was it Karl's car?* My mind raced, piecing together the fragments of the scene even as I continued my headlong dash towards the house.

The night air was filled with the chatter of neighbours who had spilled out onto the street, drawn by the commotion. Their faces and voices blurred into the background of my consciousness, insignificant in the face of my singular focus. I prayed fervently, a silent plea to whatever gods might be listening, that I wouldn't find Karl hurt — or worse.

As I neared the front door of the house, my body collided with an officer moving in the opposite direction, down the driveway. The impact was brief, barely a brush in the grand scheme of things, but in my heightened state, it felt like a jarring disruption. I barely registered his face, my eyes and mind fixated on the open doorway ahead. Information, at that moment, seemed secondary to the imperative of finding Karl. I had to see for myself, to know he was safe. The urgency was all-consuming, drowning out everything else in a tide of fear and determination.

Taking the front steps in a single, desperate leap, my determination to find Karl eclipsed all sense of protocol or caution. The officer at the door tried to block my way, but I was already past him. My only focus was to get inside, to find Karl, to see with my own eyes that he was okay.

The living room light flickered on just as I entered, momentarily blinding me. I blinked furiously, trying to force my eyes to adjust to the sudden brightness. Officers swarmed around me, attempting to restrain me, their hands grasping at my arms.

"Fuck off!" I yelled, adrenaline fuelling my strength as I pushed through them. Their voices merged into a cacophony of orders and shouts, but I tuned them out, my mind singularly focused on finding Karl.

"Karl!" I called out, my voice echoing through the house, a mixture of fear and desperation. The reality of what I might find was a weight in my stomach, a dread that tightened its grip with every step I took.

But then I stopped dead in my tracks. There, in the middle of the living room, lay a middle-aged woman on her back, her life ebbing away into a growing pool of blood. The sight was jarring, her face was unfamiliar to me, and for a moment, confusion clouded my thoughts.

"She's gone," someone said solemnly, crouching beside the lifeless body. The finality in his voice was a sharp contrast to the chaos around us.

My head was spinning, the room seemed to tilt and sway as I struggled to piece together the events. "Jenkins?" I asked the nearest officer, hoping to find a familiar face in the sea of uniformed personnel.

The officer shook her head. "Haven't seen him."

Relief, fleeting and fragile, washed over me. Karl was still out there, still alive. With nobody trying to stop me, I turned and walked briskly out of the house. My mind was a whirlwind of thoughts and emotions, struggling to make sense of the scene I had just witnessed. As I made my way back to my car, the numbness of shock began to take hold, each step feeling heavier than the last.

Gladys, leaning heavily against the side of the car, took another trembling sip of shiraz, her expression a mix of apprehension and alcohol-induced haze. "Who is it?" she asked again, her voice barely above a whisper.

I inhaled deeply, trying to quell the storm raging inside me. "I don't know," I confessed, my voice muffled as I leaned forward, resting my forehead against the cool leather of the steering wheel. The weight of uncertainty and fear pressed down on me. *Karl, where are you?*

Gladys slid into the passenger seat beside me, her movements sluggish. "I need to know," she insisted, her voice gaining a hint of urgency despite her inebriated state.

My frustration boiled over, and I couldn't hold back the outburst. "I didn't fucking recognise her!" I yelled, the harshness of my own voice startling me. I turned toward Gladys, my eyes blazing with a mix of anger and confusion.

"Her?" Gladys' voice was laced with a new layer of fear, her eyes widening.

"It's not your sister," I assured her, my voice softening as I returned my gaze to the wheel, feeling a wave of exhaustion wash over me.

Gladys took another loud gulp from the bottle, her actions more mechanical than anything. The silence in the car was heavy, filled with unspoken questions and fears. My mind was a whirlwind of thoughts — about the unknown woman, about Karl, and about the tangled web in which we found ourselves. The situation was spiralling out of control, and I felt utterly powerless to stop it.

My patience ending, "What the fuck do you want, Gladys!?" I snapped.

Gladys' words cut through the tension in the car like a knife, her plea absurd yet terrifying in its implications. "I need Cody's body," she said, her voice trembling as much as her hands.

I turned to her, incredulity etched on my face. "No. I can't help you," I replied firmly, shaking my head. The very idea was preposterous, beyond any moral boundary I had ever contemplated crossing.

Gladys, with a heavy sigh, looked at me with a seriousness that was chilling. "You know they're going to discover you were there when they find his body," she said, her gaze fixed on Luke's house. "It's inevitable."

My eyes shut tightly, a wave of despair washing over me. She was right. The reality of the situation began to dawn on me with a crushing weight. My mind raced, trying to find a way out, a solution to the impossible predicament I found myself in.

Gladys seemed to read my thoughts, her timing unnervingly precise. "If you help me, I can make your problem go away," she said, her voice steady, as if she was offering a simple transaction.

A shiver ran down my spine. *Could she really make it all disappear?* The thought was tempting, dangerously so. But the rational part of my brain screamed at me, reminding me of the line I was about to cross, a line from which there was no return. I sat there, wrestling with the moral dilemma, the weight of my decision heavy in the stillness of the car.

Uncertain, I looked back at Gladys, my mind swirling with a mix of disbelief and desperation. "How?" I asked, my voice barely above a whisper.

Gladys, reaching into her trouser pocket, retrieved a familiar device. It was small, rectangular, almost nondescript, but it sparked a memory. *Cody had that thing*, I realised, my confusion deepening at how it was now back in Gladys' possession.

"With that?" I asked, my skepticism clear. *How could such a small, unassuming object hold the power to make catastrophic problems vanish into thin air?*

Gladys nodded, her face serious, eyes locking with mine. She took another swig from the bottle, the liquid courage seemingly fuelling her resolve.

"What is it?" My curiosity about the object was overpowering my initial objection to Gladys' questionable behaviour.

Instead of answering, Gladys extended the bottle toward me. It was an unexpected gesture, almost comical under the circumstances.

"I meant the thing in your other hand," I said, my brow furrowing in frustration and curiosity.

"I know," Gladys replied, her voice steady, the bottle still outstretched in her hand.

Caving to Gladys' insistency, I took the bottle. The dregs were promptly drained from the bottle. Simultaneously, my eyes widened.

"What the fuck!" I cried, almost spitting the wine. A small ball of light shot from the end of the small object in Gladys' hand, covering the notebook that she had collected from the floor of the passenger seat. My hand reached out instinctively, curious to touch the display of swirling, hypnotic colours that danced over the notebook's surface.

But as quickly as they appeared, the colours vanished, leaving the air and the notebook devoid of any magical display. "Drive," Gladys commanded, her voice urgent as she snatched the now empty bottle from my grip.

"Drive where?" I asked, my voice laced with confusion and a rising sense of anxiety. *What was this device, and what had it just done?*

"Anywhere. Somewhere private," Gladys responded, her tone suggesting urgency and a need for discretion.

I couldn't stop the thoughts that haunted me. *Where the fuck are you, Karl?* The question echoed in my mind, a persistent reminder of the chaos and uncertainty that had wrapped itself around my life.

With a sense of resignation, I turned the key in the ignition, the car's engine coming to life with a low growl. I pulled away, driving into the night, the destination unclear, guided only by Gladys' mysterious instruction and my own tangled thoughts.

The headlights of my car illuminated the familiar contours of my driveway as I pulled in, the sense of unease growing within me. Gladys' question lingered in the air, adding to the swirling mix of uncertainty and fear that clouded my thoughts.

"Are you sure they can be trusted?" Gladys asked, her voice tinged with anxiety.

I replied with a forced steadiness, "It's my house," as I opened the car door and stepped out into the cool night air. "Get out."

As Gladys followed suit, a part of me screamed in silent protest. *What the hell am I doing?* The question gnawed at the edges of my consciousness, a nagging reminder of the absurdity and danger of the situation. *I shouldn't have brought Gladys here.* The thought flashed through my mind like a warning sign on a dark road. But it was too late for second guessing my decision now.

Standing next to Gladys in the small, dimly lit living room of my house, the weight of my decisions pressed heavily on me. My home, once a sanctuary, now felt like a stage for a play I didn't know I was a part of. The familiarity of the surroundings clashed with the surreal nature of our clandestine meeting, leaving me disoriented and on edge.

"Show me again," I demanded.

The grey wall before me transformed into a canvas of vivid, pulsating energy. I watched, mouth agape, as swirling hues of light collided and danced, creating a spectacle that defied all logic. The scene from Luke Smith's house the night Cody was killed, illuminated in bursts of ethereal light, played out on the wall like a ghostly echo of the past. An old newspaper article fluttered into view, detailing Rita's encounters with the unknown. It was all too much, too surreal. *Was this the very phenomenon Rita had witnessed?* My mind raced to connect the dots, drawing lines between the unbelievable and the undeniable.

"I need to take Cody," Gladys broke the silence, her voice quivering with emotion. Her tears glistened as they trailed down her face, reflecting the kaleidoscope of colours from the wall. "His children want him back."

"Through that?" I gestured toward the mesmerising display with a shaky hand, disbelief wrestling with the evidence of my own eyes.

"Yes," Gladys sniffled, wiping her tears with the back of her hand.

"What... where is it?" My voice was barely a whisper, my eyes fixated on the whirling spectacle before us.

Suddenly, a soft, almost inaudible voice whispered in my mind, *Clivilius*. I jerked my head towards Gladys, seeking confirmation. *Did she hear it too?*

"Clivilius," Gladys echoed.

I eyed her, a mix of suspicion and awe colouring my gaze. "Is that where Karl is, too?" I needed to know, needed to understand the incomprehensible connection between all these fragmented pieces.

Gladys nodded solemnly. "Yes."

Driven by a reckless urgency, I darted toward the mesmerising display of buzzing electrical colours, my heart pounding in my ears. But reality crashed into me with a heavy, unforgiving thud as my body collided with the dark, solid wall. Stumbling back, I blinked in disbelief. The vibrant colours had vanished, leaving nothing but a cold, bare surface.

"Gladys!" I cried out, my voice laced with growing frustration and confusion. In a flurry of emotion, I grabbed Gladys by the shoulders, shaking her violently. "What the fuck did you do that for!?" The words erupted from me, raw and unfiltered.

Gladys' eyes were wide with fear as she screeched, "He's not there! He's not there!" Her voice cracked with desperation as she struggled to push me away.

"You just said he was!" I countered, my anger boiling over. I slammed my clenched fist into the wall, the impact drawing blood from my knuckle and sending small chunks of plaster debris cascading to the floor.

Gladys, regaining some composure, spoke with a tremor in her voice. "Karl is in Clivilius, but it is a different location."

I stopped, the frustration momentarily giving way to confusion. "I don't understand." I began to pace anxiously, my mind racing to make sense of it all.

"Portal Keys," Gladys started, her voice steadier now. She held up the small, rectangular device, its significance suddenly immense in my eyes. "They open different locations in Clivilius. They can be opened from anywhere on Earth but are tied to a single place in Clivilius. Mine... and Cody's," she paused, drawing a deep, shaky breath. "Ours opens in Belkeep..."

I cut her off mid-sentence, the urgency in my voice unmistakable. "And Karl isn't in Belkeep?" Each word punctuated with a mixture of hope and desperation.

Gladys, her expression a portrait of sorrow, slowly shook her head. "No. Luke took him to Bixbus." The words hung heavy in the air, a stark reminder of the complex web in which we were entangled.

My pacing came to an abrupt halt, like a ship suddenly anchoring in turbulent seas. "Then I want to go to Bixbus," I declared, the determination in my voice belying the chaos churning within me.

"You need Luke for that," she responded, her voice a blend of helplessness and resolve.

My frustration mounting, I pressed further. "Then take me to Luke. You must know how I can find him." There was a pleading edge to my demand, a tacit acknowledgment of our mutual dependence.

A wild, desperate flame flickered behind Gladys' eyes as they glistened with tears. "Help me get Cody's body. If I take him to Belkeep, nobody on Earth will ever know what you did, Sarah. The evidence will be gone forever." Her voice trembled, betraying the gravity of her request.

Unyielding, I demanded, "I want Luke Smith." My words cut through the tension, sharp and unwavering.

Gladys responded, her voice laced with a bartering tone. "Help me get Cody's body, and I will get you Luke."

A suffocating silence enveloped us for a few long minutes. I wrestled internally with the gravity of her proposal. I longed to be reunited with Karl, to feel his presence again, but at what cost? My thoughts swirled in turmoil.

Finally, the pressure of the silence too much to bear, I blurted out, "How the hell am I supposed to get Cody's body?" The question echoed in the room, reflecting the absurdity and complexity of our situation.

Gladys' gaze met mine, unwavering, determined. "You're going to cremate him."

Her suggestion hit me like a physical blow, and I gasped loudly. "Gladys, you're insane." The words escaped me before I could restrain them, a mix of shock and disbelief colouring my tone.

In a voice soft yet unwavering, she replied, "I'm in love."

Her words, whether intentional or not, struck a chord within me. My eyes began to sting, the emotional turmoil of the moment blurring the lines between right and wrong. I realised the depth of our entanglement, the lengths to which we were both willing to go for those we loved. The decision weighed heavily on me, a testament to the complex tapestry of human emotions and the sometimes murky paths we tread in their wake.

"Fine. You've got yourself a deal," I conceded, the words heavy with a mixture of resolve and resignation.

TO BE CONTINUED…

Printed and bound by CPI Group (UK) Ltd, Croydon, CR0 4YY

21/07/2024

01020035-0006